Changing Tides

Family Secrets

Book Five

Rebekah McClew

Dedication:

To everyone brave enough to open this book and dive into my delightful word adventure, a massive thank you for granting my humble musings the opportunity to entertain- or at the very least, mildly distract-you!

Chapter One

Secrets

Over the next several months, life seemed to get more confusing by the moment. After my long depression, I had come back to find my sister had a baby. I already missed a few years of my own niece's life. As much as I tried to concentrate on what was going on here, I had a difficult time while I was being distracted by strange images of a woman I had once fallen in love with, I knew beyond reasonable doubt that she died. She died right in front of me, along with several other vampires. She saved my life as I should have been saving hers, there wasn't anything I could do. Charlie, Sophie, and I watched from the side, unable to get to her, to protect her. I began to wonder if I was losing my mind, I kept so much to myself. I knew my family was already worried about me. I used to go out in the woods to relax, unwind, or forget what was troubling me. Now I couldn't do that. One day I was running when I thought I heard a voice. Stopping to see if anyone had been out here around me, I couldn't find anyone. It would be strange for a human to be way out here; I went in the direction I thought I heard the voice. When I did get over there, the only sound I heard came from the stream, looking down at it, her face came to life. I could see her looking back at me smiling. Then another time, I had seen her in the ring, small as it had been, I knew she was sitting, crying and there was nothing I could do to comfort her. At times I wondered if I saw her in death, perhaps there was an afterlife? I hated to think of her possibly being sad in the afterlife.

I stayed with Rose and Jacob for the last few months as my parents and grandparents moved closer to us, their own home had been mysteriously searched through and partially burned down. The little town nearby seemed to have been marked and torn down with no sign as to where the humans had gone. Either way, Sophie felt it was no longer safe for them to stay there. Without hesitating, the family moved back here.

We talked to several people about the ring I wore, the average answer had been it was cursed. Most of my family wished I would hold a symbolic funeral for Harmony, hoping to have a funeral for her might help me move on. I decided that I didn't want to let go of her ring, it was the only piece of her I had left. At least with it, I felt connected to her still, even though it had done the strangest things lately. I swear I would see her face looking at me. However, over the years she had aged, as far as any of us had known, when you died, the face I should see would be her face when I last knew her, not one as if she was still around.

Most of the unusual experiences that I had, I no longer bothered sharing, even though the family had seen some of what I did and couldn't explain how it was possible. They knew how badly I had wanted to believe it, that she was alive. They had also witnessed the rather morbid scene of her being surrounded by Drealing creatures, monsters that were created by the lady in black to kill humans, who they thought would be potential guardians. I know I missed so much with my sister and her family, but I couldn't get rid of that nagging feeling that Harmony was alive out there somewhere. At times I would take off running to get away, scream, break something or get my frustrations out. I would see things happen that were rather disturbing, I no longer could tell what the truth was and what had not been. After all, when a vampire loses his sanity, what do you do with them? I tried to keep things from them, not that I had been too successful in keeping it from my aunts Dinah and Aidelle. On one of my trips out to blow off steam, they had been out also and caught as they called it, 'one of my performances.'

Usually, if I tried to sit in my room I would be reading or watching a show, painting, or just about anything to keep my mind occupied. I would have no control over what would happen. I would sit there, and I would see the ring shine, it would catch my attention, as I would look down at it. I would see her face looking back at me, at times it would feel comforting but also depressing at the same time. I convinced myself I would keep her safe as I had with Rose. I promised her. But then Doc Denthre was able to pull her to him, away from the safety of our family. I felt like a complete failure, not being able to keep my promise to her. After she died, I would see images of her going at great speeds with the Doc Denthre. Why was I seeing these images? I don't know and Rose had guessed that maybe someone very sick, knew how close I allowed myself to get to her. Perhaps they had been trying to get at me, breaking me down, using this very personal weakness against me. I had to admit if they intended to break me, they won, I only wished they would stop or finish me off.

After seven years, I couldn't stop hearing her voice. I would lay back and relax or if I was busy in the middle of a hunt, I could hear her voice whisper to me at times and it sounded happy, while at other times it sounded so sad, lonely, and even at times a bit desperate. It was gut-wrenching when I thought I heard her crying, it sounded like she had been right next to me, except no one else heard her. So now when I hear her speak or cry, I would leave the room, at least now, no one was asking where I was going. I know Grandpa Charlie was worried that he would see when I left, he more than anyone else understood the unexplainable pain of losing someone you loved. He lost Sophie, believing she had been dead for so many years and he kept after our mother, watching her from a distance, keeping her safe, and even introducing her to our father when she was older. The only difference had been Sophie was alive. We all would welcome another surprise like that, but we truly hadn't believed it would be possible. Sadly, both Charlie and I had seen it happen. After all, if she was with Doc Denthre, there would be no way she would be happy, let alone him letting her live.

There were rumors that that doc was still alive, being spotted by various creatures, I hoped that couldn't be possible, but if it had, then that would mean she was alive also. Now with the family allowing more outside influences, we broke down and bought computers. I searched on the internet for those who might have tried saying they saw the doc; however, I never did get any results, not that I expected to, how would ordinary humans know who the doc was? I didn't want to risk taking seven years and lose that much time again, after all, I had a niece to watch grow. I loved spending time with her. I hadn't realized how much time I missed with my family in general; I missed them more than I thought I would, and I didn't want to risk that again.

But what do you do when you're constantly haunted by memories, not only ones that existed but for those that are made up by the mind? Every day I was tormented by these memories, or thoughts of her, I started thinking it would be easier if I died myself, then I could finally handle it. Right now, it wasn't healthy that I spent my time this way. I knew what needed to be done, doing the right thing wasn't always the easiest choice, especially when we don't want to let go. I decided if I didn't find her this time, I was going to throw the ring out and be done with it. I hoped by getting rid of the ring, I might be free and move on with my life. As much as I loved her and wanted a piece of her, I was acting like a crazy person hiding everything, acting strange, and staying away from my family even though it was the last thing I had wanted to do. Funny how you can be around those you love and not be with them. I already missed out on so much.

I wasn't sure how I was going to break the news or begin to announce what my plans were, or how they would react the moment it hit them, or what I intended on doing. After all, it was as if I was searching for a ghost. For the family, it could be much simpler if I hadn't bothered telling them at all, but then if something were to happen, I hated to think they would find out that way, however, I hadn't wanted to tell them of a conversation I had with another vampire, or what my real intent had been. I wanted to search the area he spoke about and if there was any truth to it, if I could find any sign possible, then I would search for her further. If there were no solid signs that she still lived, then I decided once and for all, regardless of the images I would see, I had to do this. I would give up and bury the ring and let Sophie rest my mind. She offered it many times before; it was a way for vampires to forget short periods. She learned this from her friends that she once traveled with before she was united with the family again.

The vampire I spoke to, spoke of a girl named Harmony; she was with a man she called Goseck. However, to the vampire community, he was known as the doc. He hadn't been sure why she renamed him. The vampire noticed the Doc had an area where he regularly hunted creatures, that he was spotted searching for Harmony at one point near my parent's home and near the little town that mysteriously was destroyed overnight. It was a good thing my parents and grandparents had been visiting or who knows what would have happened to them. We never did get any answers to why it happened. So far, I had those two places to check and then a third, however, I was told I won't be able to get into it. That it was guarded against vampires and other creatures, and the place had been reserved for shades only, creating a shade city for their people. Somehow Harmony being human and the doc being a vampire, were allowed in. He couldn't explain too much more, but it sounded like the little place I had seen with the large gates, the night, a year ago when I came to my senses to come home.

I didn't feel like making it a family affair. I waited until most had been at their own homes in the morning, our families have usually been together during the nighttime. I waited in the living room for Nichole and Anthony to get home. When they did, they knew I had something on my mind. Asking them to sit down, I wanted to share with them something I needed to do.

"I promise I won't be gone long; I need to do something I have been putting off for a while, just because it's been difficult to deal with. I have decided to let Sophie relax my mind when I get back. I'm hoping it will help so I can move on. I plan on being gone for at least three months, no longer than five months, then I will be back. I'll be careful to keep track of time. I won't be leaving for seven years ever again, that was far too long. But I need to do this and get closure." I wasn't sure how they would take my news; let alone the way I was delivering it to them. As I told them, I think dad was happy to be sitting down.

"Your mom and I agree you need help getting over this. Do you think it's a good idea to take off on your own? Charlie has offered before to go with you. Or maybe one of your aunts, Aidelle, or even Dinah have expressed they would go with you." I knew he was questioning why it was going to take so long to do this, I hadn't wanted to explain I was looking for a ghost.

"I know you are both worried that I have let this affect me for so long, but I also wanted to see if I could find a friend. I would be in the area, and I heard my friend was over there right now, so I wanted to see if it was true. I don't know if Charlie or the aunts want to be gone that long?" I was hoping to be persistent enough to discourage anyone from coming with me.

I hadn't wanted to turn this into a family crisis, the family has finally been settling down it wasn't fair for me to uproot everyone because I couldn't let go of the love of a dead human.

"Let me ask Charlie, if he will go with you and if not then you can take off on your own for a while. You're old enough, you don't need our permission. We are happy you told us so that we don't have to worry about where you are and if you're okay. Make sure you keep your new phone on you and keep in touch no matter if you think it's upsetting, we want to hear from you." Nodding I agreed.

I went to my room to pack a few things, not that I needed too much. I could hear Anthony talking to Charlie on the phone. I was not only going to be accompanied by Charlie, but also by both Aidelle and Dinah.

Charlie hadn't planned on staying for too long, while Dinah and Aidelle were going to follow to give us privacy, then would join me once Charlie left. I would have preferred going alone, having everyone with me, was almost comforting in case I had been losing my mind. I hoped they wouldn't ask me who my friend was, just in case, I decided on a name, that way if we did find her, I would hope they would understand my covering for my possible insanity.

Soon as nightfall had come, we took off, only with Charlie nearby me. I knew Aidelle and Dinah were nearby, I had never heard or seen them for the first part of the stretch. Before we finished heading off in the direction that I had planned, we stopped by Charlie's old house to see if anything had changed since the last time he was there, looking over the burned remains. Nothing missing and nothing different, the whole situation didn't make sense. My aunts were smart not to let me know where they were located, otherwise, I could have ditched Charlie here and he never would have seen which direction I had gone. One thing I have to admit is my family was rather clever. I wished we could have moved quicker, I wanted to cover more ground, to get this over with before anyone stopped me, when they realized what I was doing.

While Charlie inspected the inside of his home, he had pulled out a necklace that Sophie wanted. She hoped it would still be there. Then for the first time, since the three days that we had taken off, I caught a glimpse of my aunts, they had both been on the far side with Charlie, distracted, trying to be light-footed as I possibly could. I had run in another direction, not one I had been planning on, but searching would be so much easier on my own. I loved my family and understood their concern, but if I was truly going to lay to rest my demons, I needed to do this on my own. I could hear my name being shouted in the distance. I kept running until the shouts were no longer even a whisper.

I should feel bad for ditching my family, but after a while, I can't help but feel tired of everything being a family matter. Yes, I understand we live around humans and that if something goes wrong, we need to figure it out ourselves, after all, we don't have doctors we can go to and certainly no psychologist to speak to. I knew I had run much further, however, I wanted to make sure if they started tracking me, I would lose them. I made it a point to cross several rivers and lakes until I was back in the correct direction. Not far from the area I had seen the people going into, I was told that Harmony and Doc Denthre had been spotted not that far from there.

So far, all I had were simple leads of a creature spotting her. I know we hadn't separated until that moment that everyone died. The only thing I worried about had been if I prove her to be alive, will the others be alive also. Will she be anything like her old self, if she has been traveling with the doc? There had been rumors of a battleground with a strange group that had been made by the lady in black, they still existed, yet people knew very little of them since they stayed on their private island, rarely coming off unless they had been called for by the lady. Since her death, no one has seen them. This would be my first place to search. I had noticed that the three areas that I was about to search were rather close to each other, forming a triangle shape, oddly enough the little place I had found had been dead center in the middle of it all.

It had only been maybe two days' travel from Charlie's house. He had only owned the house about a year before Sophie showed up again. Watching around in case my aunts or Charlie went looking around nearby, I tried to stay quiet, especially if the lady in black's creatures were still around. She may not have been here anymore to give them orders, but I could guess they might still be hostile. I heard so many stories about creatures the lady had created herself however, most have died off. We probably would have been like most vampires, not knowing much about her if we hadn't been related to her.

I preferred the colder climates, even with the snow, there was less chance of humans being out in the middle of nowhere. I admit, it had been easier to get around in the warmer climates, the downfall of warmer weather was the sun being out for longer, incredibly thick forest, difficult terrain, or rainforest might not have been easy to get through, but it was perfect for blocking the sun out. The thick forest is what I happened to be going through now. Good thing I had worn my old shoes, they were already wearing out going through the swamps getting them wet. I packed an extra pair; I usually went through quite a few pairs of shoes.

The first place I had to search had been in the center of a mountain. There had been at least four large ones in this area and the center, or rather ravines between had been trails or paths where the trees hadn't grown. Following these in, sometimes groups would set up camp, even gypsies have gone through here. The area I wanted to search had been the furthest out which meant I was going to get wet. Since I would be coming back to this spot, I had left my bag here with everything, hiding it under the leaves concealing it. Once I made my first stop at the island, I would be coming back here to get it to check the other places.

I could spot the island from here; it looked like two huge mountains surrounded by water. Not looking forward to getting wet, I got it over by jumping in quick and swimming out to the island, always keeping an eye out, making sure no one was watching me. I made it out to land quick, pulling myself out of it, it didn't seem like there were any footprints or signs there might be someone here. Finding where the vegetation grew less, I took what looked like an old path following it along the side of the first mountain, the other mountains in the distance came into view once I was higher up. I kept walking upward until I had a strange stinging sensation on my hand. Most mosquitoes died if they tried to bite me, but this didn't seem to want to go away. I still wore the ring on my finger, which is where the stinging was coming from. Looking down at the ring almost expecting to see harmony looking back at me again, instead, I saw a rather creepy-looking creature. At times, I felt like I was wearing more of a crystal ball than a ring.

Trying not to pay attention to it, I had to admit whenever I had been in an area Harmony had been, the ring would either glow or I would see some strange site. I started walking again when the slope started downward rather steeply. I first spotted some ugly-looking humans, until I realized they were experiments of the lady. Crouching down, I watched to see what they had been up to. Oddly enough, I watched the two get into an argument with each other, and eventually from fighting with each other, one died while the other seemed to walk away for a short distance before dropping dead himself. The problem with breeding so much anger, there wasn't much self-preservation. Not wanting to get near them, I went through the wooded area until I came to a clearing. It looked rather strange to have a clearing like this, I wondered if it meant there was a lookout keeping watch of it.

Sitting for a while outside of the opening, I watched carefully, waiting for any movement or for anything to make itself known. There hadn't been any animals, or people moving around other than those two stupid ones, which now I understand why they were able to be seen. Most likely sick or not capable of thinking right in their heads. Observing an area and being quiet was rather boring, especially waiting for something, anything. I stood up about to walk out into the opening, thinking if something was going to happen, I might as well help it get started. Then the ring on my finger flashed a bit. I looked down to see it, instead, I looked past it and found something on the ground, which was for once even better, the ring itself never showed something. I was starting to wonder if the ring was trying to help me find her. Picking it up, the piece was a simple ribbon, dark emerald, one of three favorite colors that Harmony used to wear. It could have been owned by any girl, however, except it had her scent on it. I wondered if this had been the place she went missing when Sophie had expected to be called to her? There were little drops of blood on the hair piece.

This could have been one of those areas she had popped into when she first had the life stone. I never knew how many times she had randomly shown up places until I ran into her myself. Looking at the stone, walking out, I should have been paying more attention. Not that anything could knock me out, but hard twine wrapped around my legs and bound my arms to my sides rather fast, as I came crashing down onto the ground. It might have worked if it had been strong enough. I broke free getting to my feet rather quickly, to see three people realize it didn't hold, and take off in a fast run. Racing after them, intending on catching at least one to question them, it had proven difficult to keep up with them. They may have been short, but they certainly were fast.

Racing across, there had been a deep ravine before coming to the other mountain where a huge waterfall cascaded down, the two people didn't seem to be scared at all from jumping off the side of the cliff. Not knowing what was on the other side, or how far the other side was, I had come to a stop at the edge to watch them disappear behind the waterfall, not coming out. I couldn't help feeling shocked at what I observed. Looking around, there hadn't been any other way down, no rope bridge, or even a decline to the side of the cliff, it had all been just straight down. They couldn't have gone anywhere else other than the waterfall. I hadn't seen any emerge unless they could hold their breath well. Normally I would risk it if I knew what it was like on the other side of the waterfall, so I decided to make my way down.

I had to find out what happened to them. Hoisting myself over the edge, holding on doing my best to make hand holds and foot holds. I was able to break into the mountain even though parts of it had still been loose. I lost my grip a few times, it hadn't been until I was about halfway down, that I lost hold and fell into the water down below. I was bracing for the worst but after hitting the water, falling under wasn't as bad as I had expected. There was such thick spongy ground to land up. Moving away from it, I swam for the waterfall staying underneath since the pressure was so strong. As I had gone under, not that far ahead there had been an opening in the cave. It wasn't difficult swimming with the current as it rushed me in. I was only worried about getting out. Following through the open tunnel, there was an area where I could see people up ahead, walking past the water. I had been in the water for a few minutes longer, watching when I had seen there was another entrance to the side of the waterfall, which most seemed to walk in and out. These didn't look like the two I had watched kill each other, not that I had ever seen these people before.

Looking around, I hadn't seen the two that I followed here. Neither did I see their bodies floating or going anywhere. Climbing up the side bank, squeezing the water out of my clothes, I had seen a bunch of people looking in my direction in sheer horror, at least I knew I looked different. They raced behind the huge gates before I could do or say anything to them, no one was visible anymore. Walking over to the gates I scanned the area, it looked like a huge city, how could this be here, and we never know about it? Onyx stone dominated the architecture everywhere, it looked so stunning. Then I heard a low-toned voice.

"What do you want?" I couldn't see where it was coming from, so I spoke in a regular voice assuming it must have been somewhat close.

"I was going to question two people I saw earlier until they dove for the waterfall, I wanted to make sure they were okay." The voice hadn't responded right away.

"They lived… go away." That was all the voice decided to say to me.

"Mind if I ask you a few questions? I'm looking for someone special and I heard she might be near here?" Waiting for a response, I wasn't sure if the voice had waited around to answer.

"Don't know anyone…. go away." The voice was rather quick to answer that one.

"I'm looking for a human. A young woman." Not wanting to give up, I wanted to know if she had been here at all.

"No humans here…. if so, they are usually dead…. now go away." The voice was getting a bit gruff, probably because I wasn't leaving as he had asked.

"Do you eat humans?" I figured I would see what they would say if I asked something basic.

Before I could ask another question, the person was now in full view with his hands on his hips asking me now.

"No! We don't eat humans…not like bloodsuckers like you, we love humans… now go away." He seemed rather upset by my question, but at least now I knew what they were afraid of, it had been the fact I was a vampire.

"Does anyone here know of a girl named Harmony? I'm looking for her, I promised to protect her, but I lost her. I wanted to know if she was here or if anyone saw her. I found her hair band not far from here." The expression of anger on his face changed to a rather strange dopey look.

"You suck as a protector. If you lost her, serves you right. Hopefully, she finds another protector, a non-vampire, now take yourself out." He had started to walk away when I put my hand on the gate door, he turned around quickly with a spear in his hand.

"I will use this, now go." He seemed serious with his threat.

I still wanted answers, but I hadn't wanted to be rude by pushing them if they were trying to safeguard themselves in their city. Taking my hand back, I figured they probably weren't any more helpful to Harmony, if she had shown up here. Walking out of the tunnel, I had taken the path that the others were walking on instead of going through the waterfall again. What I hadn't expected to see on the other side, had been Charlie, he found me. He wasn't even angry; he had a bit of a smile on his face.

"If you wanted to search you could have just told me. I don't mind exhausting every chance before we give up. Next time don't try to lose me, I'm too good at tracking. It won't take long for Dinah and Aidelle to find us, you don't exactly cover your trail that well." Charlie patted me on the shoulder with a sarcastic grin.

I knew Charlie understood what I was thinking. He had already been in my shoes, just in a different way. Walking halfway up the cliff, I showed him Harmony's hair band, that I found on my way here. As we talked, we heard steps from a distance coming up from behind us. Both of us turned to see who it had been, almost expecting my aunts to join us. I had seen a young girl looking at us slightly nervous. We figured if the others reacted the way they had, then she had to be rather brave to face both of us out here. Not wanting to scare her, Charlie sat on the grass, I leaned against the wall as I made no motion to move.

"Before I can say anything, I need to know your name first." Her voice came across as shaky, but then if you were next to something that terrified a city, you would probably react the way she had.

Her question had been fair enough to ask.

"My name is Lucian, and this is my grandfather Charlie." As soon as I said my name she smiled no longer looking nervous.

"I have something for you, news spread fast when you were spotted nearby. I tried to grab her things when I heard a vampire was outside the gate asking for her, I hoped it was you. She left behind her bracelet and the clothes she had worn. I was going to throw them out since they belonged to a detestable group, she couldn't help that she was held by them for a while. I was going to give them back once they were cleaned, but I couldn't get the blood out. That and she had left pretty quick with her friend." Handing me a bag, I could tell that even though being washed, still had the faintest hint of her. I recognized the bracelet she had worn.

"Do you know where they had gone? How might I find her? When was this that they left?" Both Charlie and I gave our full attention now that we thought there was a slight possibility of her living.

"They went to the city of the shades, I would show you, but I'm not allowed outside of the gates here. I need to get back before they notice I'm gone. The shades are straight up, northeast from here. She was traveling with her friend and the queen. The city of the shades is protected, and no other creature is allowed in." From the way she had described the man she was with, it sounded like Doc.

However, the woman she called the queen, the lady in black never wore any other color, which had been another reason she had been dubbed that name. She had always looked like she had been mourning something however, the woman she described, had been slightly older wearing all white robes. Thanking her, I promised her when I found Harmony, I would let her know her friend Mia said hello.

Now with a bit more urgency, we had taken off for the city of the shades. At least I know she was still thinking of me if this girl thought positively about my name once she heard it. We hoped they would assume we might be shades if they were fooled by the Doc. Taking off immediately for the direction, we ran into Aidelle and Dinah on the way. Charlie was correct; it wouldn't take very long for them to find me. I hadn't wanted them to think I was crazy for searching for her, since the odds had been stacked against any possibility of her surviving the blast that killed the others.

The others remembered me telling them about this new place I found when I was on my way home the first time. Now we headed back being careful not to run into anything else on our way there. It had been easier for the two of us to blend in with our surroundings, but with the four of us, we stood out more. We branched out a little trying to blend in more. As we had come closer however we regrouped. Once there, outside of the cavern, we watched a few people coming out into the daylight. We had to wait until night to make another move, so we sat here watching as people had come and gone. I hoped this wouldn't be difficult as the other place had been, but then who knows, maybe she made a friend here who might be willing to speak?

We waited patiently under the leaves of the trees, staying in the shade as much as possible, only moving as the sun started to shine in a different location. Eventually, the sun lowered to reveal a much-relieved moonlight. Walking down to the opening, we listened carefully to make sure no one was coming now. Walking down the tunnel, it was extremely dark and easy to hide since there had been several niches along the way. When we were close enough, there had been two people speaking with the guards, just before they had gone through the gate entrance. The gate had taken up the entire opening, not leaving any space for outsiders to get in. Sliding along the side wall, I had tried to move through the narrow bars of the gate

I could have squeezed in, except there was such strong pressure on the other side, keeping me out. I kept feeling searing heat as if being poked with a million needles in my skin. I know it had been nighttime, but somehow this side, it was daytime. Moving back quickly out of the burning sun, I made my way back to the cave, my skin hurt still, stinging as if I was still in the light. I even had what looked like a burn mark on my skin. Talking with Charlie, we would either wait till the sun went down on this side or talk to the guard, hoping they will listen without attacking since they looked much more prepared for a fight or rather defending their city than the other place had. Otherwise, we had to wait for the guards to be preoccupied until we could get in or get a message in somehow.

Waiting another day to get in was driving me crazy. The simple fact she could be in there and I was stuck out here. Not that we knew if the people here were friends of the Doc or the lady in black. The reception may not be that good, so we decided we would sneak in to find her. Soon as the sun had gone down, I tried to squeeze in the gate again, which I wasn't able to do. There hadn't been any other gaps, so now we were stuck trying to get in by the guards. Only one guard was standing at attention at the moment, both Dinah and Aidelle stepped out in clear view, getting his attention hoping he would chase after them, which he hadn't. Then, Charlie walked over to them trying to keep the guard's attention. The bars around the gate were wide enough for me to pass through, yet I still couldn't get in. It was as if there had been a spell or enchantment of some kind keeping us out. Giving up, I walked over to the guard. He hadn't acted worried until I started speaking with him.

"I'm here looking for a human girl. Her name is Harmony. I was told she came here with a friend and the queen." As I asked, the expression on his face never changed, at first, I wasn't sure if he was going to answer.

"No vampires allowed under any circumstances; no creatures other than shades allowed in here. If she was human, she wasn't in here. Now leave." At least what they had in common with both cities, they both seemed to want us to leave.

"Is there a way I might be able to see your queen? I am not a threat, and neither am I armed. Is there a way of speaking to someone to find out? I know she had come here. I was told by a person from the Eurubian people that she came here with your queen. Please ask her, she may wish to see us." Nodding he was replaced with another guard, while he went and asked.

He had been gone for a while. I began to wonder if he went and walked all the way there to find out or simply left us here waiting. After quite a wait, reappearing, he came back with no change in expression. Instead of the other guard leaving, he simply stood on the side as two other guards joined them.

"The queen does not wish to socialize with vampires, she has nothing to say to you. You will be killed if you try to get in." Not saying another word, he resumed his position guarding the gate.

"Have you heard of the name Harmony? Do you know where I can find her? I need to find her." I was hoping if I stalled long enough, we would catch the attention of the residents from inside.

Maybe someone from there would know about her or say something? I wanted to stall as long as I possibly could since this had been the best lead we had. I wasn't sure where to look after this. I wanted to know if she was free, or if she was being held against her will. Someone had to know if she had been here before or possibly where she was.

"We do not discuss the conditions of Shades living here or out elsewhere. If she is human, she is none of our concern. I have no further words for you." As he said this, the others noticed what crowd we were drawing to the gates.

No one tried coming out however there were even more guards standing at the gates now. All four of us stood there, not going anywhere or speaking as the guards stood still in their places watching us. I scanned the people inside, who were all lurking around out of curiosity. There had been a group of young people that gathered, whispering to each other. Keeping a close eye on them, one of the girls left a note at the far end of the gate, passing it through. That's when I guessed the enchantment must have been there to keep us out, or at least to keep vampires out. Walking away from the note, the group disappeared behind the crowd. Walking over, I grabbed the note with Charlie, Dinah, and Aidelle following behind. Simply the note said, 'we're friends of Harmony, wait at the tree line for the night on the other side, I will come out. They won't let anyone out while you're still waiting here.'

Doing as the note said, we went to the far end, at the end of the tunnel waiting for night to come. Once the sun started to go down, we crossed over to the tree line and waited for who we assumed was the girl that was going to come out to speak to us. What we hadn't expected, had been about fourteen young-looking kids, coming out of the tunnel together making a straight line for us.

Hoping not to scare the kids. I stepped forward while the others were standing not far behind. I watched as the kids elected someone to speak to us. A different girl than the one who had left the note stood forward, she had a piece of paper in her hand.

"We were looking in a crystal ball and this is who we saw, he looks identical to you." Handing over the piece of paper to me.

As I looked it over I couldn't help but smile, she had been looking at me. I was hoping she might have come out with this group unless they were here to give me unfortunate news about her?

"Is she still here? I'm trying to find her, or at least find out if she's still alive. I'm assuming she is since she has been to so many places now." I was hoping for some explanation or something, maybe they knew something about Doc.

"We heard you talking to the guards and them not wanting to tell you where she was. It's because they don't know. She was grabbed a few months ago and we didn't know if she was alive, then she had come back after her father searched for her. The queen last had her up at the palace. I only saw her walking by where I live, I didn't get a chance to talk to her that last time. She had lived here in the shade city for a while with her father. The queen is looking for her, she wants her to do something but for some reason, she left rather quickly with her father somewhere, they didn't leave any messages about where they were going. We've all been questioned by the queen, and she will know that we spoke to you." I could tell she was trying to tell me, but being watched, she had to be careful not to let out any information, she didn't want someone else to have.

What didn't make sense was referring to the Doc as her father. She kept repeating that she was staying here with her father, they seemed to be under the belief she had been a shade herself.

"I want to make sure we are talking about the same harmony, she was human. The one I'm speaking of." Nodding their heads, they had agreed she was human.

"There are things we cannot speak of because of the queen, we can't say what goes on, but there are things that have changed. If you find her father, you will find her." Most of the group started to move back towards the cave again, only leaving four of the younger ones behind, including the one who spoke to me.

"My name is Zoë this is Tara, Bridgette, and Najee, we were Harmony's closest friends. We were heading out for a bit, so if you follow us, maybe we can walk and talk? Or if you're in a hurry, you can give us a faster lift out?" Opting for the faster version, I hadn't wanted to risk anything from delaying us from finding out more information.

I hadn't known what they wanted afterward, or if there had been a place they were heading for? Taking off, the others followed. I had taken Zoë with me as the others were picked up by Charlie and my aunts. When we had gone far enough, Zoë whispered in my ear that we could stop. Getting down, I was ready to hear more than she could tell us.

"The queen has a lot of ears near the cave, that's why I didn't want to say anything there that would give out too much information. The first night that she had been at the queen's palace, apparently they upset Goseck a lot, they put Harmony in danger to test something and he was angry that they would do it again. So, they took off, without telling anyone where they were going. She used the stone to do it. When we met Harmony, she introduced herself as Goseck's daughter." After describing what the Doc looked like, they confirmed that had been Goseck.

None of us thought of him as having another name, but knowing she was with him, we didn't feel safe leaving her with him. Why would she call him her father, unless she couldn't remember who she was? The girls were trying to inform us about him, they told us about their first impression of him, being dangerous, foul-mouthed, never smiling, and always angry. He had at one time even been removed from the shade city, until recently, when he came home with his daughter. He acted like a completely different person. The girls admitted they had a chance to get closer to him, that because of Harmony, he had been a much better person.

Chapter Two

Right There

I wasn't sure how to take the information. I didn't want to share my suspicions, but I had wondered if she was becoming more attached to the Doc, not just pretending to be his daughter. Her relationship with him seemed rather close. The girls had said if we found his cabin, we would find them, they described the place the best they could, it was the only place they thought the two would go. From our experience, we matched up two ideas of where it could have been. My two aunts were going to take off and check out the first one. If she was there, they would call us and the same if we found them at the other place. The girls and the one boy had only been a few hours away from their home. At least they helped us as much as they could. When they were walking back to their home and out of sight, we took off with the information they had given us. I was hoping to find where she was and hoping she was okay and still wanted to see me.

I didn't have to voice my opinion, I wasn't the only one who had been thinking maybe the reason she hadn't contacted me, had been that she moved on herself. When Charlie called Sophie on the phone, she said she might have thought she was protecting me by staying away with the stone, not that she could understand why she would want to be with the Doc. I had to face the fact that we had never told each other we loved each other, maybe I had been the only one who fell in love? Maybe she was where she wanted to be? I started to doubt myself. I wasn't sure if I wanted to find out, even though I still had to make sure she was safe. If she was happy. I would leave her alone, but if she was sad and still wanted me, I would take her away. I was thinking way too much to myself, I couldn't help it, I wasn't paying attention to the ground below. Charlie had fallen behind because I had sprinted out so fast, I was allowing my emotions to control myself, that I finally hit a large tree root, tripping and falling at such a fast speed, I felt like I had fallen apart, hitting the ground I almost felt paralyzed mentally.

I had crashed to the ground in an emotional heap, crying at the thought that she might not want to see me. I didn't know what to think anymore. She had been around for so long; I didn't know what to think? Charlie tried comforting me, telling me we don't know what conditions she was being held under and maybe, whoever she is with, isn't the same Doc. People seem to believe he is someone else, only vampires have told us she was with the Doc. We wouldn't know how she felt until we found out, either way, it would give me the closure that I needed. That and we could find out if the stone of life was safe or not. Once I was able to get up and get going again, we took off for our destination. We hadn't found the second cabin yet, but Dinah called Charlie on the cell phone, so we had to stop to keep the connection. They were in the middle of exploring the area and the cottages that had been along the lake, but so far, no sign of them. It didn't mean they were not there; they were going to continue looking for signs or evidence of who might live in the cabins.

We arrived at our destination, a rather odd place, and empty-looking area. There wasn't another place in sight for miles and in the middle of a forest, covered with snow in every direction, there hadn't been a lake to see, except it could have been under the snow. The only cabin we did see had candles burning. No regular lights turned on, with only a fireplace going. I felt so sick I wasn't sure if I was ready, but I couldn't stop either. Charlie had me hang back while he checked it out, thinking if the Doc has softened on her, he might still be dangerous towards us. We didn't want to risk her life. Getting up close enough, Charlie could make out two people in the cabin. One person stayed in the room to the side, while the other sat on the couch, in front of the fire.

The man sitting on the couch, he identified as the Doc. The other he could only assume had been Harmony. Charley couldn't see the face of the woman; she was sitting on her bed facing away. Keeping an eye on the house, I worked my way around to the other side. Charlie called Dinah and Aidelle to come to join us, in case we needed help. After all, the Doc was notorious for fighting and two vampires wouldn't be difficult for him to handle. While we waited, I could see her in plain view from my side, looking right into her window. Charlie called mom and dad, telling them that we had found her, she was alive and with the Doc. We were careful, however, for Nichole and Anthony to be prepared, in case we called them for help. We knew they were quite a distance from us but if this lasted or others helped the Doc, we might be able to hold them off until they arrived.

I worked my way up to the window, getting even closer. It was so difficult to stay away, but I didn't want the Doc to know we were here. As I was watching her, she had the life stone in her hands, looking into it as she did, my ring glowed. I smiled, at least I knew she was thinking of me. Looking down at the ring, I wasn't sure if she would realize I was waving at her or just waving in general? She did have a bit of a puzzled look on her face. I wished I knew how to signal for her to come out if she was able to. Picking up snow, I held it by the ring, then watched her from the window, she had tilted her head, she looked like she was trying to figure out something. Making sure the snowball was small enough, I threw it at her window, trying not to hit it too hard, it caught her attention.

Closing her bedroom door, she walked back over to the window, looking out trying to figure out where the snowball had come from. Looking at the window, she could see part of it had still been there. Grabbing a coat and shoes, she slipped out her window onto the snowy ground, looking around the sides of the cabin, she still hadn't seen anyone. Then turning, she was going to climb back in, when I shot up from behind her and covered her mouth, so she wouldn't scream. Picking her up fast, I ran back to the trees before I set her down. I realized I probably scared her, I just hoped she would forgive me. Turning quickly to see who had grabbed her, she took one look at me and passed out. It was a bit overwhelming. Charlie closed the window to the cabin, and as I picked her up, taking off, we took her all the way home, hoping we were making her safe.

When she first started waking up, she thought she had been in a dream. Looking around and seeing all of us around her, until she realized it wasn't a dream. Her reaction hadn't been what I was expecting. When she saw Sophie was there, she asked for a cell phone immediately, before she even said a word to me. It felt as if I had died. I could hear her conversation on the phone. She was desperately trying to calm him down, that she was alright and hadn't been kidnapped again, she would be home soon and explain.

"You want to go back? Do you know who that is you were with?" Charlie asked, wondering if she was thinking sanely, or if maybe she was under any illusion that he was someone else?

"Yes, I know who that is. His name is Goseck, and he looks a lot like the Doc however, he's not. The Doc is a vampire and Goseck is a shade who pretended to be his identical. He's told me everything about himself, even the things he wished I hadn't known, he has been protecting me and I hate worrying him. I know he won't relax until I get back home. I was so shocked to see Lucian that I passed out. I never thought I would ever see him again, but I need to get back. I hope you understand." Nodding, Charlie agreed I could take her back, my aunt Dinah would follow behind in case we needed her. Originally Charlie was going to come with me, but I wanted some time to myself after this.

As we stepped out of the house, I noticed something different. I couldn't figure out what it was. Then as I waited for Harmony to get on my back, so I could take her there, she shook her head no, smiling at me, I thought she meant for Dinah to carry her.

"We can talk once we get to Goseck's cabin. There is so much that has happened I need to explain to you. I don't need a ride. But do try to keep up with me." Smiling again, she shot off with such speed.

It was a good thing I knew where the cabin had been and that she had wanted to talk to me still because I had lost sight of her, I was in complete shock and so was Dinah. She wasn't a vampire, but she was still human, so how was she running so fast?

Once the cabin was in sight, I could see the man standing out front with her, hugging her. My heart sank, I wasn't sure what she was going to fill me in on, I hoped she wasn't having me here as a friend. I hated to think about it, but if she had fallen for this man, then I wouldn't be able to stick around, watching the woman I loved, caring for another man. Dinah stayed closer to me when she saw Harmony hugging him. As we got closer, he seemed rather protective of her, standing in front of her quickly, as we approached closer. Harmony said something to him, he relaxed as she stepped out from behind him. We could tell just watching them they had formed a close bond. Walking over to me, she motioned for both of us to come into the house. Dinah entered first, as Harmony took my hand, pulling me in with the man walking behind.

I felt incredibly nervous, as I was sure Dinah was, seeing the Doc standing this close to us. Neither of us let our guard down, in case he was to attack us.

"Dinah, I'm going to talk to Lucian privately in my room. Goseck can keep you company out here, don't worry, he's safe and won't hurt you. Dad, we'll be back out in just a bit." Taking my hand, she led me into her room, closing the door behind me.

I hoped I hadn't walked my aunt and myself into a trap, especially if he had brainwashed her. Why was she calling him dad? Once we were in her room, she stood there looking at me with a big smile on her face.

"I'm sorry I didn't react to you better. I was shocked to see you, I never thought I would see you again. I had to get back here, Goseck's been through so much, especially in the last several months. I hate to admit it, I'm not the easiest person to protect." Taking me by the hand again, she led me over to her bed where she sat down and motioned for me to sit.

"My life had yet to slow down since finding the life stone. When it looked like the others died there, the main ones we transported to the new site, a ceremonial site. Sophie taught me what she wanted me to accomplish with the stone. Originally when I left you, I was to bring Sophie to me, she was going to finish training me, but Goseck had been waiting for me, don't worry, I was still safe, he had been a great teacher and in ways earned my trust. He has been a wonderful father to me. Because of him, we killed the lady in black, and many of her followers in another area were safely away from you. Because of him neither you or Charlie died. I thought staying away from you would keep you safe. I admit I kept checking on you more so when we had moved to the shade city, they believed I was a shade because we told them I was his daughter, and I did feel like I was. He was very much a father to me during that time. No matter how bad it was he didn't keep the truth from me. I tried to find you once but that didn't go too well. I met someone who destroyed the town. It's why I was kidnapped for a while. I don't want to go through all that again. Later I'll explain it but how did you find me? I thought you would assume I was dead?" There were so many questions I still wanted to ask her, but I could tell they hadn't been anything she wanted to get into right now. Maybe in time, we might get a chance to speak about them.

"Your grandfather's ring you left on the island I kept and wore hoping I would find you again. I honestly thought you were dead but at times I could swear I heard your voice. I would hear you laugh, scream and cry. I would even see your face in the ring, but I could watch you age as well. But there were times it was almost unbearable. I would hear you cry, or I would see these horrible creatures after you and you looked terrified so I had to find out if you were alive, I kept thinking I wouldn't see these things if you were dead. But I kept feeling like you were still around. So, I went looking for you. Charlie, Dinah, and Aidelle came with me to help to look for you. Your friend Mia wanted me to pass on her hello and Bridgette, Tara, Najee and Zoë all miss you. Your friend Zoë is the main reason I was able to find you and Mia was the first to confirm you were still alive."

"We were just about to settle down for the night. Since we left the shade city I've been watching you here every night. I didn't know you would hear or see me. I hope I didn't upset you too much." The look of sadness went across her face.

I figured she was hinting she was ready for me to leave. Standing up I still hadn't known why she was running faster than a human, but I had the main answer I wanted, she seemed safe and wasn't interested in a relationship. Walking towards the door I wanted to escape before I could touch the door handle, she grabbed my hand standing right next to me.

"Do you need to leave? There's a guest room that Dinah can stay in if she wishes. I know she doesn't sleep but it would give her some privacy and Goseck needs sleep he's had a long night, so if you don't mind you can stay in here with me. I know you don't need sleep but I'm tired and I'm afraid I'll fall asleep on you, but I don't want you to leave yet. I just got you back." I could hear the desperate sound in her voice. Maybe she was right she was treating him like a father? But did that mean she wanted me? I felt so stupid for not knowing how to handle this.

"Let me ask Dinah she may just want to go back home and Goseck may not want me staying here?" Walking out of the room we joined Dinah and Goseck in the living room. They had been deep in conversation.

"Dinah, did you want to stay here, or did you need to head back?" I was hoping she might be able to decide for me.

But her answer hadn't helped any. Taking a bunch of papers that Goseck had given her to read while he went to sleep, she went into the guest room to have privacy to look over the papers. She didn't mind me staying here but wanted to stick around for a while, something had piqued her curiosity. Also, she was going to call Charlie to let him know what was going on. Even I knew my parents would be worrying about now. Smiling and happy everyone was staying. Harmony pulled me back into her bedroom closing the door.

"It will almost be like old times." Climbing into the bed pulling the covers back. I sat on top like I used to. I had felt like I was a friend now instead of anything else. Wrapping her arms around me as she laid down to sleep. This had been as painful to endure as it had been before I found her when I would hear her crying.

"I'm glad you didn't give up believing I was alive. I tried to find you, but I didn't know where else to look after I stopped at Charlie's house. I was worried something happened to you until I saw you in the stone again. I could always see you, but I didn't know where you were?" As she spoke, I put my arm around her.

"I just wished I could have protected you better. Our situation could have been different." Rubbing her arm, I could feel something strange, moving the shirt sleeve I had seen several deep laceration marks on her arm. Cringing I hated knowing she was in pain that I couldn't stop or prevent. Now she relied on this guy to protect her.

"There are things I wished were different but if they had been I never would have met all the people I did. I never would have been through what I had good or bad, I hate to say I wouldn't have traded any of it and most important you didn't get hurt during it. At least I hope you hadn't I'm sorry for making you worry about me." I wasn't sure if I wanted to tell her it was more than worry, I lost seven years of my life because I couldn't stand the thought of her being dead and that I lost my sanity because I was hearing her voice all the time. Then something I learned from Rose. She told Jacob what pained her, and she let him know how she felt she made it clear she loved him but wasn't going to hold back. I decided I needed to do the same.

"I spent seven years trying to cope with your death hidden away in a cabin, in the middle of the woods, and under piles of snow until I could barely make it out. I was losing my sanity every time I thought I heard you cry, and I couldn't console you. I was positive you were alive and in pain and I had no way of stopping it. I had seen this image of you with these creatures about to attack you and all I could do was watch. I don't want you to feel bad but trust me, if it had been me dying to protect you or going through that again I would rather die." I didn't want to make her feel guilty, but I had to let her know how I felt especially if she wanted this to be a friendship. I wanted what would make her happy. No longer laying down, she sat up. I wasn't sure what she was going to do.

Pushing the covers back I almost thought she was going to leave the room. Sitting directly in front of me I could see the tears stream down her face, and I felt horrible that I said all of that to her and wished I could take it back. Except I couldn't deny what I went through, it would be saying the loss of her wasn't great, except it was, it changed the way I was able to look at the world, and how I looked at others. She straddled my legs as she sat down on my lap getting closer to me. Placing her right hand on my cheek, placing her forehead against mine then speaking in the lightest whisper.

"I'm sorry. I was hoping to prevent you from getting hurt. I didn't want to risk leaving you in the cabin, so I took you back to the island where we first met because I knew you could get back to your family safely. I wanted to protect and keep you safe. If I had followed what Sophie told me to do, either her or you and Charley would have died, possibly all three. I did what I thought was best, I didn't have much time to decide. I haven't had one day go by that I didn't think of you. I loved you so much, but I never knew if I was doing the right thing by staying away from you. I wasn't thinking straight. I should have thrown my arms around you when I first saw you instead, I fainted and the first thing I thought had been when Goseck finds I'm missing again, he was going to panic. I'm sorry this wasn't done differently. I thought of so many ways I would have responded when I saw you again, but I messed it up. I love you so much." Leaning towards me, she kissed me on the lips.

Pulling her closer to me wrapping my arms around her holding her close not daring to let go I said the words I wanted to say. "I love you." Kissing her, I wasn't going to let her go, not after she was finally mine again.

"I promise no matter what happens I will bring you with me." One of the things I had loved about her human side, no matter how she tried to fight to stay awake she always managed to fall asleep eventually. As I lay there by her side holding her in my arms, I would never let her out of my sight again.

Imagine what it looked like for my parents and other relatives who thought the doc was dead only to see him brought back to life by looking like another man. Over the next several years we learned how Goseck impersonated the doc and what happened those days that Harmony disappeared when Sophie waited for Harmony to summon her. It seemed no matter what happened the life stone would be discovered and either it or Harmony would be forced to use it for various reasons. One of those reasons had been the shade city. As much as she found she loved living there it wasn't fair for the queen to use her in the ways she did. Gifting Harmony powers of a shade no doubt was to gain her trust.

We made a special effort to visit both of Harmony's friends Mia and Zoë, being careful who had seen us come and go. I had even run into the vampire who alerted us she had still been around. I no longer felt divided as if I lost my mind. I was able to concentrate on being with my family again instead of my heart wishing it was elsewhere. Learned about Harmony's secret gift that had been given to her as she was still discovering what it meant to be a shade.

Instead of moving in with my parents as I had done in the last few years, I wound up moving in where I never would have thought possible before. I moved in with both Harmony and Goseck. After getting to know him and how much he did to protect Harmony. I couldn't help but feel respect towards him even after a short time I started calling him dad like a real father-in-law. Originally, I had been the only one who moved in however with Dinah spending so much time here it seemed like she never left. Dinah and Goseck had become close friends discussing life. They seemed rather fascinated even by the discoveries he had made over the years. Eventually, Dinah claimed the guest room as her own.

As Charlie once said to Sophie, they kept to themselves as a family because it was easier to protect each other, they had been a relatively small family, but after a while, you cannot control the natural desires of even vampires. The family has expanded over the years expanded adding new little ones to the family as well as ones we never thought possible. A man we never would have assumed us accepting had now become a regular in our family.

Chapter Three

Blending in

Over the next several years we heard the rumors of a vampire king. A self-proclaimed title a vampire made for himself. We hadn't been familiar with him however we assumed he might be someone that might cause problems later. For the most part, Harmony found she liked going to work with Rose and Jacob on the tropical tours that took people through the rainforest and explaining the various vegetation and animals. Sophie immersed herself in her old way of life being a gypsy which had been strange for Charlie to get used to but had also grown more interested the more he learned about it. Nichole and Anthony had taken a second honeymoon while Goseck and Dinah had taken their first. They had a rather small impromptu wedding on the beach. We were spending time as a family; Charlie made the mistake of saying it was nice to everyone together. Harmony and I guessed immediately the look both Goseck and Dinah shared, and they had Charley officiate the wedding after he made the statement. Harmony and I had taken some time out to make a vacation out of it. We stayed in her old room in the Eurubian city. As much as they used to fear vampires, they had grown to trust our family.

The Eurubian people had been such an accepting group even taking in perishing or struggling groups into their homes. They only refused a few groups out of fear of what they might do to others however our family earned their right to be part of the city as they grew to know us and not fear us. It slowly became our second home. The queen occasionally visited from the shade city; she was impressed how our family blended in with the others however still did not allow for mixing in her city but certainly was welcoming here.

The Eurubian people were getting ready to celebrate their yearly life festival. The place looked amazing as they strung lights everywhere. Anything against the black onyx background made every color stand out. Over time Lucian met many of Harmony's friends she made along the way. It wasn't difficult to see why they were naturally drawn to her. She had always been rather friendly and comforting. Our entire family made it for the festivities, all sixteen of us. Not a usual family when most vampires preferred smaller groups of two or three but then most hadn't had their full families as vampires either. Some added other family members from outsiders, ours had original family and still counting.

We had been busy getting things ready that we hadn't noticed much of the activity outside of the city. We had been enjoying others' company as our family over the next few years joined Mia and her family in what we still liked to refer to as the palace. Some of us were working in the hospital helping others. Aiden found he was rather skilled in working with illness and injuries. Even Lewis found areas his experience could help establish classes for the children starting a school within the city. As most of us hadn't needed sleep we had been awake as Zoë made her way into the city followed by several of her friends from the shade city. She shared the horrifying news that the queen had gone missing while the other royals had no idea where she had gone. While the city was still to be guarded the other royals had gone into hiding fearing the worst. Most assumed they used the portals to hide in various worlds while only a few of us knew the truth.

Sophie had gone to the shade city making every intention to find out what had been happening. The people there were very nervous about attacks now that the royal family left even though they were worried about their safety they worried if they knew something they had not been sharing with the rest of the city. The protection chants had still been in place as Sophie tested them however, she found she could also manipulate them. Word of the vampire lord became much stronger letting others know he planned on taking over the shade city only to control the portal. If the portal could have been closed it would have been however no magick seemed to affect it. At first many had been nervous about having vampires in and out of the city however it had only been our family as they knew we were there to help protect them.

Charlie decided it was time to collect information to find out what others knew about the vampire lord and what he was planning on doing with the portal and how it would affect us and the humans of the earth. As we found he had been grabbing others changing them without their consent leaving many unguarded and tutored in the ways of living as a vampire. The vampire lord had been one of the lady's many creatures she created. Only he had been changed as a mere human eventually getting away from the lady no longer wanting to be controlled but wanting control for himself. With her gone, there was nothing to stop him as he wanted control over the shade city.

Over the several months, Sophie had been studying the two large portals in the hidden part of the palace. She had only found them when she and Charlie had gone walking exploring through the many caverns and tunnels until they came across it. We all expected some shiny glowing thing that a person might walk through. However, we had no idea how it would work? On the back wall, a large round stone-forming outward of black onyx surrounded by the white crystal-looking material that the rest of the city had been designed in. The same black onyx from its sister city. We both wondered if they might have one similar to this? We know we had been told this was the only spot, but would it be possible to have two and not know about the second one? Not wanting to risk touching it they waited for Goseck to come in case it only responded to a shades touch. The stone glowed to the point we could see through it; however, we couldn't get through ourselves.

As Goseck explained the only way in had been with the royals all together opening the stone. This was to safeguard the earth, the city of the shades, as well as the other worlds in case the one controlling it had been coerced by evil. Each had their role as we found the queen had left herself neutral so that she would only be opening and closing it as the others allowed it. The shade city had been capable of protecting itself for centuries until now. That's when we found out the stone of life urgently needed to be protected once more. The alternative had been to use the life stone to call yourself to another person on the other side, as being a shade, the stone recognized the person as a human still. Whether or not a non-guardian could use it no one had tested that theory yet. It had been so difficult to trust anyone however we did have Goseck now.

One of the guards that had been sent out a while ago came back with news, the information we wanted but not exactly what we planned on hearing. The vampire had been searching for any evidence that the stone was not destroyed. Somehow, he had been informed that it might be in use. Not sure if the queen would give up that information if it meant her life or if someone else had been on the inside that gave out the information. Even though few still knew it existed. Somehow it leaked out. We hated to think there was someone in the shade city we couldn't trust. After deliberating for a while, we decided to keep alert to anything unusual and hope for the best. Charlie and Sophie left a few minutes ago to go to the sister city to search for a replica or at least possibly the reverse of the onyx stone in the Eurubian city.

Back in our room Harmony and I had been talking about the stone and what she wanted to do to keep it safe. So far, we felt the safest place to keep it was in the closet of the shade city home however all the royals had known it worked its way back home the first time. With the royals' gone Sophie was able to control the ban on vampires allowing our family in. However, it left the city vulnerable to others who might attack so we didn't stay there very often. Only when Charlie and Sophie had been there having the defenses been down but not for long. We stayed behind in the Eurubian city when Charlie called us letting us know they were on their way back. They were able to confirm there were replica stones in each palace. The one in the Eurubian city was a similar stone to the onyx stone. It was in the same area however instead of the prime stone being made of onyx, it was a white crystal with black onyx outlining it.

Harmony had been holding the life stone as the rest of the family had been filling up the living room to talk about the life stone and the best way to protect it. Lucian sat behind harmony out of habit not wanting to risk a flash in case she focused on something too hard. She had been able to heal him but avoiding the pain had been much better. Looking into the stone she had seen one of the robed royals. Harmony didn't know where the place was that she was seeing, the royal was crouching behind a bush trying not to be noticed. Keeping an eye on her I wanted to know if she was alright. As the family said only, if she could come back through the stone would be unable to go there to save her. I watched as she moved to hide trying not to be seen.

Then as she turned quickly something surprised her from behind as she felt the jolt, I had slightly jumped myself from the surprise. I had been concentrating on her so much that when her attacker had come after her she phased out right in front of him. I could see the person who had been so angry almost being able to catch her until she was gone from his grasp in a puff of smoke, she appeared shocked in front of us. She appeared without her guard, not that I had seen any with her as I watched her.

"Who are you, what do you want with me?" Standing back, I knew she had recognized where she was, however, she had never been aware of any power being used here before.

"Sorry, I concentrated on you so strong when he almost attacked you, I guess I called you to me. I'm Harmony. I met you about seven years ago in the palace when I first moved there with Goseck my father." Lucian had been standing behind me, he was as surprised as all of us had been having the royal standing before us. Not that she seemed to know how to react to having a vampire in her midst.

"Thank you for saving me however I cannot stay here. They will be searching for me as they do my brothers and sisters. We must not be found; do you have any of the guards here?" She must have left before Sophie ever stepped foot inside the shade city with Charlie even though the citizens themselves holed themselves up in their homes while he had been there.

"There aren't any guards here in the Eurubian city, as far as we understood the queen went missing and all of the other royals had gone into hiding, guards are watching over the shade city but that's about it. You can hide here until we can find a safe way of moving you, I could even move you around using the stone."

"I need to find my brothers and sisters. They were to meet me and the queen. I fear the worst for them if the queen has gone missing. There was a disturbance when we had taken off. The queen was to join us later but none of us wound up at the proper destination." She looked worried that she may be the last one to protect the gate to other worlds far inside the palace.

"I pulled you to me. I could always try and call them. I haven't been able to enter myself but maybe I could call them all here and then we can find a place to hide you? Lucian?" Not even having to voice too much he agreed to try to call the others that he would get Charlie to see if he had any idea how to safely hide the royals from discovery.

With Lucian taking off. I sat there with Mia next to us as I concentrated on the other royals. I had been thankful that I remembered what their faces looked like since I had only seen them twice, but I had seen the queen more often than that. One by one, surprised as the others appeared in front of me. My room had begun to get rather crowded as Mia slowly walked each one to a larger room in her parents' home where they would be a little more comfortable.

Charlie and Sophie hadn't taken too long to show up. Everyone had been offering suggestions until Rose stood up and said the one we all agreed on.

"The one place that is the hardest to find someone is in plain sight, why not hide them in different locations but among humans? I blended in rather well and there are enough of us that can watch over them. At least if they blend in no one would ever think they would be with humans. Most would assume they would try to hide with other shades." We all nodded in agreement, figuring this would be the safest way since there had been enough guards to protect the city however not enough to follow the royals around. We tried figuring out how to split them up and who would get them.

It had been decided that Goseck and Dinah would take Lucas and Madison with them to the cabin. Rose and Jacob with Larissa had taken Gabriella and James with them while Lewis and Evangeline took Logan and Elija with them. Deciding to leave the city for a while, Lucian and I moved out to Charlie's winter cabin for a while with Victoria and Natalie. Making sure in case the city had been watched we kept it as silent as possible only having my new family leaving and heading to their homes as I would transport one group to each place using the stone and then come back the last time to collect Lucian and the others. Charlie and Sophie decided to stick around a little longer.

I tried to find the queen however I couldn't seem to find her. Either she had been under a protection spell to not show where she had gone, or she did not wish to be seen or found blocking any others from looking for her or finding her. I tried several times, and every so often I would search in the stone looking for her. One of the nights I had been looking at the stone after searching and not finding anything and relaxing holding it in my hands. Natalie had come into the room sitting on the bed with me.

"It's been a long time since I had last seen the life stone this close. As beautiful as it looks it is one sight I don't miss. The last person who held it the way you do, had been Iuliana. She would spend hours gazing at it almost as if she was stroking a favorite cat of hers, almost motherly. Mind if I take a look?" She hadn't made a move for the stone, but I felt it was alright for her to look.

Waving her hand over the stone almost cupping the smoke as it had come out of the stone facing herself, she alone saw the vision she was looking for.

"I have to admit I never liked this thing, but it serves its purpose. I am thankful you do not see the things I do when I look into it. Never a pleasant sight or memory. I was always thankful not to be a guardian." Not even explaining the sight that made her smiling face change to one of almost sadness, she stood up walking out of the room with her sister in tow.

For the next several months, we had been fortunate not to have any attacks on the cities even though there had been whispering among vampires wondering where the royals had gone. At least the shade city had been safe however those who wanted to gain control of its power still searched for the royals but for now, had been rather silent about their searching being careful not to be found out. No one could give us information as to who the self-proclaimed vampire lord had been or where his location was, so for all we know he could have been quietly watching us.

I wasn't worried about how Rose would be doing with the ones staying with her since she had been around other humans for so long. The only thing we had to worry about was how to occupy them since we had no idea how long this was going to be? Gabriella and James started working on the tour with Jacob and Rose to find they liked it. James had been fascinated by humans and the way they looked at the world. He seemed to enjoy their persistence more than anything. Larissa had loved having the extra company which meant more attention for her. Both Gabriella and James spent time spoiling her. Even speaking to her in their native tongue. She seemed to be picking it up much faster than English. On one of the days, they had been playing with her Gabriella commented to Rose.

"It's funny how different age is here; she is considered the child and yet in our homeland, we were the children. Perhaps it's because we live for so long?"

There had been a bit more privacy where Jacob and Rose lived even though most of the time instead of staying at home, they had chosen to go with each other to help on the tours. After the first run-through, James had the entire tour memorized.

On one of the mornings that James and Gabriella hadn't felt like going to work, they stayed at the house playing with Larissa. Taking her outside to play, they were curiously watching her almost as if she had been a rarity taking out of her pocket a red stone glowing bright crimson red. It caught Larissa's attention wanting to play with it. Life was rather quiet with not much going on. Life was more laid back here.

Goseck and Dinah had their hands full since Lucas and Madison seemed more interested in exploring as one almost drowned in the nearby lake and the other not watching for cars was almost run over. Even if they wanted to get out on their own, they had to be constantly watched. At least Dinah had experience with her nephew and niece being sneaky and clever. Madison had a temporary cloaking spell she would use to hide to get out however she still couldn't cover her footprints. They acted more like partners in crime rather than the calm royals we had all seen them as. The longer we had gotten to know them they were more like innocent children than anything. When they were in the palace every move or decision had been made for them. While here, they were learning to make their own choices no longer dictated by anything other than those that were to protect them.

At times we would get phone calls from Madison and Lucas letting us know that Dinah and Goseck had been bickering like children with each other. Being married, their friendship was much stronger, they also knew exactly how to get under each other's skin. We thought about joining them a few times however it was safer keeping the royals separated or it would have been easier to spot or detect them if they had been together or an easier more dangerous target if all had been captured at once.

Lucian stayed at home as I took the girls out shopping for clothing. With all the moving around I found other than what I was wearing, and one other outfit Mia had given me. I only had those to wear. At least we wouldn't have a problem going out in the sunlight to go shopping. Not being used to wearing anything other than robes it had been difficult to pick out clothing that would fit and blend in with the others around. The styles changed so much but I agreed I wouldn't make them wear anything that I wasn't wearing either. After searching several of the stores and frustrating countless salesclerks, we finally had a few outfits for all of us as we brought them home. Lucian was happy he couldn't go out during the day. He hadn't wanted to get stuck shopping even though I still picked up a couple of outfits for him.

Every night I would search in the stone looking for the queen but no such luck. At least now Natalie and Victoria looked like normal human girls and from the way they were dressed no one would have assumed otherwise.

It had been difficult knowing what to do with them hoping we wouldn't insult or degrade them. The two girls with us had been the youngest so it had been hard hiding their age since a few asked about their schooling when they first moved here. I had a diploma at least to show them if I had to but the girls hadn't been to a traditional human school. Natalie seemed interested and had no problem blending in with the others while Victoria fought it a little more.

I admit I would have complained about going to school at her age also, but it was either that or getting a part-time job. No one would assume the royals to be working. Figuring learning would be easier they had chosen school. As much as Victoria said she hated school it was hard to get her away from it. Every event she could get into, she did. She joined the cheerleaders, debate club as well as committee for homecoming. Any event that went on she seemed to get into and take over the control of it. On an average night, our home seemed like it had been packed full of teenagers.

The town had grown so much since Charlie had last been here, he thought we would still have privacy. What he hadn't realized was if he didn't buy the several acres he did, he would have a neighbor even closer. We were surrounded by houses in town. The old asylum that had once been here has been dug up and removed for housing and apartments. Part of the town had grown bringing with it thankfully more jobs. While the girls went to school to pass time, we had both taken on part-time jobs also.

At least the last time we heard from Charlie he reported they knew where the vampire lord had been, sadly it hadn't been too far from the shade city. They had been keeping an eye on it for any of the royals or anyone else who might know anything. At least no one was getting hurt yet however very rarely did anyone bother leaving anymore. At least the girls that were with us had blended in even speaking more like the teenagers here. I felt tired and wanted a break from the loud music and the kids goofing off. Sad when I used to be one and I was more tired now. I wondered what my life would have been like if I had still been with Beth? I felt as if my life and the way I looked at things changed when I had been introduced to this new world. But then who wouldn't. I wondered if not knowing the human world was having the same influence on the royals as their world had on me?

Lucian had been out as he told others for a solitude walk when I knew personally, he was hunting and getting away from the crowd. Closing the door, I had pulled out the stone looking at it wondering when it would change my life next. It must have realized I was going crazy waiting not knowing when this was going to be over. I didn't want to seem ungrateful or self-centered, but I had yet to be alone with Lucian since we found each other, even during our vacation we had others with us. Looking at the stone I wasn't sure how the royals were going to take this, and Lucian hadn't answered his cell phone but then when it rang, I heard it ring in his jacket pocket in the closet. I tried to call Charlie however there were times they kept their phone off. Instead, I wound up calling Goseck on his cell phone. I tried to remain calm because I could have misunderstood what I was seeing but it seemed so strange.

As I told Goseck I figured he knew the queen better than I had but even still it didn't prepare him for what I told him. I had seen her speaking almost as if holding an assembly of people around her. It was rather dark, and she didn't have her cloak on her. At first, I thought it was someone else oddly showing up in the stone. I hadn't realized who she was until she put the white robe on. I saw her face and I knew immediately who she was, but she had been wearing the clothing of a demon hunter. She didn't look as if she was in trouble however I couldn't tell if she was the vampire lord or if she was speaking for him? How could she turn on her people, her own family? If she planned on taking over, she already had control. She could have come and gone when she wanted to not that the others would have allowed her to take others with her. Maybe she wanted full control over it? The stone could pull others out but couldn't transport them directly into it. I was still trying to figure out why she would still want the stone? She had at one time wanted me to leave the stone while she had me control some creatures. That's when I realized the creatures had been hers and not the midnight madam. I wasn't the only one who couldn't get a message to Charlie and Sophie; Lorah tried calling them for the last week as she didn't want to try to get too close since there had been a lot of activity outside of both cities.

I felt nervous waiting for Lucian to get back at night. I know he liked going out longer because during the day he's cooped up for so long. I couldn't help but worry about him. Keeping an eye on the girls I was worried about what was going on. I hoped no one found any of the royals but then I also worried about my friends in the shade city would be killed. After many of the kids had gone home leaving me with our two. I sat down on the couch with the girls asking them a question that made them wonder why I was asking it.

"I don't mean to bother you but if the vampire lord wanted to take over the city and managed to get in, is there any way other than having your siblings open it together. Is there another way of controlling the portal?" I didn't want to worry them, but I did want to know if there had been another way of controlling the portal.

I felt bad for spoiling their fun night with grim news, but they seemed to take the question alright.

"If we die. Our powers shift to our surviving siblings and if we are all gone the queen inherits our powers so there should always be someone protecting the city. This had been put in place by a very young mind. You made friends with him; his name is Najee. He is very limited in the use of magick but what he has figured out has been amazing. He wanted to be kept silent and out of it in case anyone was to find out, but Victoria and I are the only ones that know he did this magick, which is why he knew you had the life stone, and the queen knew you had it." When she said this, I was surprised and not at all what I understood before.

"I thought the queen did the protection enchantments over the shade city protecting it from vampires. That to keep both worlds safe she closed off the portal so that nothing can get in or out without her control?" I was getting more confused by the minute by this.

"We as the royalty are from another world and control the portal. We open and close it as we deem fit. The queen governs over the earth's domain, she was to protect the shade people and by doing this she would be given privileges by our people; however our own home had been destroyed by vampires. We had not felt she was ready to have control over the portal power, similar to the life stone, it does strange things to people. Even ourselves we had forgotten what it was like to loosen up and live. We have been so reserved for so long out of fear that we might lose control and become harmful with the power of the portal. You realize most of the stone's potential yet is nowhere near as powerful as the portal. Yet the stone itself can yield power over it that not even we can. The life stone has far more powers even in other worlds or slightly less in the lesser magical worlds." After talking for a while, the girls went into their rooms to get ready for the next day.

I didn't have the heart to tell them they had been correct about not giving power to the queen. At times when I saw them goofing off with the teenagers, I had forgotten how serious and controlled they could be. They had forgotten what it was like to be children.

Sitting in my room. I waited patiently for Lucian to come back home while the rest of the family worried about what was going on with Charlie and Sophie since neither could be reached. If the city had been taken over it was more important now than ever to keep everyone hidden and safe. It was driving me crazy while I waited for Lucian to get back home, and I knew it had been late however in case anything was happening. I wanted the others to know also. I called Rose letting her know what I had seen along with what the girls told me. She said she would pass on the information to the rest of the family and would let me know as soon as they could find out what was going on with Charlie and Sophie. Lewis changed out of his human form and into his natural wolf form to scout out the area to find out what was going on.

Before Lucian had a chance to open the door, I grabbed a hold and hugged him. I had been so worried I thought about using the life stone to call him to me, but I refrained from using it for personal gain, my guilt stopped me from using it when it had not been called for. Trying not to let fear rule me was difficult, especially when the fear is losing someone you already lost once. At least I didn't have to say a word for Lucian to understand what I was feeling. Wrapping his arms around me I felt safe for the moment. I knew things were going to keep changing and I doubted I would like most of them. Especially for some of the scenes, the life stone showed me that I couldn't get myself to explain to anyone else, especially since they were things I could not even imagine myself doing.

Chapter Four

Missing with a twist

A few more months passed and still no signs of Charlie or Sophie. It had been almost as if they vanished into thin air. At least we know why we hadn't been able to contact them. Their cell phones and personal belongings had still been in the Eurubian city however the city itself seemed to be deserted without a trace, they must have gone missing when we left. Lewis had scouted out the entire area. None of them had gone to the sister city while theirs had been emptied as if no one had ever been there. I hadn't heard from Mia in a long time, and neither had she indicated there were any problems the last time we spoke. The only reason we found any belongings of Charlie and Sophie had been the location where they left them. In the lowest part of the castle in front of the black onyx stone, they must have dropped their cell phones in front of it either on purpose to show they were there or by accident.

We guessed maybe they were walking down here either surprised or somehow the stone itself played a role. Either way, it doesn't explain why everyone else disappeared or why there hadn't been any hint of where they had gone to. I know if Mia knew she was leaving she would have said something to me. It was either sudden or forced but there had been no sign of a struggle or anything. When most creatures or people move, there would be something left behind. However, if you were to look at this place you would never know anyone ever lived there before.

Until we heard otherwise or had a sign to take off, we would stay put blending in as we hoped it would throw off those who would pose a threat. Keeping a closer eye on the girls we were more careful about where they were and who they were around, making sure they were safe. Instead of explaining it to them, we had shown them the stone, letting them see for themselves what the queen had been doing. Talking amongst themselves they were able to speak to each other without using their phones or anyone listening in on their conversation other than who they chose. They cut short some of their new activities to be at home feeling safer and closer to us.

When it was prom night, we thought that Victoria would at least spend time at the dance after all the hard work she had put into it. However, she felt the kids would be busy enough at least that they would not be missed. Her reasoning was there were too many people, and something could happen. Natalie shared something with her sister, not wanting to worry as we assumed they had seen something. We didn't push the matter feeling if they wanted us to know they would have said something. Natalie had come close to saying it once or twice but held her tongue.

Keeping an eye on any new people in town there had only been one gentleman and his son that moved in. To be on the safe side we were careful around them not to let on about any of us being new. They hadn't stuck around for too long. Supposedly his job relocated him for a short time and then removed them as quickly.

We made it a regular habit to go to the movies together with a few of the girl's friends trying to blend in more as a family. One of the afternoons we had been shopping picking up a few things at the store when Nichole called us to let us know that Lewis was now missing. He had been out with Logan, but neither had come home. Evangeline panicked, not sure if they were being watched. She had seen extra steps around the house in the snow. So, Evangeline and Elija were making their way to us. I tried hard as I could to concentrate on finding them with the stone except, I couldn't get a sense of them, it was as if they evaporated into thin air also. Where were they all going? If they had found a better hiding place, they wouldn't have left Evangeline behind with the young boy to defend themselves so something must have happened, and I hated sitting back not knowing what was going on.

The people in the shade city hadn't seen the queen or heard from the sister city. Neither had any of the family been there recently. I talked to Zoë, and she said the city had been rather quiet, not that anyone risked leaving once they heard the sister city disappeared. Lucian had grown even more protective making sure when he hunted, he hadn't gone too far and always careful to make sure he might be able to leave a mark or something behind to let me know where he was in case anything was to happen. It made me sick knowing he could disappear on me.

In a few days, Evangeline showed up with Elija. That's when we noticed an increase in vampires in the area. When Lucian had gone hunting one night, he had to be careful at first. He hadn't been sure if humans were out walking at night even though it had been rather strange to be out this late. That's when he realized they had been vampires also keeping an eye on him. Not being able to hunt for a while we started to feel like prisoners in our own homes. The girls didn't bother going to school instead we called in sick for them so we wouldn't draw attention from the school. The family disappeared across the street being filled with neighbors we didn't know, even though we pretended not to notice them, they kept a close eye on us. Feeling it had been time to move out of the area we tried to think of a place that might be safe. All the places we had been associated with started being watched by others, even Nichole let us know they were staying at home now not venturing out because of the spies. Nichole had always been good at eavesdropping on or finding out information. At one time she thought of being a spy herself finding it rather intriguing. She kept herself hidden when spying on her neighbors when she found they were vampires discussing how they had not found who they were looking for and that they needed more time. We could only guess these were ones working for the queen or as we learned her name Nevaeh, this is the name the vampires referred to her as.

As they had done this, I kept vigilant with the life stone watching her and the others who had shown up in the neighborhood. It helped to be able to spy on them from a safe distance, then the time came when I had seen them creeping up to the house in a rather large group. Instead of risking it, we transported ourselves to Nichole. I hadn't moved so many people before at once, it was much harder. At least with the girls, the flash wouldn't affect however Lucian had to hold on from behind, it would have affected him much more. I had also gone to get Rose, Jacob, and the ones who had been staying with them. We felt at one time it would have been better to stay separated for the sake of the royals. However now not knowing what is happening to the ones missing, we figured we might have a better fighting chance if we stuck together.

We knew we couldn't stay here for too long. We had to find a safe place that had not been searched yet. Then I had an idea. Checking first to make sure it had still been there. I doubted any of those looking for the royals would know of this place. After moving everyone into a few groups, I moved us to the best temporary place possible. My old training bunker. It had still been there, no one had the chance to take it apart. For being a battle zone and having fire burn the inside it had still stayed intact.

The only ones that had been determined to stay put were Dinah and Goseck feeling they were still safe. No one had even come close to where they had been. I didn't want to risk anything happening to him but at least I knew he could defend himself and the others safely, after all, I know I wasn't the easiest to watch over and he managed to keep me alive. At the first chance, they needed us, Goseck promised me he would call. The only time I had been here I had my other instructors here. Focusing on them I wondered if they knew anything. Sitting in the center of the room I worked on creating a dreamscape, something I knew Jacob had been familiar with and insisted on coming with in case there had been trouble inside of it. He wanted to help protect me while the others kept an eye on our bodies. Once in, I called Mikhail to us, I hadn't been able to focus enough on the others as Mikhail said they were busy. It's why I was able to call him to me when he heard my voice.

He heard from Sophie a few days before the people went missing in the sister city. He said he sensed an enchantment spell over the city cloaking it, that the people were still there however they were in hiding. Probably why Lewis hadn't noticed it. He hadn't been too experienced with cloaking spells, not that I would have picked up on it if it had been done by someone more experienced than myself, which I guessed Sophie had done, however that does not explain their disappearance. She was a vampire also and couldn't enter the city unless she dropped the protection of the city which she was able to do with the queen gone, but they hadn't been there they were in the sister city which did not have the same enchantment on it.

Looking directly at me he asked, "are you sure you cannot think of one place the queen seemed interested in that you knew of? You told Iuliana about the creatures and how the queen wanted you to leave the stone on the side. How you trapped the creatures in the crystal because of an enchantment you put on them. Have you ever been able to see them in your stone or are they blocked from you also?" After reminding me I felt so stupid.

How I could have forgotten something as simple as that. I was thankful I kept up with my teachers as they kept trying to teach me more ways of using the stone. The reason they could disappear into thin air would be if they had been trapped in a crystal, since it's not like the queen had control over the portal and couldn't hide them in there. At some point, I was going to have to use the stone against Nevaeh. There had to be some way of tricking her. I knew how to get rid of her vampire followers but how could the life stone, work against a shade if I had been one now and the stone accepted me still?

By now she must have known we were hiding the rest of the royal family, however, the others let us know they had yet to absorb their brother's powers. So, he still must have been kept alive. Najee must not have let her know she would have total control if they all had been dead. At least this way it would keep them alive if she had her hands on them. As far as Nevaeh understood, Najee had been a simple shade of the people with a higher standing handpicked to assist the royals because he was trustworthy and put their wishes first at all costs.

What they hadn't realized as Mikhail filled us in on, that even the royals were not sharing with us had been that he was their king, their very own father. He was believed to have died when their hometown had been destroyed. He took on an entirely different image when they escaped to our world. The queen stated it was a vampire who decimated their home world however, Najee had known it was a shade that had done it which is why he came here searching for that one to be brought to justice. The royals were not shades but shapeshifters, ones that proved themselves worthy of protecting shades, humans, vampires, and other creatures from destroying each other. The royals were not shapeshifters in the way that Lewis had been where he could turn into an owl or a wolf, they were only able to take on appearances such as people which made it so easy for them to blend in since their form had been so similar.

Unable to destroy the portal to prevent other stronger entities from other worlds from coming through to destroy other worlds, they had been stuck here hoping to find a way of stopping it while they fell in love with the earth. Now making earth their new home they decided to stay knowing while they were in the shade city, they could control the portal, until the queen had gone crazy with power hoping she could accomplish the one thing that the lady in black hadn't been able to do. Mikhail and the other guardians have been learning how exactly the queen fit into all of this, and why the royals hadn't wanted to share this information. After all, queen Nevaeh had been the mother to the lady in black. When I learned this, my head started to swim. I hadn't been the only one watching her as Mikhail pointed out. He had been learning much over the last several years putting things together.

"I thought shades could die. I don't understand how some can live to be so old and yet not die, when does immortality kick in? And how did she get into the shade city if it's protected against vampires?" I probably should have been able to answer this one myself, but I felt so overwhelmed.

Smiling back at me he understood how I was feeling and never once made me feel stupid or told me that I should have known this or thought it through before asking. Mikhail and my other teachers had indeed been patient with me. At least I didn't feel bad if they had been around for so long and still were learning the truth of what was going on.

"In truth, the protection was never there. It only blocked out other vampires that did not have her permission or those creatures she didn't wish to have come in. That way she could protect herself from attack from others. She wanted control over the portal and so did her daughter. She kept her out hoping not to have competition getting to it however she also wanted the life stone and waited for her daughter to get it as she planned on stealing it from her." Looking down at the stone that I held in my hands, I wondered how a stone like this could become such a sought-after object?

Was I so blind not to notice the power, or had I not been educated enough about it? I wished I could have met her sister, the one who created this in the first place. She had to be such an incredibly intelligent person. I was in awe of her and had uncontested respect for her. Without having to ask him he answered in a rather strange way.

"All worlds have their secrets. Even demons and angels have their secrets along with raising the dead. Sometimes we think death is the end and we are surprised when death had not come to us at all. There is a world in which her body had been sent to that as near-death as you can be, then by miracle chance brought the impossible back to life. The one truly who can stop all of this would be the creator of the stone. We only protect using the stone until the rightful owner assumes full authority again." Was he telling me she was alive?

Even the lady in black said she killed her sister trying to take the stone. There had been several stories that were spread about it, that her sister handed it off in time to others when it recognized her as dead. It passed itself onto the next guardian as it had the last several centuries. Or was she never considered a guardian to begin with? I was beginning to wonder if death ever existed anymore.

"I think what he's meaning to say is that you need to find her. Maybe she has been stuck in another world unable to get here again or been prevented from entering because the portal has been locked? There must be some way for you to get in there, not that I want to risk the royal's life, but you may be able to control it. Sadly, we don't have a way for you to practice and if it's done wrong, you could die. The protection might fire against you. We can't risk the royals. They could be captured and used against us but then if they caught you, they could take over with the life stone itself." I know Jacob was making sense.

I needed to think this through. There was so much information I hadn't been ready for, not knowing how to handle it. Even Mikhail didn't have any answers to how I would get in or where to start searching.

"Then I have one last question, how does my friend Najee fit in all of this?" I couldn't help but wonder since the royals had spoken of him as controlling power and being involved with the portal.

"That is a very good question. He is a very good friend of yours and made it a point to be so. He is the only one that truly knows Katherine's sister. He alone hid her which is why his world had been destroyed. The one who destroyed the connection of the three portals, the power dispersed. There were several stones and crystals dispersed around the earth from the portal. The madam hid one of the largest stones which was the main source of the portal, it had tremendous power. She went after the power which belonged to the stone which was dispersed among his children. He is older than you think. He is not the person as you think yet a very strong part of the portal. He is the same. There is a reason you won't find a third matching stone in the Lipedian city, Najee was born from the stone while you and Goseck destroyed what was left of that stone." Smiling he simply turned and excused himself from the dreamscape leaving Jacob to look at me wondering what he meant. At that point I understood.

No one knew what Katherine Hawthorn's sister looked like let alone a name to call her by. Only Najee knew and I had to find him if I were to have any chance of finding her. As much as Lucian wanted to come with me, I needed to be alone for a while closing myself off in one of the rooms. Jacob had been filling them in on what we discussed. As the royals listened, they were surprised also that Najee survived. They hadn't known he renamed himself. They assumed this was to protect them as well as himself and the other woman. Now I had another person to look for. I had to find Najee and he even seemed to be missing, my one strong link to the portal.

I felt I was running out of time. I had to find him. At least I knew the royals were safe with so many looking after them. I had to find a way of making sure the others who disappeared were alright. The horrible thoughts that kept running through my mind had been if Nevaeh locked the missing away in a crystal with her horrible creatures. I had contact with the crystals not that I could call them to me but maybe I could see where they had been? When I looked at the portal there had been guards around it, so I knew I had to find Najee if I planned on getting in to search. I was hoping with his help he would link me directly to her not that I knew how the portal worked. The others understood about my not being interrupted. I kept struggling and getting frustrated trying to locate the crystals, they had to be protected. I had to somehow get close to them or under the protection unless they had been in the city itself under partial protection. If I were to go in, would she know I entered?

I started to wonder if I was going to have to risk it. I knew Lucian would hate the idea, but I didn't know what else to do. I kept feeling like I was running into a brick wall. I was running out of options even though I knew he would always say there has to be another way. Even now I wanted to move in quickly hoping if only I went in, it would be easier to hide but I made a promise never to put Lucian through the pain I caused him before. I still wanted to protect him keeping him from the pain. Besides once I went into the portal if it's how it worked, I may not be able to bring him with me anyway? Getting up and joining the others I knew they were still trying to come up with ideas. The look on Lucian's face couldn't be masked even if he understood what might happen.

"I had my theory of what might need to be done and thought it might help him cope with the idea if I presented it first, but ultimately it would be up to you." Jacob had been thinking the same thing.

At least while I went to the shade city, Nichole, Anthony, Rose, Jacob, and Evangeline would stay here with the remaining royals. I wanted to check on Goseck to see if they wanted to stay here as well while I did this. I figured he wasn't going to be happy about it, he always worried any time he thought I might be hurt or always trying to protect me.

His cell phone rang repeatedly with no one answering. I panicked pulling out the stone and looking for them. The cabin was empty as if no one had ever lived there. The guest room no longer contained Dinah's belongings. Neither had anything that Goseck owned, it was all gone. There had been no sign of the royals. Both Lucas and Madison were gone also. I wished I made them come here. They thought it was safe and now I've lost them. Lucian held onto me since he was worried I was going to transport myself but if it had been a trap or been caught. I couldn't risk any mistakes on my part. I knew what I had to do. I had to make sure I did it right. The only reason Nevaeh knew the life stone had been there, was she had seen me with it. She could have been spying on us as we did with her.

Searching around the room looking for anything that might give away our location or that might be spied on. I gathered and put them inside of a burlap sack covering them, then I put the life stone inside of my backpack hoping to keep anyone from watching me from it even though Sophic reassured me many times, only I could use it right now to watch from within, but then I wondered if perhaps the maker of the stone had that power and if so I wished she could see me.

I wasn't sure if I could get Lucian in or not but as I promised I would take him. The others were to stay here until we could come back. I had been hoping I might find the crystals or Najee, hoping he would know what to do, and then somehow if I couldn't find him maybe I could find some way to use the portal. Sadly, with only a few remaining royals the control over the portal, the power to run it wouldn't be the same since they had not absorbed the power from the others. At least we knew they were not dead, which left hope that our family was alive as well. While I was trying to think our plans over, I looked up at Lucian.

"What's wrong?" He was wondering why I stopped.

I must have had a strange look on my face. I kept hearing a voice calling me, one I hadn't heard in a long time. Not a matter of one voice, it had been two girls' voices. At first, I thought the royals were calling me, but no one here had been.

"I'm not sure but I think I hear someone calling me. But I don't know who?" I kept trying to place who it would be, who exactly would be calling me?

This was not the time to get frustrated overhearing voices. If this frustrated me now, then I must have put Lucian through the wringer when he heard me all the time. Leaning forward I hugged Lucian. I don't think he quite understood why unless he thought I heard something sad, then he let me know he understood exactly.

"Just think, I knew who was speaking with me and I was helpless to do anything. I understand what you're feeling." Then it hit me who I was hearing, Mia and Zoë.

Concentrating on them looking into the life stone. I could see them; they were hiding together in the shade city with another person. The one voice I didn't hear that was with them also had been Lorah. It looked as if she was trying to hide the girls. I wished I knew how she had gotten herself in. There must be a way to get in without alerting anyone there, even though I would prefer to call them out to keep them safe. The problem is it might give away our location pulling them from there to us.

I wanted to practice on an inanimate object. I knew I could affect other objects I just wasn't sure if I could call myself to an object that didn't have a life? As I watched them in the life stone. I had seen Zoë's bracelet I had given to her resting on the counter. First, I figured I would practice with something minor.

At least when they saw this hopefully, they would assume it was me that had been controlling it. As I watched moving it to another location, they watched seeing it untouched by anyone but moving by itself. I then concentrated on something I hoped would work if I knew I could get in, then I could move them out and then get back in myself without having to find another way of sneaking in.

Trying to picture the object in my mind I pictured myself in their room with it. Usually, when I did this, I would transport. I already learned how to show up where I needed to go except I hadn't been able to show up where there was a magickal shield, or to a physical object, it was usually a person or place. Unfortunately, It hadn't worked as the object wound up coming to me. Jacob had been watching me practice for a while when he came over and sat down next to me.

"In dreamscapes, there are many ways of controlling them. Either pulling people into them and leaving a body behind, which is spirit walking, or you can go into a dreamscape and pull their physical body in and pull it through to where you physically are. It is much more difficult to bring your own physical body into the dreamscape. I know you can do this; you've done this with the royals, you get results from emotional reactions so now that you're trying, it's difficult because you're not being affected by emotion. You won't get anywhere rushing yourself." I know Jacob was correct, I was forcing myself too much.

Taking a deep breath, I still wasn't good at creating a dreamscape, so I used the one Sophie never fully closed. I thought about the girls, first Zoe. I felt sick she was scared waiting there hoping for help. Jacob was right, I reacted much better on emotion. I know I had done this before, but it always seemed to work when I wasn't trying, usually surprising myself by the reaction. The room around me vanished as I reached out. I had taken Zoë by the hand. I was able to pull her to our location where she saw my body sitting there in a meditative state. I couldn't get over how amazing this looked but I didn't have time to enjoy it for now. Moving Lorah and Mia out of the room then, thankfully it was safer moving Lorah this way instead of the life stone which would have stripped her flesh. Jacob stayed in the dreamscape in case I needed any help.

I accomplished what I wanted, they were safe, and I found a way in not that I was able to get Lucian to join me. For some reason I hadn't been able to get him into the dreamscape, Jacob thought maybe his mind hadn't worked that way, he had remembered when Katherine Hawthorne tried to get some vampires in but couldn't, or even students however their minds worked on a different wavelength. He had to settle with looking after my body as I walked around in my spirit body. I didn't want to risk using the life stone until I knew what we were up against.

Mia explained how she had been out walking collecting herbs, when she came back the entire city vanished in a matter of hours showing no sign of life. Worried, she went to the shade city to see if they had still been there. At least she had shade qualities she was allowed into the city as she went to see Zoë, hoping she might have heard something. The guards had been coming and going all day from the city making people wonder what was going on? The guards had been bringing in bags full of what looked like crystals into the palace when one dropped from their bag. They waited for the guards to leave not noticing they dropped one, they picked it up bringing it back to their room with them. They had seen Lorah in the crystal with a group of others who had been locked in the crystal. At first, they thought they killed her and the others when they dropped the crystal, except when it broke open it freed them.

"Have you seen Najee? I need to find him." Both girls looked at me answering at the same time.

"He was in the crystal, he said you would be looking for him and he's waiting for you in the city." At least if he was waiting for me then I knew I had to get there.

I didn't know if it would have to be the physical form or if I could walk in my spirit body and do the same?

"You don't have to use your spirit body to get in there. Use the dreamscape and walk through it physically. I know Katherine Hawthorne did that when she snagged me from my parents when I was a baby." I was thankful Jacob was still here.

I didn't like being separated from my body for that long besides if anything happened here it makes it harder for them to protect me making me at risk in two ways.

"I don't want you going alone. I'm sure we can find some other way of getting in." I understood Lucian's panic.

I wouldn't have wanted him to go alone either but honestly, it would be safer and easier for one person than two. Without having to ask, Jacob volunteered to come with me. At least this way if I had a problem with the dreamscape, he could help me the best he knew how.

"With Jacob coming with me I won't be alone. I know you wanted to come but this is the safer way. As soon as we can. We will be back." I hadn't wanted to leave him either.

I kept feeling if we separated again one of these times, I might not see him again but if this did work, I could find Najee and hopefully find the others who had already been trapped.

Instead of sitting, and going into a meditative state, we stood focusing on the dreamscape that Sophie created. Normally no one else would see the dreamscape other than those drawn to it, this one was created in the physical room we were in, anyone around us could see it. The room in front of us became foggy with an arched color aura in front of us. The hazy fog was incredibly thick, and the colors have barely showed through it. No matter how many times I did this. I was never going to get used to the fact that a human like me was doing this! I wished

Beth could have seen this. Someday I'm going to have to surprise her even if it does give her a heart attack.

As with anything, it had taken me a while to get in. Once the dreamscape opened, as we walked in Jacob was more of a pro than I had been. Once in it took a little longer to focus on the room the girls had been in feeling it would be a safe place to start from. While we were in the center. I could look back and see the others still watching the fog that set in until they could no longer see us. We were in Zoë's parents' home. Stepping out of the fog I couldn't believe what happened. Long as I had the stone, I was going to be continuously amazed at what it could do. I wished I could have made a graceful entrance as Jacob had. Stepping in with my body had been a bit awkward but stepping out was like stepping on a slippery floor. I slipped and fell on my butt. Getting up and recouping whatever dignity I had, we made sure no one had been in the room.

The girls said Najee would be hanging out in the tavern. Since the queen disappeared, he hadn't been in the palace once. Not wanting to draw attention to himself, he stayed with the other shades. The city had been bustling like it normally would but more seemed skittish or fearful knowing what was coming. They feared someone taking over so no one risked leaving the city that they might be ambushed outside since anyone that had, has yet to come back. At least we had some cover, we could walk around with others. We needed to be careful not to let them see who we were especially the guards. It helped living here for a while, at least I knew a few of the back ways to getting around here. Always making sure I hadn't lost Jacob, yet we made our way for the back stairs. We didn't see any guards patrolling the back areas so we guessed it would be a safer route for now. Only a few people acknowledged they knew who we were but never once alerted anyone that they had seen us. One person handed Jacob a piece of paper however kept walking. On the paper it had a picture of me, they were looking for me.

We took the back stairs as far as we could. Stopping at the back end of the shop, it figures I would end up behind this one. It was where she gave me the crystal ball, entering and going through the shop. All the shop owner had done was nod in my direction. Before letting us go, she stood outside for a moment then stepped back in whispering there were no guards she could see and let us slip out.

Making our way halfway through the city keeping a constant watch on things, there had been a few guards making their way past us heading for the palace. As they had we turned to look at the stores hoping they wouldn't see our faces as they passed. They were working on something; we could have been standing in front of them and they wouldn't have noticed because of whatever it was that occupied them. There had been an open stretch I was worried that we would have been spotted. I wasn't sure if there would be those that were loyal to the queen assuming I had done something with her from the way we disappeared without warning, or if they would be angry if they noticed that Jacob was a half-breed? At least he blended in much better than Lucian would have.

Stopping for a moment I noticed there was a crowd of kids coming up and heading to the tavern. The old group I used to hang out with when I lived here. As they had gotten closer hoping none of them would fuss over the fact I was back, we seemed to blend in fine. I hoped once we were in, I would be able to spot Najee. Standing in the center it would have been difficult for anyone to see us, then as the group split into two groups, one group heading for the bar and the other group for our old table. We continued to walk to the bar with the others. I hadn't wanted to sit at the booth, or it would have been easier to spot us there. Up at the bar, there had been others, and it was easier to blend in. Looking around I hadn't seen Najee anywhere, but I wasn't sure if he would stay there all the time or if he was hiding at other times? If no one else understood how important he was to all of this, at least he would be safe and be able to walk around everyone.

At least we knew he would still be coming back here if he had been waiting for us. Sitting at the bar waiting for him to show, one of my friends started working as a bartender. He waved for us to follow him. Jacob wasn't sure but I knew we could trust him. As I got up Jacob was right behind me, I walked over following my friend past the bar and into a back room.

Chapter Five

Beyond this world

Entering the room with all the lights off, the door closed behind us. I knew Jacob worried if we walked into a trap, I trusted my friend. I knew he wouldn't do anything to us. As soon as the door closed, the lights turned on, and right in front of me was Najee. Looking the same as I left him last time. Jacob was about to step out in front of me to protect me, but I grabbed him by the arm whispering this is Najee. This is who I was hoping to find. It felt strange being here again especially now that I knew the truth about him.

"Took you long enough, I was beginning to wonder if I should have dropped some hints? Follow me, we have a distance to walk." Heading over to the wall, the slab of stone slid out of the way when he touched it with his hand.

"If you knew she was still alive and that I would need to find her, why haven't you located her? Do you know where she is and if so, I have no idea what she looks like or what to call her if I were to find her?" Nodding his head in agreement, Najee never seemed stressed but was always calm.

"Panic makes a person react before they should. You may have learned how to meditate but it has not become you. I do know who she is however you will know her when you see her, besides, if I go looking for her, she will most likely want to kill me." Smiling he was holding back something he didn't want to say.

"Why would she want to kill you?" I wasn't going to ask I had learned that if Najee wanted to tell you something he did and if he didn't you always wound up with riddles which is why most didn't talk to him too often.

Even though it was Jacob asking him I was curious about the same question.

"I fear before I could explain to her what she is being brought back for, she would outright kill me, she has every right to. I was the one who accidentally killed her. Sort of. It's not as if I was the only one. Make a mistake and get branded for life, what's a person going to do?" Shrugging his shoulders, he was taking it rather well, not that I expected him to respond.

There was more about Najee than I realized but I couldn't help it. I always liked him as I saw Jacob was starting to like him also. At least he was right, we did have a long way to walk. It felt as if we were going straight down until there had been a little bit of water running in the center walkway. When the tunnel evened out, we started walking straight forward which I guessed must be leading us under the palace. I wondered if the queen knew this was down here. Without speaking to him in mind Najee answered.

"No, the queen is not aware of this. I built it much later. You need to consider thinking less and accepting more. It is fine to be rational or think problems through but not all need to be thought through." Why did I always feel as if I was getting a life lesson from Najee?

"I thought it was a rumor you were consorting with vampires. How did you meet the broken person?" Najee said this with a smile and a sarcastic tone to his voice.

"This is Lucian's friend and brother-in-law. I've told you about Lucian. This is Jacob and he's not broken but he is a partial vampire and has part of his human side still." It sounded strange hearing Jacob be called broken even if he meant it sarcastically.

"I should have known better than to ask a broken person about another broken person. At least you weren't broken when I first met you. Not that it would have mattered. I still would have tolerated you anyway. When we get down here, I'll explain what you need to do." We walked for what felt like an eternity and then I realized what we did.

We walked upward again; he built a tunnel to the other side of the stone.

"This is why the queen has only seen one side of the portal to multiple worlds and not what lays behind the prying eyes of its master. This is the better half, almost like an éclair, most of the stuff it's filled with is on the far other side, the better side. She had only seen the side that is missing the best part." I loved waiting to see what he was going to compare some things to, Najee was intelligent but also rather amusing and never dull.

When we were standing next to the stone itself Najee reached out saying something to it in another language, I hadn't understood causing the stone to glow.

"Won't they know something is happening from the glowing?" I felt nervous when it started hoping he would be safe waiting behind for us.

"It only glows where the hand opened the door, it will not glow on the other side. Now all you must do is step in. I will direct it and then you search for her, but remember, don't touch the fuzzy little guys on the other side. They look cute but they're like sharks, nasty little things. In you go." I must have missed something.

I kept thinking over what he said, and I knew not to touch the little things but how do I get in? How do you step into a stone?

"Like I said you think too much. Step in, it's not solid, it only appears that way. Should I give you a manual? Walk-in and the other one follows, simple as that. I do the rest of the work." At least I wasn't the only one who didn't have a clue what we were doing other than looking for a person who was female and had no idea what she looked like.

"I don't even know what she looks like. Where do I start looking when I get in there? Is it huge or is there only so much space? If it's huge it could take us a long time and I don't think we have that long? Maybe if you come with us, she won't kill you?" I knew he understood my worry.

"It's an entire world, of course it's going to be big! Trust me when you see her you will know it, we all have something like us out there. She will come to you once she senses the stone, like a moth to light, bzzzzzap. Now as you said you don't have much time to get going. I'll be waiting here for you." Najee still appeared calm.

I started walking in almost tripping as I had gone into the stone. Jacob stepped over the bottom as if there had been a lip I tripped over. I may have liked Najee, but he did wear on your nerves after a while.

"At least the second figured it out. I told him to step in." Shaking his head Najee sat on the floor waiting for us.

I couldn't help but worry. Stepping in, it looked like a basic alcove. Following the light, in the end, we emerged to see nothing but a wide-open field. It had both been breathtaking and a bit strange to have such a powerful stone unguarded which appeared to be out in the middle of nowhere. Holding the stone close, not that I knew anywhere here to transport to unless I pulled a beginner move like I had when I first had the stone. It would bring us to safety wherever that might be. I found at the beginning it had its consequences, not knowing exactly where I would land. It could either be good or worse than the situation I was already in.

Jacob looked outside first as I followed walking out into the bright sunlight. The grass had been as tall as my knees, neither of us could see the ground it had been so thick but at least it hadn't been wet.

"If she senses the stone, I wonder how long we will have to wait. I hope I don't mistake her for something else and pop us somewhere." Jacob nodded his head agreeing.

"Make sure if you transport somewhere you take me with you. I don't want to be left here. I should have asked what dangers we should be looking for. After all, if it was this easy to come in here there must be a reason she hasn't come back through herself having a guardian of the stone bring it back to her. There has to be something that Najee isn't telling us." Not sure where we were heading other than walking forward.

We hoped something would stand out letting us know we were doing the right thing. The field felt as if it would keep going on until we had come across a thick area of trees. Still being cautious we walked carefully.

The main thing that Jacob wanted to do was find a safe place to wait. That way if she would come to it, then she would come to us instead of having us get lost in case she was to take the stone and leave us behind. Jacob didn't want to be too far from the cave getting lost. I glanced at the life stone a few times hoping it might show a sign of something or even a face, but nothing even glimmered in the stone. I hoped it still worked here in case we needed it. As it had started to rain, we turned back heading for the cave to avoid getting rained on, neither of us had a set plan of where to go but it had been made difficult not being able to see in the rain. It had been coming down so hard. Inside the cave out of the rain, we could see what looked like very furry tumbleweeds rolling in the cave when we remembered not to touch them. Najee had been right; they were cute but neither of us wanted to risk the dangerous side. If we left them alone, they left us alone.

After the rain let up, we took off in another direction not sure if this world had known about people like us or if they had their strangeness. We still had to be cautious hoping not to attract attention to ourselves other than what was necessary to get her attention. I wished I had the name of the woman we were looking for. Off in the distance, it looked like an ordinary town like the ones on earth, nothing too strange. Then we noticed what the difference had been. As we watched a shapeshifter change shape right in broad daylight and no one flinched. Even though we wanted to avoid drawing attention to ourselves we must have stood out as outsiders, perhaps they were used to who lived here and who hadn't?

Jacob thought it was a good idea to bring the stone, that way I could hold it easily but also keep it covered. I used the same backpack so often when transporting it around others when I hadn't wanted them to see what I had. It felt so strange wandering around not having a direction to go. As we walked through town there had been what looked like a coffee shop. Jacob picked up a piece of paper to look at it that was laying on a table outside. Nothing special on the pages. It looked like a simple newspaper much like our own.

It looked like any other average town, but this had interesting-looking people. One of the locals, a woman stepped out in front of us smiling at us. I immediately wondered if this had been her even though I couldn't help but feel it was a little soon?

"I couldn't help but notice you two looked a little lost? We haven't had anyone new to our town in a long time." Smiling she was waiting for an answer.

I was glad that Jacob spoke up. I wasn't sure what to say if we should admit the truth or not.

"We are new. We were wondering how close the next town would be from here?" Jacob sounded rather casual about the question he asked.

"We are a long way from any other towns. There are only a few towns scattered with a few surviving cities. We had a natural disaster recently wiping out half the world. Rather strange you don't know that even if you are new to our town?"

She seemed a little hesitant now with her smile slowly going away.

Speaking up, I pulled a piece of paper out of my pocket that Victoria had written an address on. At least it was something.

"Would you by any chance know where this address is or if we are close to it?" Handing the paper over to the lady, she looked at it and started smiling once again.

"Yes, this place has been deserted for years. The family disappeared many centuries ago. If you follow the road to your right. Follow that until it joins the dirt road. Follow that and it will loop to your left a little. Just keep following it and it's about two hours out of town." The lady kept smiling except she looked more curious than anything

"Thank you for your help. That's the place we were looking for." Handing me back the piece of paper she said goodbye.

As we walked across the street now with everyone watching us. I wished the others hadn't known where we were headed, but she had spoken loud enough. We had to act as normal about it hoping no one would guess why we were there unless it would help us find her faster?

As far as we could tell no one had followed us. We hoped this would give us a place to start or at least wait until she was to find us. We hadn't wanted to walk around too long in case when we moved, she would miss us. As far as Najee was concerned, I had nothing to fear. She would be protective of me because the stone recognized me as a guardian. He didn't know how she would react to my having a half-breed with me. Either way, I was determined to make sure I brought Jacob home in one piece also, even though I had a feeling he could protect himself better than I could. I was getting tired of walking. I knew Jacob could keep walking for hours, but I still wore out easily. We were getting closer as we could see part of the house towering over the trees. The dirt path led out into a tree-lined road with only one house at the far end and it was enormous looking from a distance and even more intimidating as we got closer.

For being deserted for centuries it hadn't looked too bad with the black iron gates around the house. Its looks were deceiving. We pushed the gate door as it simply fell over from having its hinges rust out. Walking up to the front door Jacob had me peek at the stone to see if it would show anything. As I looked it remained the same with no clues ahead. From the outside, the house had the appearance of two large homes being connected, as part of the design looked much older and different from the other side. Jacob pushed the front door open before we went in surveying the inside. The entrance had been empty, it only had dirty drapes barely hanging onto the walls. Faded wood floor with dingy orangey white walls. Being careful where we stepped since there had been a few places the flooring had been soft even with a hole in the far corner leading down to the basement. There were four floors. As solid as it looked, there were a few structural faults from aging and not being cared for. The place smelled so moldy and full of dusty cobwebs. I didn't care for spider webs as I was hoping not to find out what their spiders were like here.

Figuring we had time we explored every floor from top to bottom, at least Jacob liked exploring as much as I had. We found which room belonged to each of the kids with their names printed clearly on their bedroom doors. Jacob decided we would wait for a while on the second floor hoping she might find us here. At least we had a good view from up here of the outside and would hear anything coming up the stairs since they creaked so loud. Jacob had rather sound reasoning with his choices. I wasn't going to argue with him. Besides, it didn't matter to me where we waited, I was nervous wanting this to be over even though there were so many times I kept hoping for things to be over just to be surprised by more when I finally relaxed. Maybe if I didn't allow myself to relax no more horrible things would happen? Nice thinking but I was sure I was wrong.

We had already been here for a few hours waiting not that anything was happening, and I was getting impatient. I looked in the stone a few times. At least I know I could still see our world. Jacob caught me using the stone to view Lucian. Smiling, he hadn't said anything, but I knew he would be thinking of Rose. At least we knew the group was still safe, but I could tell from the worried look on Lucian's face I wished I could comfort him. I wondered how my life would be without the stone. I had gotten so used to it having my life changed or dependent on it and now I would be handing it over to its rightful owner? Why hadn't the other guardians before me done this unless they had never known Najee? At times I wondered if I was doing the right thing or if we had fallen into a trap? I trusted the royals, but I couldn't shake that nervous feeling in the pit of my stomach. I wasn't the only one thinking this now. Jacob also expressed to me his concern.

After a few more hours the stone started to glow catching our attention. I looked at it, a person was walking around in the house however it hadn't been female it was a male. Looking closer we could see that it was Najee, why was he here when he made it a point not to come in with us? Now I was starting to think we couldn't trust him. I hoped it hadn't been too late. Were they all in on it? Getting up being careful not to make any noise we went out the window, out on one of the many porches that wrapped around the old house. Slowly lowering ourselves down. I was thankful we hadn't stayed up any higher or it would have been harder to get down. With the backpack on securely, we had taken off running to a shed outside Jacob thought we could hide out there until we could find why he had come through after us, or if there had been any others with him.

The shed didn't have anything in it other than empty shelving. Watching the house, we could see there were several people walking around inside now. Najee hadn't been the only one. How could I have misjudged him so badly? Or had someone disguised themselves as him? After all, there had been shapeshifters here and they did nothing to hide that fact. We had been waiting for the opportunity to take off when the floor beneath us had given way. Jacob was able to land with ease as I again fell flat on my butt which was getting sore now. Looking around there wasn't a way back up leaving us with little choice other than to find where the tunnel would lead us. I held Jacob's hand leading him through the tunnel when the light left completely, his human side made it difficult for him to see, at least my gift made it possible for me to see. Finally, something I could use.

The tunnel through here had been rather narrow so I let Jacob know he was going to scrape through a few spots, even for me they had been rather tight until we came to a larger part where there was more space. Jacob pulled at my hand a bit to indicate he wanted me to walk a little slower now that we could both see a light ahead, not wanting to walk into a trap. In the distance there were a few people walking around. I hoped we could get out of here, but it looked like we were trapped, the last thing we wanted would be for anyone to know we were here. To keep from being seen or making noise we walked back a little and sat down on the cold hard floor.

In case they could see in the dark we hoped they wouldn't be looking on the floor for anyone. Listening, we tried to hear their voices to see if we recognized them. The voices had been far too faint to hear. Looking at the stone hoping it would alert me. I wondered why my amulet had not turned from its gray to more of a black or red warning. The stone itself showed something I hadn't expected. I watched as the others left walking upstairs closing a door behind them, I got up quickly motioning for Jacob to stay put. I had taken out a few of the crystals I planned on enchanting when I had time. I took them out of the backpack and went to the far end making sure I looked around the corner in case the stone had not shown everyone. On the table under the light had been several other crystals, replacing them with the ones I had. I took those and hurried back to Jacob placing the other ones back in the backpack. I knew he was wondering what I had done. It looked like I brought back the same crystals. All I could do was say, I'll explain later as I zipped the bag back up.

Hoping not to run into the others we made our way up the stairs. We had seen the others when they left open the door carefully peeking around the corners not seeing anyone. Guessing at a way out we had seen a window, this time we were going to try to get far away from the house as we could. Slipping out of the window, there was nothing on this side of the house. The tunnel led us to the basement of the oldest-looking part of the house. Moving away from the house this side had been closer to the trees carefully keeping an eye on the only two windows that faced this direction. We had taken off as fast as we could, hoping we could get to the cave, maybe back into the shade city assuming Najee hopefully hadn't trapped us in this world? So far, I knew I could use the life stone in the shade city however I wasn't sure if I could use it to leave this place.

Keeping up with Jacob, we darted quickly through the trees heading back to the cave when I felt myself lift right off my feet. Jacob grabbed a hold of me when he stopped suddenly placing me back on the ground. He put his finger over his lips indicating for me to be silent. Looking ahead I hadn't seen what he was looking at as we crouched down making our way in another direction. Slowly Jacob put his hand on my shoulder indicating to stop again. This time I had seen it and before if it had not been for Jacob, I would have run right into it. There was a woman in the woods. She looked insane, her hair massively matted, messed up with twigs and other leaves that had tangled in her hair. It was wild and hung around her shoulders and down her back. She looked rather messy almost as if she had been dragged through the mud and dried. Her black long robe was shredded in pieces revealing another robe only it had been a very dingy white robe. Leaning over she had a creature of sorts that was dying in front of her, she was breathing some thick powered looking substance at him almost turning him to dust. He hadn't bled, he dried out and blew away. I could feel a shiver go all the way down my back as we watched in horror. We couldn't imagine that if she had this kind of power what power the others had. I had been so nervous out of old habit. I was rubbing my ring showing the whole situation through a stone back in our world where the others could see what was going on. I hated myself for doing this and if we lived. I was going to have to learn to stop playing with my ring when I was nervous!

Grabbing the stone, I held onto Jacob, I hoped it would send up somewhere safe. Anything had to be better than this as the stone transported us. We could see the wild woman coming running for us as we popped out. I was wrong about anything is better than the situation we were in. Instead of the stone transporting us to a safer location, it re-deposited us behind the woman. Moments ago, she seemed rather crazy in the way she reacted when she had seen us, even staring at Lucian more than she had with me. Now she stood straight up almost shocked as we transported behind her. Starting to walk over to us I had still been holding onto Jacob's arm just in case we had to transport again. If anything, I hoped we would wear her out or she would quit if she realized she wasn't going to get a hold of us.

Trying to launch at us again she wound up flying to the ground as we transported again. I hoped this time we would end up farther away. At least that way we would have a chance to run from her, not that we knew how fast she could run. Instead, we again wound up not that far from her. I wasn't sure if the stone wasn't working that well here or if there hadn't been anywhere else safe to transport us? As we looked at her, she was starting to look more frustrated than anything.

"Will you stop doing that and standstill?" She yelled at us as we had been standing only a few feet from her.

"Then stop trying to attack us and we will, otherwise I can do this all day." I hoped my threat would work. I could do it all day but then after a while, she could guess what area we were about to end up and wait there for us. Eventually, we would have to stop. Instead of looking angry she not only smiled but she was laughing finding us rather humorous.

"I haven't met anyone here so far that has a personality like that. You see a creature that can kill you and you think you can make a threat?" Laughing so hard she sat down on the ground.

I hadn't thought I sounded that ridiculous but then Jacob warned me that it could be a trap. She might be trying to make us comfortable enough to let our guard down.

"So human why are you listening to that twit? Don't you know he's a vampire? Not the best combination if you asked me." As she was still sitting on the ground, she was sizing us up almost surprised by the fact I was with him.

"Yes, I know he's a partial vampire and not broken like one person likes to say. My name is Harmony, and this is Jacob." I was hoping by making that comment she might let us know who she was? Not that I was sure if I still wanted to locate the woman we were searching for.

"I don't remember asking you for your names. I don't care! What are you doing here if you don't want death from me? Neither of you belongs in this world." Now she was staring at Jacob even more intently.

"We are not here to die; I want to know who you are? We are looking for someone and we don't know her name." Looking at us, she shook her head.

"I don't have time for this, there are enough others around that will kill you both off, if not, I rather not deal with stupid people." Starting to walk away from us I tried to get her attention in the only way I could think too.

For some reason, I kept getting the urgency she was who we were looking for and needed.

"Are you Katherine hawthorns sister the creator of the life stone?" I almost shouted it.

I was hoping she wouldn't go running off, but I had to find or say something that we might get answers from her. I was right it had caught her attention. Jacob whispered, 'probably shouldn't have said that. I already know she doesn't like me. We should leave.'

"You speak of that traitor? No wonder why you consort with vampires, perhaps when they are done with you, they will have a nice meal afterward? What do you know of the life stone pathetic human. you are as much a traitor as anyone searching for it? I won't help you." She hadn't made a move to leave even though I was pretty sure I pissed her off enough that if we moved, she would attack us.

"We are not looking for the life stone. We need to find the woman who made it. Najee helped us go through the portal to search for her here and I think you know who she is. I realize you don't like vampires but not all are bad. No matter what creature or human, you will find good or evil, sometimes even both. Jacob here is trying to help me save a lot of people who are in need. The Eurubian people have disappeared, and the shade city is about to be taken over putting the royals at risk. We need her to help our family members that are missing." I was hoping by at least giving her some information and at least being honest with her she might consider helping.

"Don't say you do not search for the stone, everyone wants it; do you think she will create another like it? I don't help vampires, and I certainly don't help Najee. He should have died years ago for what he did." Taking it from her comment I guessed this had been her.

One glance at Jacob he nodded his head in agreement. We both confirmed it was her. She started to walk away from us again.

"I am the current guardian of the stone that you created. When I was told about you by Najee, he regretted almost killing you which is why he was helping us get here. I thought I could trust him but now we don't know if he walked us into a trap?" The second I said I was the current guardian she stopped and immediately turned back around to face me.

Not even looking at Jacob now I couldn't help but feel extremely nervous as she looked me over, and figured I had the stone securely held in my arms in my backpack with the straps wrapped around my arms. If someone wanted to steal it from me, they would be taking my arms with it. Even though I thought Najee said she would be attracted to the stone and that we wouldn't have to go looking for her.

"Najee knows better than to come in here without permission from me. At least I know why I felt this headache come on so quickly. Why do you consort with vampires? Najee I could understand, it was an uneducated mistake but vampires? One day I will rid them of the earth. That I stand behind, there is no place for them." She had only taken a step closer to us.

"I am not here to take you back to wipe out the vampires, Jacob here is with me to protect me and the life stone and has done nothing to deserve your contempt neither has the vampire I have fallen in love with or his family and many others out there. Maybe you're soured by what your sister did to you, but you cannot hold it against an entire race! We will find another way." I took a step back hoping she wouldn't come after us.

When she stood there watching us, she let us leave running again for the cave hoping we might still be able to get through it. How could I have been so wrong about my assumption about her? But then I guess I hadn't made the right choice about Najee either.

Closing in on the cave there had been three people that entered the mouth of the cave. Stopping quickly, the only way we could have run would have been straight back even though within minutes that way had been blocked also. Holding the stone tightly I knew even Jacob was getting worried. he wasn't sure if we would be able to fight them not knowing what their gift or fighting style was. Hoping the stone would not transport us near them again we popped out quickly only to end up in the place we ran to within inches of the woman we were previously speaking to.

"Took you long enough to get back here. Where did you think you were going anyway? Now if you look behind you. See those people off in the distance coming this way, and the one in the front that looks like Najee?" She nodded towards the path behind us I could hear them long before I could see them. Jacob confirmed it much earlier than I could.

"The man to the side of them is Najee. He's the one who helped us get here." As Jacob supplied her with the answer, we looked to see what she was doing, she had already been standing right next to us.

"That's not Najee. He's a shapeshifter probably hoping he could have tricked you into believing him. Besides, my husband knows if he steps foot in here, I would be like a moth on a flame killing him. Now we need to get going or they will get us." She said as she tilted her single finger over the stone not even trying to take it from me, she simply set her finger on the tip of it before we popped out.

I managed to get in 'he said the same comment about you being drawn to the stone' which was all I had the chance to get out. She tried bumping Jacob off to leave him behind except I looped my other hand quickly around his waist making sure he was still safe with me.

At least we hadn't kept transporting to the same spot, but I couldn't get over the fact all she needed was her finger to make the stone respond to her and we were where she pictured. Looking around it looked like the forest had been torched, the ground was blackened along with what trees barely stood up as we walked to a stone-looking house that was blackened also. I couldn't help but start to cough from the smoke still in the air. Following behind her we walked into the house not that we stayed on the first floor, we went down the stairs to a door that blocked the upstairs to the area we would spend some time in.

"I see you still brought him. You have a much-displaced loyalty." As she pointed over at Jacob looking rather disgusted.

"I would never leave him behind. You as a person blinded by so much hate happen to be the last person who should be telling me whether or not my loyalties are displaced." Walking away from us still with a scowl on her face, sitting down in a chair near her fireplace.

"I could kill you very easily. After all, you saw what I did to that last person. I'd watch my tongue if I were you." With a snap of her fingers, the fireplace roared to life.

Still standing away from her taking in our surroundings Jacob whispered to me 'if we don't find out something we can use then we need to take off and find another way. We can't wait for her to make up her mind if she's helping or not' I knew he was right. I was also feeling like our time was being wasted.

She hadn't liked the fact we kept standing there next to each other watching for her next move. Waving her hand towards a couch she expected us to sit down. With Jacob protectively keeping his arm around me, we sat down waiting for her to say or do something which she hadn't. She simply sat there staring at the fire. I had seen Sophie do this before, but I never found out why she did it.

"What are you planning on doing with the vampires in your backpack if you like them so much? Just a hint, don't ever try it with me. I'm powerful enough to keep myself out and I'll kill you much faster than you can stick me in one of those." She spoke to us without even looking in our direction.

Growing impatient I tried to control the tone of my voice, but I didn't want to waste any more time. I hadn't wanted to answer her question since I didn't know what I was going to do with the crystals yet. At least I wasn't going to risk releasing them here. Hearing this Jacob understood why I grabbed them. With the royals assisting or not somehow, they were able to pass them through the portal without it being opened by all the royals.

"How is waiting here going to help? What are you going to do that the guardians before me haven't done?" At some point, I was going to piss her off, but I might lose everything anyway if I must rely on her.

"Spoken like a true human always impatient, the longer we wait the more frustrated the others get trying to find you thus sending more people here to search for us. Then we find out who are friends and foes. When I say it is time, we will use the life stone to transport to the other world. We do not need the portal from this side to get out. I know what I need to do but are you determined to seal your death to protect those people?" As she waved her hand toward Jacob saying this.

"I can't bring you to the other side. I can't risk one race for another." Standing up I hoped for a miracle, not that I knew what I had been searching for anymore.

"Then follow in the steps of the guardian. Only a powerful enough enchanter can kill one of the same, you can try but how many are you willing to risk for it? Is your family truly worth the risk when eventually they will die anyway? You're a very frustrating human, don't worry you don't need to remind me that I'll want to kill you after all of this is done." Sitting back in her chair she seemed so relaxed and self-assured of herself.

"You're no better than your sister once you're done. I won't let you kill the others. I will fight you every step of the way." As I spoke, she stood showing no emotion either way.

"At least I won't be bored. I like killing feisty people, it's time to go." I hated feeling like this.

I felt like I traded one evil for an even worse one. As she placed a single finger on the stone Jacob held onto me as the three of us were transported out and directly into the palace sleeping chambers of our world. No one had been waiting in here for us. I almost wondered if it would be safer if people had been safely hidden in crystals rather than be made easy targets and if it had, would they forgive me? After all, it's difficult to kill what you can't find. When we transported in. I no longer had been holding the stone, she had it in her hands. I knew we were screwed. Motioning for us to leave I hoped we had done the right thing trusting her this far.

Opening the door to walk out, there had been no one in the hallway as we made our way through not sure where to go not that I wanted to leave the life stone alone. I didn't want to end up in the middle of the showdown with those two women. I wanted to make sure Lucian was safe. There had to be a reason or a way of making the portal work unless they found out about Najee?

Chapter Six

Fight for Family

Not an option that we had, if you're meant to be somewhere in the middle of something then it was going to happen regardless of whether you planned to or not. Neither of us expected it to happen this soon. I was hoping to at least find a way of getting Jacob out of the city but for now, I was going to have to wait for the opportunity to present itself. I truly wished someone made me a helmet. I was going to make it one of my new priorities. After standing in the hallway with Jacob. I had no memories after that. I had been hit so hard I couldn't even remember who I was or where I had been for that matter. Standing up, I reached for the door trying to get out to find it had been locked, no one else was in the room with me.

Someone must have been waiting for me since the door opened rather slowly showing someone on the other side looking at me rather intently as I tried to figure out who this person was. Walking in relaxed putting her arm around me hugging me looking me over.

"Sorry about locking the door on you. I had to make sure you didn't leave and harm yourself again. I did it for your good dear." As she stepped back, I knew the voice, I just couldn't place the face.

"Where am I? I don't remember getting here or who you are for that matter?" As she went and sat down, I had a flash of an image of another woman sitting down the same way except the face was different.

I couldn't remember why I was thinking of this other woman. Motioning for me to sit next to her. I sat down on the bed next to her.

"I'm your mother silly, you hit your head horribly this time. I know you lost some of your memory but don't worry I'll help you regain it. Then you will be back to normal. You will soon forget those suicidal thoughts, now you're needed for important duties, they need to be carried out or no one else will Aimee." Standing up, holding my hand she led me behind her as I did nothing to resist.

Following her trying to at least remember something. Why is it that when she had said Aimee, I hadn't liked the sound of it? Walking into a rather large room there were so many guards surrounding the sides. I almost couldn't see the two exits on either side of the room as we entered from the center.

On a table in the far corner had been a huge pile of crystals. As I looked at them, I had a huge memory flash of little creatures coming at me and then in a flash they were gone. Why was I remembering something like that, is there a reason I tried to die? I can't help but think I wouldn't do something like that but for now, I wasn't too sure, so I followed the woman who called herself my mother. As I watched her make her way to a row of thrones, I couldn't help but notice the bite mark on her back arm. It looked like a human bite but why would someone bite her? Did I do that? Waving her arm towards another throne for me to sit down on I obediently listened and sat down as I was told.

Sitting back watching everyone else I was curious about what we were doing as the whole row of thrones moved forward. I could now see over the balcony that had been in the distance. The guards blocking the view moved aside when I looked to see what was over the side. There had only been one person down there. A woman standing alone. We had been overlooking an entire city with only one person representing it.

At the top of her lungs, all I could hear had been 'now we will find where your loyalties naturally belong' looking at the woman next to me she looked rather angry. Now she stood up from her seat walking behind it out of the way. All I could see had been a bright flash of light coming at me from down below knocking me back through the seats. It was a good thing they were wooden. Anything stronger and I would have been smashed to death. If there were only the two of us up here who were the other thrones for? Getting up quickly I saw that I was the only one left as the others went out the back exits leaving me to face this woman not knowing what to do.

Wasting no time coming up she already made her way as a brilliant flash of light dissipated revealing her standing right next to me.

"They run because they have no way of fighting me, I have no time to deal with you right now, especially one with no memory, however, you are coming with me." As she grabbed my arm, we transported out ahead of the others who were trying to run away.

I had figured out they were trying to use me as a human shield. In yet another large room there had been a few that tried to attack the new woman however not very successfully as they were either thrown to the side or slain. The room was covered with blood. Stepping backward, I felt stressed not knowing what to do. I didn't know if I should try to defend these people or run? Without making a choice one of the guards came up from behind me as the woman tried to nail him with a shot of light from the stone. It launched off me as we both flew backward into the wall behind. He used me as a shield against the stone she was using. Was I immune to it? Why were they trying to avoid it? As we were flung closer to the others the woman who called herself my mother dropped a white powder that filled the floor around us filling the room, it transported only a handful of us to another location. I couldn't help it, but I was tired of all of this. I wanted someone to explain what was happening.

In our new location mother sat me down at a table with a few of the guards surrounding me, all eyes on me had been making me very nervous.

"For now, I forgive you for losing the stone. But you will get it back. I can't use it anymore. I'm no longer human. You can thank your friend for that. You can help make up for it by getting my kingdom back. The stone won't hurt you, it's why you have to get it back, we have no way of fighting for ourselves, but she can't use it against you. Make her trust you. Pretend to work for her. But get that stone back." Still staring intently, I think she was almost expecting me to object.

"Where is my friend? If I'm going to figure out something it seems I would need my friend's help. What makes you think she's going to believe that I would help her out if I'm with you. After all, you are my mother, doesn't it seem like I would side with you?" I wasn't sure what I was supposed to do if they couldn't fight her, how was I supposed to especially if she didn't leave the stone not that I knew what I was supposed to do with it?

"When you accomplish this, you get your friend back. Right now, you can say he's being well preserved." Smiling at me, she made me sick.

"My friend better be alright, before I do anything I need to see this person." I didn't even know if my friend was male or female, but she didn't seem to want to offer any suggestions if my friend bit her then the person must have had a reason. There had to be more to this than what she was telling me. Taking out a crystal from her robe she placed it on the table. I could see something moving around inside of it. Picking it up no one stopped me. I could see a face that looked panicked looking back at me. Placing it in my pocket I wasn't going to give it back.

"No worries, you don't know how to release him without me. Get the stone or I kill you. Simple as that, no mother needs a daughter who serves little use. I can stay hidden for as long as it takes but I won't preserve you if you don't obey. Don't forget we are fighting for our lives, against an evil being. There are reasons she will trust you but don't forget where your loyalties are for!" Since waking up, this had been the second time in a short time, I had my loyalties questioned.

I wished I could remember something. I wasn't sure what I was going to do but it didn't seem like I had much of a choice so I might as well go see what this other person says to me otherwise, I might be dead no matter what I do?

Taking off with two guards to make sure I made it back to the palace safely they turned around leaving as soon as I could see the gates, they were afraid of dying. I started to feel like I was playing a game of cat and mouse. The once mammoth gates were laying on their sides destroyed as I walked in. I wondered what I would be walking into. There had been no people around, no sound or movement of any kind. As I walked straight back to the palace nothing slowed me down, no obstacles to walk around just a straight shot back. I was wondering when I would get stopped or when I would run into her, hopefully not poised to kill me.

I made it through the majority of the town, and I could see the stairs heading upward leading to the palace. I heard a voice speaking. 'What do you think you're doing? How could you forget me?' I stopped to look around.

I hadn't seen anyone. Pulling the crystal out from my pocket to look at it, the voice hadn't been from it.

"Who said that?" Waiting to see if someone would announce themselves. No one spoke as I started walking again then the voice became clearer again. 'Aren't you going to speak to me? Remember how we speak to each other? Speak in your mind to me, we used to be connected.' I did for a moment think I was losing my mind, maybe I could be capable of trying suicide?

'Suicide, are you insane? You would never do that. Jacob said they hit you over the head, but I didn't think they hit you that hard? Please, you must remember me. I was like a father to you. Trust me, you need to save yourself.' Looking around still not too convinced I figured I would humor myself, fine if the voice is coming from my head, then I was going to ask it a few questions.

'If you're speaking to me then where are you right now and who is Jacob?" Standing still I waited for the voice to speak to me again.

'I'm stuck in a crystal, Lucian is missing. They caught the rest of us, the royals are here with us also, and neither side can be trusted. I would tell you what to do but I don't even know?'

Thinking in my mind to whoever it was speaking with me, 'if you don't know then it can't hurt if I at least try, one of these sides has to be right and I need to find out who. I can't even remember who I am.'

Walking up the stairs, there was no one still to stop me, even as I entered the main room of the palace. There had been a single throne detached from the others sitting in the center stopping where I stood. The throne turned around with her sitting in the seat smiling at me as she had her arms resting on the sides of the chair.

"I'm surprised your back?" She hadn't said much not that there was much to say.

"I don't know what side to trust so I thought I would see what you have to offer?" Standing there I hoped if she was going to kill me it was going to be quick.

I hoped the voice didn't pop back into my mind at this moment otherwise I was going to have to make an excuse she would buy.

"Poor little you not knowing who you are. At least you know when to question things however how is it that she let you out of her sight? After all, if I use the life stone you are the only one that can stop it from killing her?" Still leaning back in the chair, I expected this question and thought it is best answered with full honesty.

"She told me she was my mother which I doubt, it doesn't feel right. Besides, she wants to kill you also and has cloaked herself to hide where she is, I know where she is." I knew I didn't have any leverage at all and nothing to offer her other than to serve up the other person, not that I knew how I would get the stone away from her as I watched her holding it in her hands.

"First let me remind you a bit of your life then you help me find and kill the others. I'll see if I have any need of you after all of this, if you're smart you will." Standing up she walked over to a crystal ball set up on a stand in the center of the room.

I wasn't sure but this looked familiar somehow. I kept picturing this older gentleman that had been with me standing next to it. Then the voice kicked in, 'that was me, we have been there a few times together,' watching her I was wondering what she was going to do even though the voice almost felt comforting this time. I felt I was remembering at least the voice.

As she placed her hand over the crystal ball it formed a smokescreen filling the entire side of the room as a few scenes flashed across it. One of myself resting on someone's back racing across the countryside. I seemed rather happy with him. I couldn't remember who he was. Then there were flashes of other faces than one. I remembered it was of Najee only this wasn't something I remembered seeing either he was in front of a glowing stone looking behind him as the woman who told me she was my mother struck him down killing him. The people looked rather happy, however, each time. I would see a city full of people, the background looked different. I couldn't figure out why. Some of the faces looked familiar. I still can't remember why.

"This woman who said she is your mother lies to you; she is my mother. You are simply a human that was made a guardian of a stone I created. She intends on killing off the vampires as I would have. We both want to rule the portal and now I can, but if there is any potential threat out there. I need to rid myself of it, so I have no worries of anything ever getting in my way again. Maybe if you get your memory back you can answer why the stone seems weaker? But first, let me show you where your journey is about to begin." As the smoke cleared, the crystals I had seen earlier were all piled up on the floor as she waved her hand over them with the life stone still in her hands, smoke escaped from the crystals releasing a crowd of people.

Many of the faces looked familiar. I wished I knew how I knew them all. What was she planning with them? 'I'm over here on the far-left side. Please don't go with her, she's only going to kill you anyway.' As the voice spoke to me, I looked over to where it directed me. I remembered him a little just not as much as I would have liked to. Speaking back, I said, 'If you taught me well then you're going to have to trust me.' Turning to face the woman I wanted to see what she was going to do.

"Now do as I order you and kill them. Place your hands on the crystal and watch them. It will suffocate them until they die, now to show your loyalty." I had such a sharp pain in my chest that I couldn't explain but I knew looking at the face of so many people I couldn't do this. Moving away from the crystal ball standing between them and her I made my stand.

"I won't kill them; you can ask me to kill this other woman or even show you where she is, and you do what you wish, but I will not kill my family and friends. I may not remember everything, but I will not kill them." Standing there she tilted her head as if she was trying to figure out something.

"I'm impressed. I might keep you around for fun. At least kill the bloodsuckers, they kill humans, shades, and other creatures." It almost felt as if she was staring right through me making more of a point than anything.

"I won't kill any of them, especially the vampires. If you want my help, then we leave but promise us, that if you still chose to kill me, at least let them go." I started fidgeting with my ring hoping she wouldn't notice how nervous I was.

I had been trying to control my nerves by playing with my ring. As I saw the life stone shudder. I rubbed the ring harder, and the stone shuddered even harder catching her attention. Taking my hand away from my ring I didn't want her to know, at least maybe I could fake some leverage?

"How are you doing that. Tell me this instant or I kill all of them along with you." She raised her hand as if she was about to do something.

"You can't use the stone against me. It won't let you kill me remember, I'm a guardian and I'm the one with amnesia. Now if you attack them then I'll have to protect them. As for how I'm messing with the stone, there are things I remember that you don't so if you want my help, you're going to have to work with me at least. Leave them alive and I will help you, deal?" Watching her I could see the frustration on her face, but I could also see a rather cryptic smile appear.

"I think I'm going to either enjoy this adventure with you or enjoy killing you. Either way, I benefit from some enjoyment. Let's go." Tossing the crystal that had been in my pocket to the man who spoke to me, he held it nodding his head.

I could only assume he was going to try to trust me. As she walked over to me, I could see the worry on everyone's faces. At least they could remember who I was now if I could just figure out what I was doing? Transporting out we popped into a rather strange place.

"Isn't this the place we were just at?" But then looking closer I could see there had been a few differences.

The guards somewhat blocked my view when we left, not seeing where it was until we entered the city. Looking around I recognized where we were and knew where I needed to take her.

"Never mind. I know where we are, this way up here." Walking in the lead she simply followed a few steps behind being careful the whole time in case there had been an ambush.

I probably should feel guilty for turning her over, but she had killed a friend of mine, or at least it looked like it. Najee was dead now and she was willing to put me in the line of fire to save herself. If she had been my mother, she would have protected me like the man who had spoken to me in my head.

Walking up carefully I avoided the main entrance room preferring to walk around to the back taking the smaller tunnel, not sure why I remembered this, but it felt like the right way. Following it down as it led around, we passed the black stone where I thought we would find it. Placing my hand on the stone it glowed like the white one had, looking at me the woman seemed a little shocked as she had never seen the black onyx stone glow before. What she hadn't known had been the large piece that chipped off from the corner, the majority no longer existed other than the tiny piece I added to my ring, a piece of stone that also connected to the life stone. I liked the idea of the ying and yang theory, I felt good that I was remembering something, not exactly what I needed to know yet.

Walking past another room. I kept getting these images in my head of this place almost feeling like I needed to flee. Walking downward even further I stopped before going any further and I turned to face the woman.

"Do you need me in there? As far as I know, they are still in there waiting for me to show up with the stone, even though this is rather soon. If I hold the stone, they may feel vulnerable enough to believe a story I could tell them. It's up to you. I'm here to work for you so let me know what you want me to do." As soon as I said that she relaxed a little, but I could still feel her hesitating not wanting to hand over the stone.

"How do I know you won't turn against me also and take the stone for yourself?" She held the stone closer to her being overly protective of it.

"I've had the stone this whole time. If I wanted what either of you two searched for, I could have had it already. I hate to say it, but I believe I'm the one that can be trusted out of all of this. Besides, as I almost remember in your words you don't know if I will turn traitor on you?" Standing there it felt good to use something of her own against her even in this situation.

"Then I guess I have to trust you; I'll wait here until you call me." Moving back a little in case anyone was to look out in the tunnel they wouldn't see her.

I walked into the room announcing myself first so I wouldn't be ambushed. As I suspected they have been cloaked and hiding, now surrounding me as I held the stone in my hands or at least an illusion of the stone, even I could feel the difference. Playing with my ring again. I was ready to call on the small amount of power I still had over the life stone. The woman still held onto the life stone as it trembled in her hands as I played with my ring, I hoped it would work.

Making herself the woman who had announced herself as my mother made herself seen. As she walked over to me eyeing the stone with amazement. I knew she was wondering how I captured it so fast. So, I made up an excuse on my way over here.

"I struck a deal with her, she thought she had the real stone. I traded stones with her, I made her believe I had the real one and she had the fake one. She wanted me to prove the power of the stone so I killed a few vampires, no one will miss them anyway." Keeping a straight face along with monotone as if there was no big deal killing a few others, no matter who they happened to be, at least with losing my memory she might not know if I would do this or not?

"How are we supposed to know that you have the life stone and that she doesn't still have it? It couldn't have been that easy?" I knew she would question it, but I hoped I would be able to bring the woman to me even if I was using the ring instead of the fake stone connecting to the real-life stone.

"Simple enough, want me to call her to us?" As I had the guards were all positioning themselves around being ready even though I knew they hadn't stood a chance.

The supposed mother stood over to the side keeping an eye out in case she had a chance to escape. Holding the stone over my hand with the ring I started playing with it again.

"Call her here, as soon as you do then we kill her, and you will have served your mother well." Giving me an evil smile in response she stood there waiting to hold something in her hand.

I knew she was ready with something. I wasn't sure what it was? I did as the woman asked, I called her to us but with a twist. Instead of bringing her here, I brought her spirit body here pulling it out of her, doing this almost out of instinct that it caused such a shock to everyone else around.

"See, I told you I control her now, what would you like done?" Standing there with a smug look on my face the mother thought I had done quite well while the other thought I crossed her.

However, I didn't have it planned what to do when she was in the room. The other woman was prepared to kill her immediately.

"May I suggest something that would be rather fun for all of us?" Letting my voice take on a rather snide tone to it.

I was bringing out more of an evil side or at least as much as I could as the one woman looked on in horror. I winked at her hoping she would pick up on it, giving me one nod, I hoped she still trusted me.

"Now if you will I need plenty of space. I'm about to show you something even more powerful than the life stone." Walking to one end of the room I could see the mother sitting down in a chair to watch thinking it was safe with only a spirit body here.

As I pretended to prepare, I mainly waited for the mother to set down what she was prepared to kill her with. Then I focused on the real-life stone playing with the ring hoping this would work. I brought her body in front of me standing frozen as her spirit body walked around it, her physical body had been holding the real stone. As she had, the ring shot out a bolt of light connected with the bolt of light from the life stone bringing her into her physical body. The blow from the light threw me back into the wall. I pretended to be knocked out. Laying against the floor with what looked like real blood dripping from my nose and mouth.

It had been hard to force the liquid up my nose it burned so badly trying not to make any sounds. I lay there hoping she would know what to do at this point. What they hadn't been paying attention to had been when I was pretending to set up, I summoned red berries into my mouth hoping to use them as substitutes for blood. As far as I could tell it was working. I could hear the other side get up as a bolt of hot liquid shot across the room spraying even the guards in their midst. The mother didn't care who she killed if it preserved her. As I was hit with some of it, I had to try not to flinch and pretend to be dead.

Even through closed eyes I could tell how illuminated the room had become with obvious results as the stone of life had been used, eventually the mother had slumped down to the floor not pretending but before she had one last bolt run past out of her hand, she hit me with it. At that point, I was only aware of thinking I could no longer feel my body. Neither had I felt the air rushing around me or been aware of how far I had traveled assisted. At least she had kept her word. I think she was amazed I had done exactly as I said I would. Bringing me far away from the others we headed for where she knew I would eventually be cured.

After a while I started to feel searing pain, I could not stop or figure out what was causing it. I couldn't see or hear anything other than the occasional crackle sound almost like fire and then I found she was burning me alive. I was engulfed with fire as it burned through me, I felt every nerve in my body responding to it. As a human, this was not a good thing, but I hadn't been sure how the shade half of myself would react? I wasn't sure if he could hear me or not but at least I knew with no doubt they would live.

'Are you there?' I had thought as loud as I could. 'Yes, I am always here with you,' it felt so comforting to hear him again. I felt so bad for letting him down, but I knew he was safe now. 'I'm sorry, I'm making sure everyone leaves the shade city, I won't be back." As I said this, I could hear a scream from him, 'no, you can't go, come back here.'

I know what he wanted but I didn't think I could honestly give it, even if I wanted to. 'I'm already dying, at least it isn't in vain. Say goodbye to everyone for me' that had been the last I remembered before I blacked out. I accepted I was dying, after all how many lives does a human live even with gifts?

Chapter Seven

Death never comes easy

Sitting down at the kitchen table with her coffee cup staring straight over at her mother shaking her head and letting out a sigh loud enough for more than those seated at the table to hear.

"Mom, how long do you intend on leaving him in there? It's not fair, he needs to be let out. If he takes off, you need to let him do it. I don't think he will this time. Either way, you can't leave him cooped up in that crystal any longer, no matter how much safer you seem to think he is in there." Standing up to pick up Larissa, Rose took her very sleepy daughter to bed, leaving her parents to watch over the last crystal that hadn't been freed.

"I know we have to at some point. Sophie, do you think you can do it?" Nichole picked up the crystal and handed it to Sophie.

Sophie hadn't wanted to force it earlier however Rose wasn't the only one to comment on it. Charlie patted Nichole on the shoulder trying to reassure her.

"I'm sure with us available he's going to be fine but either way he needs to be allowed to deal with it himself, it can't be easy to lose someone twice even though I haven't been through that yet." Holding the crystal out Sophie waved her hand over it chanting a few words allowing the smoke to release him in a much easier way than breaking the crystal and dropping him on the floor.

Standing there looking at everyone with a shocked look on his face and stretching getting the kink out of his neck.

"I get it that everyone is worried. Thinking I'm going to run or be worse than I was last time, but seriously, did you have to leave me in that cramped thing for so long," looking to each person for a reply except all he received had been guilty glances, "while everyone kept me in there Goseck made the offer that I could stay with him and Dinah, so I am taking him up on the offer. I'm not running away just moving in with a different family for now." Heading off to Larissa's room to say goodbye to Rose, explaining where he was going for now.

Over the last few months, our family moved out of the Eurubian city, and the people moved into the shade city, their own homes had been destroyed in the powerful fight between the two sorceresses. No longer fearful of attack over the portal the stone that represented it was missing from the wall. Not that anyone knew what had happened to it or where it had gone. We searched under the ruble only finding the bodies of the guards and one woman who died but nothing of Harmony or the woman she had taken off with. Neither did we have leads so hoping if she still existed, she would try to contact us herself. As far as we knew she had amnesia but still could contact Goseck if she wanted to. Our family scattered a little, some moving back into old homes. No one had seen the woman that had last been seen with Harmony and neither had anyone seen or heard of rumors of her. No one knew if she truly had been dead or not, other than her last contact with Goseck.

Over the last several months the family heard again about the group that was trying to take over a powerful empire among vampires. Their goal would be to control the actions of vampires to prevent killings of humans and savage attacks on societies that might have powerful magick. However, they made it clear that if there had been any powerful magic, they would be the ones to protect and look over it. As rumors go supposedly, they ripped the black onyx stone and the white crystal stone from the walls hiding them somewhere guarding them. For centuries we as vampires had been left to ourselves with no hierarchy. However now with so much going on and senseless human attacks, many were warming up to the idea of having a higher-up group take over, but no one could agree who should do it. A battle warred as to who had the right to govern, our family did our best to stay out of their way.

No one had a clue who this group had been other than to say they resembled shades. The royal family of the shade city denied being a part of these rumors. There had been rumors of different ones disappearing and not to be seen or heard from again as some assumed they might have been taken into this new group forming, or they might have been killed for standing against them, however, the truth will be difficult to prove until they step forward with their intentions.

Quite a few miles away from the family Alana had been preparing various creams adding them into the large tub as the young woman-soaked waiting for her wounds to heal. Not sure what to expect, it hadn't been a possibility that she had been ready for, even though she had been the one who created the stone of life. Even she had not known this was a possible result. Alana found the portal after an earthquake broke off a chunk from the one portal. It's when she first met Najee, that was so long ago. Now that he was killed, his body was absorbed into the remaining stone. He was the figure drawn in the stone that she brought to life as she ran her fingers over the lines of his body.

When the bolt of light from Nevaeh hit Harmony along with the bolt from Alana meant for the other, the life stone called both strikes to itself exploding the room but protecting the very person it had been made to protect, which was the guardian preserving as much as possible absorbing itself into Harmony. The fire that erupted charred her to a completely blackened-looking corpse except after a few days as the outer shell had broken off, it revealed a paler pink skin underneath completely healing her from the outside while the life stone existed now inside Harmony. Alana had been anxious to find out if it still worked or rather how it would work now?

At one point Alana had to be careful when Lucian had come nearby looking for Harmony with Charlie and Aidelle, the family searched this time before giving up or at least until Alana had planted an item of Harmony's at the Eurubian city so they would know that had been the last place she went to. Now they could assume she perished with everyone else in there and Alana was free to follow her goals without anything slowing her down.

After a month of the constant watch over her, she started stirring awake. Waiting for her to speak felt as if a lifetime passed. Watching Harmony sit up looking over her own body. Bewildered this hadn't been what she thought death would be like as she looked at the woman standing over her.

"I'm dead, aren't I? This isn't what I expected it to be like." Looking around the room, I felt strange.

Waking up to find yourself in a bedroom but then I couldn't remember my name so maybe forgetting was part of it?

"Yes, you're dead, now shower and get ready. We have a lot of work to do and already we are far behind what I wanted to accomplish." Even though I believed I was dead just out of natural reaction, I checked for a pulse and felt shocked when I found one.

"If I'm dead, why do I have a pulse?" Looking at me disgusted I could only assume I was irritating her.

"You have a pulse because you are alive, if you believed me would you have needed to check?" I had to agree, if I thought I was dead there wouldn't have been a reason to worry if I had a pulse or not.

"I'm alive? You were going to kill me. I was set on fire?" I looked over at her as the woman sat on a chair next to me shaking her head in disbelief.

"No, I didn't set you on fire. The life stone did that. I took care of you while you were healing, we've wasted a lot of time and have a lot to catch up on. Stop looking at me all shocked. Yes, you're alive, now get out of the tub and get dressed, your clothing is laying on the back of the chair here." Standing up she left the room giving me enough time to get showered off and dressed.

I had been in a rather small room not knowing where I was but then I still hadn't been able to remember much over the next several months. I started wondering if I would want to? We had lived underground in a rather large building that had been constructed using abandoned tunnels turning this into our headquarters.

Over the next several months we spent time building up the training grounds as well as searching for recruits. Some had been rather easy, others were difficult at first to find whether they would be in favor, for now, we wanted to get our numbers up as silently as possible before we started using force. We made it possible to change the outcomes of humans, vampires, shades, and other creatures out there. There had to be order, even if we had to force it. During this time, I had been taught fighting styles from Alana and a few others including a couple from the original order. All those years she kept up with them knowing if she were to take over, not that she ever wanted the shade city. Alana had only wanted its power to rule with. Not that I could remember much but I would have safely assumed this was nothing like I had ever seen.

Natural tunnels that had led under cities that were once used but over many years were built over, some cities had more tunnels than there was city space. We had taken over tunnels and open natural cave areas that had been abandoned adding more, to make space for what we needed. We built underneath the city right below their very feet and they had no idea what was happening. Neither would any creature get the idea it was here and come searching for it, we chose the best place at the center of everything.

Shades were easier to find than willing vampires as Alana already attached herself to several strong and reliable shades over the centuries, however, vampires were much less convincible. As the two of us would be ruling we needed strong guards who represented both sides even though I would have liked to find a vampire to rule with us. After all, we would be setting rules and regulations for their people as well even though most of their rules consist of the old ways only with a few changes. For as much as we worked on and organized, the only thing that seemed to be giving us a problem had been the simple fact that the life stone infused itself inside of me.

As much as Alana didn't want to admit it, I knew this was the only reason she hadn't killed me yet. She didn't want to risk losing the power now that it was in me, and she had no idea how to reverse the power to herself. On top of working, I was learning to fight as a shade, I was still trying to control the power inside me. I no longer had to hold it in my hands at a moment's whim I could be thinking of something or have a flashback moment kick in and instantly I was standing wherever that event happened. I tried to hide much of it. However, when I had a shade coming to attack me there would be that moment and whoosh, I would be gone as they would tackle nothing but air as I evaporated to another place. Some thought I did it as a fighting technique and liked it. Only Alana knew I didn't have control over it.

Sadly, if I had been taught about the life stone at one time. I hadn't remembered much since I lost my memory not that I even knew how that happened. Alana knew her design quite well even knowing her sister the lady in black understood the magical properties better than her. Over the years with the stone being passed among guardians she knew it would never fall into the hands of vampires. That without fail, it would one day make its way back to her. She hadn't been born a shade until Najee had taken her to the other world where they healed her, giving her the gift as she lived there explaining what she wanted to do once she was out. Najee locked her inside taking himself and their children out into the other world, her old world. He couldn't take them to his old world, a group of vampires decimated his entire world. They were permanently trapped in there when they killed all other forms of life, he hadn't dared once to see what they had done with his beloved homeland.

The one thing she never shared with anyone had been the simple fact she had taken credit for creating the life stone, only Najee figured out the fact that a powerful sorceress had taken her in, teaching her the craft believing she would uphold its values only to end up dying by the hand of her student, who had been the best deception she had ever been faced with. Not until a few days ago that she told me this secret when I had enough. I was angry over the fact she didn't seem to know how to control it for being the maker. She had been vague and secretive. At first, I thought she was doing this so she would have some control over me until the truth came out.

I spent most of my time in the training room even if I wasn't practicing. I loved watching the others battle with each other or teaching new tricks. Ways of manipulating the air around them to control the moisture or even the lack of it helped with the way they fought. As much as we had trained not many of the shades fought against vampires or some of the various creatures out there. We knew there had been easy assaults we could use; however, they were not always in a position where they could be used. We had to make sure our guards were capable of not allowing anything to get past them to get to us. So, learning many styles and mixing them even outside of the physical we had to research and find as much information as we could about other creatures. To know what they were capable of and what gifts might be out there that we might have to contend with.

There would be times I would wait until everyone left to practice in case I was to accidentally kill someone. No one would be around to watch as I would place things around the room, I would imagine scenes in my head almost like running a movie. I would picture myself going through an area searching for a debased vampire or another type of creature who had been hunting the city exposing humans to gifts without proper training or mentor to guide them or otherwise without their consent. We had to make sure humans were not aware of our existence. In the past they would kill or hunt us, now we could control our numbers. We worked on getting people into the city that passed for humans, setting them up, and preparing them for important use later in case the need ever arises. We could keep our world a secret as well as the other worlds that existed well beyond our world. All of this felt so overwhelming to me as I felt we needed more but Alana insisted that we could handle it.

I never explained to anyone why the walls in our training rooms were jet black. I hadn't wanted to let them know I had been torching it, however eventually some had finally seen what power I did control as Alana said it helped those to fear me, they would be less likely to attempt to overstep me. I think I earned the trust and worthiness of the others simply by practicing and working hard alongside the others without being treated differently by our trainers. Besides, there was bound to be someone that would challenge me, and I wanted to make sure I was ready to handle it when the time came.

One of the only complaints was from a few shades who were used to eating meat. While we wanted to stay low profile, we also needed to be completely self-dependent on ourselves as a group. A major part had been those who worked for us that tended to the gardens as lavish as they looked, it had been our main food supply. Some on the outside had the option of providing their food but for the most part, we were vegetarian, animals didn't exactly do well living underground except for the few cats that were determined to be cared for. I would call them pets, but I swear they were more cunning than that. We also wanted to keep as undetectable from humans as possible using our solar energy as well as digging our water wells. We also set up businesses in the human world to help blend some in more as we went from simply twenty people finally to eight hundred who all worked or at least reported directly to Alana and me. After a while I no longer had time to train. I was busy tending to the needs of those who worked under us.

After spending a solid year of this, we set out to make those outside aware of our presence and to let them know we were watching them. Our main court only had eighty people, as most were workers either inside the coven or outside in the human world being required to check in every two weeks. To distinguish ourselves from others to show who worked with us in our groups we had a color code. Alana and I had worn nothing else but solid black as the rest wore black mixed with red. We needed some way of tracking creatures down so that we would be able to see where they were all the time, especially since vampires were known to move around a lot being nomadic. Over the past year, we killed many of the demon hunters that had been controlled by the Doc and Katherine, they refused to follow anyone else. Only two joined the out-group. Alana no longer wished to admit to her existence anymore discussing her other than what we needed to do to move ahead.

Alana attempted many times to create something that would memorize where every creature was or to find out what was happening or where they were going. Most of what we could do was to listen to the human news as certain events would unfold searching out the results at times, we found it was natural, human control, or on the few occasions started by creatures. I hadn't been sure this would work and even presented an idea close to it to test what Alana had thought about it, dismissing it as I thought she would. I thought I would give it a try myself. I found over time the life stone that absorbed into me offered more power than I could have imagined.

I sat down with one of the shades who seemed to like meditating. She tried to teach me. I found that I was a natural. Later when we talked about this, she felt that I may have already been able to do this however because of my memory. I had forgotten all about it. She was positive that at some point there would be something that would bring it all back to me. Never voicing it out loud I had been afraid to find out what my former life was or if I even wanted to know what it was.

We had a chance to prove ourselves as other creatures would find out our strength and power. One of the vampires who made quite a name for himself over the centuries had been out making younger followers, not discriminating who he chose or if they wanted the change to begin with. The town had been afraid of a serial killer being on the loose as more were staying in late at night in fear, that they would be next. There hadn't been any rational way he was choosing his victims which made it much more difficult to track him, as he also did not appear in the crystal balls to give away his location. He had been covering his tracks rather well. Leaving lookouts in as many areas as we had available. Eventually, we cornered him as Alana, and I made our way with our top guards. This time he struck in the heart of the city. Keeping him penned in guessing what was coming after him, he hadn't been afraid of our watchers; however, he had become aware of the fact so many of us closed in on him.

"If you wish to make me an example then why don't you do the dirty work yourself, or are you so weak you need all your little henchman?" As he announced this, we knew there had been two others who were with him.

However, we allowed them to slip by for now, much easier for them to pass on the news rather than anything else.

Getting closer Alana and I silently agreed I would go after him first, if there were any problems than any of our guards could move in to attack.

"I'll take that challenge; you won't be difficult for me at all." As I walked out from the darkness so he could see me.

Only the streetlight illuminated the night with the moon hidden behind clouds. I could tell that in the nearby building a few people were looking out their windows. At least they only looked like a few teenagers, nothing we had to fear yet. We preferred keeping this in silence, not allowing humans to see for fear of hunts again.

"You're far too confidant and far too eager my friend." As he simply stood there showing no fear of attack.

I wanted him to make the first move so even I stood there carefully hoping he would grow impatient.

"What would you know about eagerness? There may be nothing wrong with expanding your group, yet you have no criteria, consent, or reason for changing anyone let alone the ways you ditch them if they are not working out for you. Leaving them for humans to deal with exposes us leaving a great risk to our way of life." Not that he needed a lecture, but I felt it was a good way to stall waiting for him to strike first.

This vampire had been around when the original vampire court was still in place. It's not as if the rules changed any however now there is a new order taking control now.

"I could teach you a few things, who knows, maybe teach you to survive long enough that your friend when she no longer needs you, your life will still be capable of living." I wasn't too surprised he was trying to undermine my confidence in Alana.

"I'm not here to strike a deal. If you wish to die, I will honor you otherwise we can finish this rather quickly." Now instead of standing there a small smile spread across his face as if he thought of something important. Now whispering so that only I could hear him.

"Then, by all means, kill me. I could link you to your past and bring you to your love but then who knows, perhaps you have no heart any longer now that you've joined the side of evil." As he said this he looked over at Alana.

She was shifting uncomfortably now probably wondering if he was going to lure me away with a tidbit from my past. It would be sad if it could happen that easily.

"Before I do, there's something that doesn't make sense? You've been around pretty much forever, why expose yourself now. If anything, you lived by the old rules when no one else was. Why be so careless. Everything I've found out about you doesn't make sense from what you're doing?" I knew Alana and the others were getting anxious, growing tired of my conversation with him.

However, I couldn't help but feel this was too easy even if it had taken us a while to find him.

"You're right to assume there's more to this, after all, I should know better than to risk exposing myself to humans, rather interesting though there's a new group taking control. I heard stories about you thinking if I found you, I might find the truth. I rather hoped you would be one of those who lived among the humans. I wanted to find out if the power would transfer out of you or if you would die when it no longer recognized you. Do you honestly think that a veteran vampire such as myself would pretend to need followers when I am normally a nomad? I'm here to seize power from you, no one should rule over vampires. Even if the lines between vamps and shades are crossing more, that's over now. We no longer need shades to carry on our historical legacy, we are here to regain rightful power." It certainly felt like a trap, I had to figure out how to get us out of it.

In my mind, I could flash an instant image of where every one of my people was standing. I had never moved this many people without touching them, but I had concentrated the best I could, mentally I was picking up on it, I could see an ambush coming in. As they leapt from the shadows landing on their feet about to attack, Alana and my guards landed on their feet confused as if nothing happened, but mere dust stood between myself and them. I hoped it worked, at least I knew they were no longer here in danger, I only hoped they all arrived back at the training center.

"I'm surprised you chose to stay, unless of course, you are choosing to convert. I couldn't promise you would live but at least you would no longer be a filthy shade." As he spoke the others crowded in much closer more curious how the others had done the vanishing act, but I stayed behind.

"Besides the fact that you are a vampire, what makes you think you should rule over vampires when you're willing to flush out someone as stupidly as this? I only stayed because I do not fear you." As I stood there, I could tell the others who questioned why I would stay here alone on my own.

They hadn't detected any shades in breathing distance. I intended on standing behind my statement that I felt no fear let alone will show none. For some reason I felt whatever I had been in my past I doubted it was anything like the way I was now.

"It's my birthright. Simple as that. My family had ruled over vampires for centuries. Besides, I have no need for or regard for humans. I simply humor them, some are rather skilled and can do a lot of damage hunting us during the daylight hours when we are defenseless, shades are no different and if you were truly aware of what your friend was up to, you would see she is killing vampires. Not protecting them, but then she's been killing innocent shades as well. If you're not converting it was rather stupid for you to stick around." Nodding towards someone behind me I felt a stabbing pain shoot through me.

I looked down, one of his men pierced me by slicing their hand right through me, ripping their hand back out towards themselves again. I hadn't bled as much as I thought I would. Blood dripped from my back and front as I felt the pain slowly kick in after the adrenaline had given up trying to fight the pain. I wished I left with the others now. I wasn't sure what I had been waiting for other than feeling an electric shock searing through my body now as fire erupted from the piercing, forcing the vampires back from the fire that now engulfed me. Painful as it had been. I never once lost my balance as they watched on in horror. I think they were more afraid that I wasn't dying. I knew the fire from the stone was healing me in a way no vampire would heal, and neither would an ordinary shade. Now making my way over to a stunned creature, I had done my part attacking the vampire setting him on fire with my painful agony of healing as his followers watched him writhe in pain not able to put it out. I transported us both far enough away so they could not help him.

What I hadn't been prepared for had been those three vampires who had been watching from the new area I had taken him to. For some reason I knew I had been here before out in the middle of nowhere, I couldn't remember why or exactly when. As I watched the other vampire waste away, I collapsed in pain from the fire consuming me as it had before. I was aware of the three others racing toward me. I could barely make their faces out as I closed my eyes focusing on Alana calling myself to her. One of my problems had been that if the stone's power would heal me or if I had been injured it would be hard to concentrate on staying put. I would find myself transporting all over hoping to stay concealed unnoticed. Something that Alana had me working on hoping to find a way of controlling myself if I felt pain. A particular training I hated. Being stabbed intentionally or various injuries inflicted intentionally to practice restraint.

I found it much easier to be anywhere she was simply by concentrating on the ring I had given her to wear. Not that she knew this was the purpose. I had given it to her but keeping tabs on her location made finding the groups much easier. As the group had gotten closer, I phased out showing up burning in front of Alana who wasted no time moving me. Not that she could touch me but she had made a rolling stone table I could lay on so she could safely move me into a room that I could stay in until I was fully healed.

At least we made our point as the news of our encounter spread amongst other creatures, not just vampires and shades. But then it also spread to the ears of others I had at one time known. Feeling too tired and still feeling my nerves twitch as I started to get feeling back again. I laid back trying to clear my mind hoping for this to be over quickly. At least this time I stayed put as the pain slowly worked its way out. I could feel every nerve and muscle in my body. I knew as soon as I woke Alana would have a lot of questions for me.

Chapter Eight

A different kind of life

The three individuals stood there in utter shock at what they had seen, not sure at first what it was, not until it had the characteristic flash except there had been no visible stone around, or the one they were familiar with for controlling it. Looking at each other they had been as confused as each other. They had heard of a group trying to take over control or at least attempting to re-establish the old order. At first, our family had been worried about it since most either kept to themselves governing over their species as shades kept to themselves as well as vampires, it was forbidden by the former order for classes to mix but over the centuries it had been relaxed. Other than the fact our own family was well mixed we had already lived by many of the simple rules based on common sense and experience. The main thing we would be concerned with had been a new little girl with whom we had join our family.

Most of all we hadn't ever thought we would see her still alive let alone fighting a rather powerful vampire and succeeding at that, which also made us wonder why was she attacking him or being attacked by him in the first place? Until they had all come to the same understanding she must have joined or been a rather important part of the new order, after all, it would explain the odd clothing she was wearing, the only reason they hadn't recognized her immediately. The vampire she left there to die and barely been able to crawl away as soon as she disappeared herself. Others were there immediately to remove him from the area. We could only assume he would die later or might survive, but either way, this wasn't going to get any better especially since it had been a very old legendary vampire who rarely was spotted out, Luther Augustus.

Not wanting to share it with everyone right away they felt there was one person who had been the best at handling matters like this. Racing home quickly cutting their hunt short, they were taking a vacation in this area for a change however after what happened, it was rather urgent to get back.

It had taken us a few days longer than normal to get home. As Aiden, Emma and Lorah made their way back to the family they tried to slow down before they had come to Charlie's house, not wanting to alert the others there was something up, knowing they would wonder since they had not been expected back yet. More so in the last few years, it seemed like some creatures were either getting out of control or crazed with a disease. Even our own family had to watch ourselves not to be caught or infected by those. But there also seemed to be more senseless killings. Strange as it may seem many feared the lady in black almost following her as if she was the order. Once she was gone it seemed no one had that same sense of fear or dread. Either from a feeling of comfort or being self-assured, trying to make names for themselves and exerting power over lower forms.

From the point that the new order started taking over there was a rash of attacks which after a month they quickly stopped as the rumor spread while only the three of us had the real answer to why as we explained to Charlie.

One of the things our family felt deeply saddened as most vampires knew almost as an unwritten rule how important it is to safeguard our secret, keeping it silent about our world however there was also to be no changing of children. We know of families who had but they waited for their children to finish growing or at least to reach a certain age before they were changed. Most were still careful to stay within the unwritten law. However, we wound up with a small child who for an eternity would be cursed in the body of a child not that any of us would know whether or not the mind of the child would someday grow beyond the mind of a child, an adult in a child's body or if it would eternally be a child. At one time these children would have been considered a burden and left for humans to deal with or destroy. Our family simply didn't have the heart to turn our backs on something that was not given a choice or no control of its own. Vampire children were treated much differently than any other creature. They had the potential for so much dangerous chaos or if you were lucky extremely sweet and kind.

We may not have broken any rules however no one would be able to prove it had not been us who changed the child unless they knew what we were like, so to safeguard the child we had to be careful. She became our immortal child of the night. After a short time, we found she was not the only immortal child that had been found that was being protected. Oddly enough the others had more of an idea of who had been behind it which shocked us all. We never thought we would hear his name in connection with this. It had been Luther Augustus, one of the last remaining vampires from the higher-order centuries ago.

Six months ago, Lewis and Evangeline had been out when they first came across her. Not sure what they would run into, there had been a rather mangled carcass of an animal with a long line of blood dripping as they followed it, the trail led them to a small child around the age of eight years old sitting in the cold snow with a dead animal in front of her. Tiny as she had been she could have easily passed for five or six. Sitting in the snow with no shoes or socks, just a little shirt and sweatpants on she seemed un-phased by the cold. She was soaking in blood as her hair also brightly shined with matted hair and bloodstains.

At first, they thought maybe the animal died protecting her and she was stuck out here lost from her family until they had seen her quickly divert her attention from them back to the animal draining it of the remaining blood it had. When she was done the expression changed on her face. She seemed excited to see us, standing up and smiling as she walked towards us holding her arms out to be held. Not feeling threatened by the child Evangeline picked her up taking her home letting her get cleaned. There had been no rumors of a vampire missing a child not that anyone would want to admit they changed a child so young. Sadly, even if it had been to save their life it was barely a life to be stuck at this age for eternity, death would have been chosen long before this option would have been made.

When it had been decided that Evangeline and Lewis would be keeping her in the family, they made sure she was given an education, as she had been tutored by Lewis who used to work as a schoolteacher at one time. Lewis had forgotten how much he missed teaching deciding to take on a part-time position teaching in a local school. When they felt she was able to control herself enough to be around mortals she enrolled in elementary school. At least she hadn't attacked a mortal however she had tried against Lewis and even Evangeline when she had a moment of weakness but after a short time, she was able to learn to control those feelings.

It helped that she was able to learn quicker than an average child but still slower than an average vampire adult. To account for her small size, it had been explained that she was physically challenged, had possible dwarfism, and was not expected to grow much leaving it as an unknown condition to the mortals they had to give the excuse to. Many were sympathetic towards them never giving her a problem. They assumed they would home school her for junior high and high school once it came time. It came to the point she had more than one set of parents as everyone passed her around however, she primarily lived with Evangeline and Lewis. Not sure how she would do out on a hunting trip she stayed behind with Charlie and Sophie.

She was the first to welcome them back, not worried they had come back early just excited that they had. So far there had been no name to refer to the little girl and to help teach her they needed a way of letting her know when someone was calling or speaking to her. To give her a special feeling of importance with a name of her own. We had her choose her name. She also picked out a middle name, calling herself Savannah Aubrey. She stood out from the rest of the family however she was loved, cared for, and taught the same as the rest of the family. After brushing out her hair getting all the dirt and other things that had been trapped and built up in her hair, it shined in the sun a dark sable color matching her smooth skin as her eyes were even darker as a jet black, she had been the most amazing child the family had ever set their eyes on. She was just as loving and kind-hearted as anyone could have hoped for, and we all loved having the chance to get to know her better. Larissa and Savannah loved playing together, for now, they were relatively close in age for appearances.

Sophie had been out gathering the few herbs they could find in the cold weather leaving Savannah at home with Charlie. Watching as she had raced out the door, he was there within seconds to see what Savannah had gotten so excited over. Not that she was concerned, Charlie knew from experience the look on their faces, he could tell there was something of concern.

It almost seems as soon as the family is settled in something throws a wrench in just to mess things up. As much as we love Sophie, we love to tease her that ever since she made Charlie fall under her spell the family has either been in turmoil, or a massive event changed everything making us wonder if we will make it through it or if we will just grow stronger from it. So far it seems we don't know when to quit as we do keep growing not just stronger but with more family as time goes on.

"What brings you home so soon? Hopefully nothing too serious?" We all knew Charlie was waiting for things to settle down.

We were all thankful that this time Lucian hadn't sunk into a depression as he had the last time. He spent much of his time either with his niece Larissa or our newest family member Savannah. He had also been taking lessons from Sophie. He had never really been that interested in plants, herbs, or witchcraft for that matter, not that Sophie ever called it that, most mortals did. Sophie preferred to call it her potions or remedies as she had been taught by her teachers the gypsies.

The family spent a lot of time helping the shades rebuild their city even though they were unable to rebuild the city of the Eurubian people, it had been far too destroyed leaving nothing usable behind. Once they left, they were ready to settle down as a family trying to live for a while. As we debated, we knew Charlie was still waiting for an answer until finally Lewis decided to be the one to explain.

"It has to do somewhat with Luther Augustus. We were out hunting as it had only been Aiden, Lorah, and I. Emma and Evangeline had been back at the temporary camping site we set up. We were in the middle of the field when we were tracking a deer when a few yards from us appeared a bright blazing fire with two individuals appearing out of it. One had been on fire more so than the other. The one left Luther behind, we could only assume she thought he was dead or as good as dead. When she left, he had his followers pick him up immediately leaving with him. The only thing is we know who she was. We can't figure out why she would be messing with a vampire-like Luther." Taking a breather, I looked around to make sure we were alone so that no one else would hear the rest of the news.

"Lewis, who was she? Was it Katherine or the other woman who had taken Harmony?" Charlies was curious why they were taking so long to get to the point.

Savannah had been oblivious to all of this as she made her way next door to play with Larissa being bored from our conversation.

"It wasn't Katherine and certainly not that other woman that took Harmony, even though we are pretty certain we can count on her being alive as well. But we were shocked when we saw it was Harmony. She's not dead as we assumed, there may have been a burnt outline of her even with pieces of her flesh left behind, but when we saw her ablaze, she was certainly alive. She was also wearing a certain outfit. The same that was rumored to be distinguishing the new order. If ranking fits, I would say she is the highest. She wore all black with the slightest hints of red." Charlie was baffled by this, not sure what to say.

"Before we figure out the meaning behind this, we won't say a word to Lucian. I don't want to put him through all of that again." Charlie had run his hand through his hair more out of frustration wondering what was going on and why she would be staying with the new order?

"What are we not telling Lucian?" As Nichole walked in the door with Larissa in one arm and holding savannah with the other.

"We found out something that might be disturbing to him, which is to us, but I wanted to talk to Goseck first before we say a word to him." Not sure what they were talking about Nichole learned Charlie usually had his reasons for not explaining things right away so that eventually, she would find out.

Charlie hadn't wasted any time calling Goseck hoping to figure this out before this situation happened again, possibly in front of Lucian and have him disappear into who knows what possibly getting harmed. Goseck hadn't answered the phone, Lucian did.

"Did I dial the wrong number? I was trying to get in touch with Goseck, is he around you by any chance Lucian?" Charlie was surprised that he had gotten Lucian instead.

"Don't worry you're not losing your mind, this is Goseck's number. My cell phone had an unfortunate accident, it never saw that cliff coming at it. I guess I wasn't meant to have one. He's out with Dinah right now, some exploring thing for some reason. Members of the new order have been snooping around up further and they wanted to find out more about it if they could. Not to worry I'm sure they're being careful. Anything I can tell them when they get back? Dinah left her cell phone here also; they didn't want the phones going off in case someone was to call them when they took off." Making sure he didn't give Lucian any reason to worry although he would be curious about what they found out.

"I just had a question for him, when they get back have them call me. I'm curious myself about the new order if they do find anything out." Charley hoped he would keep his voice sounding calm and composed.

"Okay, no problem I was about to head out so leaving the cell phones here. I'll leave a message in case they get back early. I don't expect to see them until tomorrow morning if they work their way back early, could be a while. Anything I can help with?" Hesitating a little Charlie wasn't sure how to respond to it without tipping Lucian off. After all, he was smart and could read him well.

"It's not anything that can't wait. Just some things I was curious about that Goseck would know. I was left here with the kids, and they seem to be getting anxious or rather bored so I'm going to let you go and entertain them for a while. I'll talk to you later Lucian." Turning off the phone Charlie hoped he sounded casual enough not to pique Lucian's curiosity.

Charlie decided he might as well make his way up north. He would be able to track down Goseck and Dinah from this side safely enough. Being careful not to go too close to the cabin, Charlie made his way outward a little before trying to pick up on the trail. There was an old trail that Lucian had taken, he hoped this is where he had gone, hoping he would not see Charlie or that certainly would raise his suspicions.

It had taken a few hours, both had been around in these areas many times in the past, however, now locating a single trail leading northward. Following this it seemed more likely they were still on this one. Being careful not to be caught by anyone else heading up this way while keeping his attention out for Goseck and Dinah not to sneak up on them, Charlie hadn't been watching out quite for everyone as much as he thought he might have been. There was only one person he had known that would be able to sneak up on him, face plant him in the snow and stick around to laugh about it, Lucian.

"So, wasn't that important that you needed to come up here searching for them? I made it look like I took off in a few directions depending on how close you wanted to get to the cabin. I wasn't sure if you would come or not? Gotta be big if you're hunting them down to speak with them. Are they in danger or something, 'cause you're taking a lot of precautions?" Standing up next to Charlie, Lucian had offered a hand.

Instead, Charlie pulled him down while swiping a huge handful of snow in his face.

Laughing Charlie said, "you're not always going to get away without being seen. And yes, it is important. I didn't want you to follow, but now that you're with me you might as well stay. It seems like we are rather close. I have some things to talk to Goseck about then later with you." As he said that Charlie looked pained but also very serious.

For the rest of the way, neither of us had spoken although there had been a lot of thoughts running through Lucian's head as Charlie thought there might be. Dinah must have heard us coming as she caught up to us before we could go any further.

"They will notice all of us if we go up there; they are already suspicious enough that they are possibly being watched. I'll take you back to our spot. We have been staying at night then we will be back later to discuss what we have found so far. I wish Lucian hadn't been with you because I don't think you're going to like hearing this." Dinah had the same expression that Charlie had shown before making Lucian even more curious about what was going on.

As Dinah had shown us to the small cave, we watched her take off to rejoin Goseck. I knew Charlie wasn't in the mood to talk as I could tell whatever it was, he would have preferred me to go back home than face me with whatever was going to be so horrible.

Whatever was troubling Charlie the simple fact we hadn't talked in the last several hours didn't seem to occur to him. After a while, I wasn't sure if it was something I wanted to find out? They all seemed to be taking care of it assuming they would speak to me later if they had to but now that I was here, they had no choice but to speak of it in front of me before they were ready. At first, I thought all of this had to do with the rising of the new order but if they were all worried about me and how I was going to take it unless they thought it scared me? They should have known me better than that.

I was happy to have nightfall but then also worried about what Dinah and Goseck were about to say. I had gotten rather used to Goseck's habits so I could see why Harmony felt safe and comfortable traveling with him when she was around. When they left, I thought nothing of it and now it was more than just an interest if Charlie was getting involved. There were other little things over the past year that popped up except we stayed out of it for the most part. It wasn't our place to meddle but only to know the information to be prepared in case there was something that could affect our family and from the sounds of it, this was getting to be that way.

In the distance, we could see the two of them coming closer as we watched only Charlie had stood up, I wasn't sure if I wanted to get involved right away and I think Charlie was glad that I decided to stay put while they first talked. I knew they were speaking to each other in rather hushed tones even though I could pick up a few words and as I had one, in particular, caught my attention letting me know why this had anything to do with me. Only once Charlie looked back at me with a saddened look on his face shaking his head as if he didn't know what to say anymore. Even Goseck was visibly upset as he seemed to finally speak the words. Before they were to fill me in, they had chosen to head home instead of speaking it further here. They were not sure how to take it themselves and wanted Sophie to be spoken to when I was.

We had taken off for Charlie's home noticing the activity at the house picked up. Both Lewis and Evangeline were still there talking to Sophie as she was planting seeds for her indoor herb garden. Nichole and Rose were talking to each other on the couch with Larissa and savannah. Jacob and Anthony were having their serious discussion in the corner except had stopped once they saw the rest of us coming in. Lorah and Emma had taken off for a while but explained she would be back later. For the most part, it was like a packed family reunion again. Everyone was sitting around waiting to find out what was going on. Only a few had known while the others sat in quiet curiosity waiting to be filled in. Sitting down, I sat with my mom and sister while Charlie asked Sophie to finish tending to her herbs. Later he wanted to discuss this with everyone in the room before he lost the nerve to be able to talk about it at all.

As Charlie stood near Sophie in the front living room so that everyone could see him. Aiden quietly slipped into the room with Emma, Lorah, and Aidelle not far behind. Taking his time deciding how he wanted to break parts of the information to the family since others knew either bits or pieces or nothing at all. This way nothing would be missed, and all would be caught up to the same information before he broke into the difficult news. Waiting for everyone to be settled Charlie started to speak.

"I know we are all aware of the new order that has been getting established with a rather furious push in the last year. Our own family has finally been settling in during this last year. It's been three years since the last situation our family had been involved with however from experience, we always need to be prepared in case we need to pick up and move or protect ourselves. Most of the information would be basic and nothing to alert or bother us as it would apply the same to any other family. However, we have an unusual connection to a person involved in it so it's why we need to take extra precautions." As soon as he said that everyone looked at Lucian.

"I know we are used to Lucian getting into trouble or starting something however this isn't something he started. Not that he's not connected, not even he knows himself about it. If anything, Goseck and Sophie are more connected than anyone." Charlie kept stopping wanting to word things right, not to put blame anywhere but to let the family hopefully feel rest assured that life could go on as it always has but that we needed to be more careful about things.

"Goseck and Dinah had gone up further observing a group from the new order. From what we can find, they distinguish themselves by dressing according to ranking as the old order had centuries ago. The highest of the order seem to wear all black with a slight hint of red along with the higher-end guards. Lower-end guards or others who happen to work directly with them wear all black very similar to the demon hunters. In the old days, vampires would have been ruled and been kept clean by no intermingling with others, not even mortals. It was forbidden. More than half of our family would have been sentenced to death according to the old rules." Charlie hated admitting it but then it had also been another reason his siblings and family stayed to themselves fearing they might break a rule.

Life had become much more difficult trying to live outside than it had to simply stay cooped up minding one's own business than mingle with the outside world.

"We have found that the new order has made a few changes from the original where this one allows intermingling of classes. However, they still do not allow mortals to know about us other than those that are of human descent from shades. That means they would be against Rose, Jacob, Larissa, Savannah, Aiden, Anthony, Evangeline, Lewis, Goseck, and Sophie from mingling with the rest of us. They have made it clear that they will decide if it is not hidden whether to allow certain one's rights such as us, since we have lived quietly with each other for so long blending in and not letting others know about us. Even though ultimately, they could decide to rule favor against us and attempt to have us destroyed, that would be all of us and not just the ones they felt disobeyed them." As Charlie took his time, we were all in shock at what he was informing us of.

Then as we had all suspected at that point not sure if savannah understood or not. Charlie finished explaining to the rest of us what we already knew just had not voiced yet.

"Any child such as savannah according to the new order is considered dangerous and marked to be destroyed. I know how everyone feels towards her as I do myself and we will do what is needed to protect her. We know she is not a danger regardless of how the new order feels. I understand how mortals have an order to their lives, they have a government system set up to protect the rights of the citizens however the way this is being done denies far too many their rights by deciding they are not worthy of life, even in death." Charlie placed his arm around

Sophie moving her over to the other couch sitting down with her holding her hand as Goseck was about to finish explaining.

Goseck had taken just as long trying to form his words since it was very personal to him what he was about to say.

"This isn't easy no matter how I word it other than to start explaining what we understand so far. There are primarily two people running the new order with several beneath them and both are very powerful as this has been seen by several different creatures. One of them we all know is the woman who had taken Harmony, her name as we have found out is Alana, she is the sister to Katherine Hawthorne. The one who died in the Eurubian city was their mother who posed as the queen for many years in the shade city. Alana is a trained sorceress; she is also a shade that had been trapped in another world until she was freed to come back here." As his voice started to lower, most assumed it had just been hard on him losing Harmony as it had been for Lucian except there was much more.

"As we all know Harmony had been with Jacob until they had been knocked out. Jacob was placed in a crystal with many of us as they left Harmony out because of her memory loss. Both sides tried to use her and as we found pieces left behind, we believed she was dead in the city along with Nevaeh the queen of the shade city. Some have spoken of the life stone being absorbed into her body, at first believing that she was killed and destroyed along with it. I know this is very difficult for Lucian and me to hear. I would love to say I have good news coming from this but as far as we know, we could still be wrong. I still want to confirm it." Taking another breather this time longer, even as Charlie put his face in his hands not wanting to hear the news. Lucian inched forward in his seat as Nichole placed her hand on his shoulder.

"Harmony is still alive. I have not personally heard from her, but she is ruling with Alana, she is the other person representing the new order. As far as we have heard from others speaking or have come across her, she does not remember anything from her past but has moments when these memories do come in. We don't know if Alana is keeping them from her or if she is choosing not to remember them. The life stone is infused in her so there is no longer a physical object she uses; it is a physical part of her. She is the main power forcing the fast drive behind the order and protecting Alana. So far, the new order seems logical and, in all senses, needed in some ways. It may not be evil unfortunately they force their reasons for control and are not exactly interested in protecting everyone. When it's left to such a small group to decide who has the right to exist and who does not." Taking a deep breath Goseck hadn't wanted to look around the room since he was sure their expressions would have displayed what he felt earlier when he found out she was alive.

Noticing that Goseck couldn't finish, Lewis had over-explained what prompted the meeting for today.

"Many of us are familiar with the Augustus family. We had been out hunting when out of nowhere came a bright flash of fire surrounding two people. It took us a few minutes to recognize who they were because of being engulfed in flames, and we thought his family might have been wiped out some years ago. Far too many theories and stories around that, however, Luther was there with Harmony, it looked like she attacked him leaving him for dead. Why she was attacking or possibly defending him she had seen us, we don't know if she recognized us, she seemed more intent on getting somewhere else. So far, the life stone is working inside of her still. We can only assume our venom would kill her if the stone decided to reject her as its host. There's still a lot to learn about this." Taking a moment for the family especially Goseck, Sophie, and Lucian to take in the news they were hearing which couldn't have been any easier for anyone else either.

"But for the most part, we need to stay low-key for now because many of our family members need to be protected right now. We don't know if she will go against us or if we might have to fight her if she comes at us. As close as we had gotten to her, we might have to kill her if she tries to kill us. I know it's not something any of us want to consider but that's for the worst scenario possible." Lewis said with his voice lowering.

Just from the sound of his voice, we all knew he hoped it wouldn't come to this. No one moved for quite a while, it seemed everyone was far too stunned or still trying to comprehend what they heard. It almost felt safer to keep everyone here for now, not that it was the most logical. We would blend better in our own homes especially Rose and Jacob, most might not even give them a second glance since they lived around mortals that hadn't noticed a difference. The first to leave had been Aiden and Emma. Emma aged a little since she first joined our family. There had been talk before about changing her, however, nothing had been done about it yet, not that we knew if we could.

The lady in black at one point had bitten her and she hadn't changed, not that anyone understood why. Aiden still didn't like the idea of testing it on her again in case it didn't take. We knew what discussions they would be having tonight however whichever choice they were to make she would still be in as much danger as the rest of us. Then slowly different ones left for different reasons. No one had spoken the whole time, even choosing to leave in silence. Before they had each given Lucian, Goseck, and Sophie a hug, not having to say a word, we understood what they were feeling.

Waiting until almost everyone left Charlie sat down next to Lucian curious about how he was taking all of this since he had not moved or spoken during the whole night. Rose wanted to stay but she knew he would be alright with Charlie and Sophie for now. Making it clear if he wanted to talk at all. Before she left, she told him just to come over.

"I wanted to know if you intend on looking for Harmony?" With a soft-spoken voice Charlie wanted to find out what Lucian was thinking since he stayed silent even after the others left, he hadn't moved from his place.

"She can't remember who she is. I doubt she will remember who I am? As much as I want to see her or at least make sure she's okay. I would put the family at risk this time if I went looking for her. So, in a way, I can't find her even if I wanted to but if I don't then she could remember us and not come after us for the right reason. I'm just really confused." At least Lucian was thinking it through before he took off.

Not that any of us would have blamed him since none of us knew how we would have reacted finding out again the one we loved was alive, just this time in a possibly dangerous situation. Let alone the possibility that would mean having to fight her. That alone was confusing Lucian. He wasn't sure if he could admit if he could make himself do something about it if she tried to kill him. Lucian thought about it and was positive if it had come to that he would simply let her. The only way he could harm her is if she came after his family, not that he wanted to think about that.

"For now, there's a lot we won't know. We must be patient and wait, hope for the best. If you do decide to let me or your father know first, we will go with you. This isn't the time to be searching on your own." Patting Lucian on the back Charlie had gone into the other room to talk with Sophie.

Chapter Nine

Vampire Children

Over the next few days, both Lewis and Evangeline spent more time at home with savannah when they heard the news of a few vampire children who had been killed. Luther had been intentionally looking for Harmony hoping to disgust her, he changed a few of the children to one of the largest cities of mortals that she had been rumored to be close to. At least according to rumors only the high-ranking guards and followers knew where they had stationed themselves. Now that he knew somewhat of where to find her or where their headquarters was located in the vicinity, he no longer needed to try to flush them out. The fledgling humans who had been changed were dumped along the side not wanting to waste time with them or the children, they had been littered everywhere.

Some handled the change well preserving their lives however a few lost their sanity, lost control, or had no idea how to control what they had become. Even a few after the change simply died from the venom not taking effect correctly killing them off. This is what Luther meant for the majority, however, the children fared much better than the older ones.

On one of the days that Lewis was teaching his class, he noticed that Savannah made close friends with another girl named Amanda Lynn. Even though they both had been friendly to the others in class they acted more like sisters just the same way that savannah acted around Larissa. Both acting their age trading secrets between the two, it had been nice seeing her having fun blending in with the other children. After a few weeks of watching them spend every minute together, they even started sharing the same table while they simply added another chair to the table that was meant for one child. Her parents had been rather friendly as they always made a point to wave goodbye to savannah when they picked up Amanda.

"Lewis, Amanda was telling me about a slumber party she went to last weekend. I was wondering if I could have a slumber party. I don't care if anyone else shows up. I just want to have Amanda over. Do you think Evangeline would let us?" She looked so hopeful Lewis hadn't wanted to say no to her which had been so difficult to do, but he knew he should let Evangeline know first before they made any choices.

"We can ask when we get home, I already know my opinion, but I need to speak with Evangeline first to make sure it's okay." Gathering what they had both needed they headed home.

Getting out of the car as fast as she could since she was holding onto the excitement as much as she could. She rushed to find Evangeline who happened to be folding laundry.

"Evangeline, Evangeline, can I, can I? Amanda gets to spend the night at a friend's house, and I want her to stay here. Can she? Lewis said we had to ask you first. Please say yes." Her eyes were huge in anticipation hoping Evangeline wouldn't say no.

"Before I can decide either way there's something we need to discuss first. I'm sure Amanda is a little more like your cousin Larissa, they both sleep, and she may wonder why you don't sleep the entire weekend?" Wrinkling her nose, savannah hadn't been too happy with the way that Evangeline answered her, not that she said no yet.

"I can pretend to sleep. Besides, I doubt she will sleep either. We could have Larissa over, she would like her, then we could have a regular slumber party." Savannah seemed rather excited over her plan as she tried to show Evangeline that she could pretend to sleep.

"Very cute, now go to your room and work on your homework while I talk to Lewis, your idea of having Larissa over also might not be a bad idea. We will let you know our answer in a few minutes." Savannah grabbed her bag running to her bedroom closing the door behind her.

We could guess she was too excited to do any homework.

"I know she had been doing rather well at school around other humans and we have had Larissa here overnight, but do you think it's safe having a human spend the night here? What if she does find out that savannah doesn't sleep, what excuse are we going to use?" Evangeline looked concerned not that she didn't mind her spending time as a regular little girl.

However, her concern had been more for covering up for the fact that savannah was not your average little girl. She was much more relaxed and might have let something slip.

"It's a good way for her to learn and behave like a regular girl. This could be a good thing for her. Besides we could explain that she had a sleeping disorder, it's common. I doubt her friend will notice how much sleep she doesn't get if she notices at all. Her parents like savannah and have been very friendly." Lewis seemed alright with it; I knew I could trust his judgment call; he did spend more time around her with mortals all day at school than I did.

"Then I think we made our choice; do you think we need to tell her, or do you guess she already knows?" We both knew she was listening at the door as we heard her scream in excitement rushing out of her room to give both of us a hug and then racing for the phone to call Amanda.

Leaning against Lewis as he hugged me, it was nice having a little one living with us but then it still felt sad knowing we would never see her grow. At least we could make her life as comfortable and normal as we possibly could. Rather give her something that was taken from her.

As soon as she was done speaking with her friend, she handed the phone over as Amanda's parents had questions. Feeling comfortable, her parents simply said that it would be fine as an equal squeal of excitement from their end erupted. As soon as school ended the next day, she would be coming home for her first spend-the-night party, now to speak to Nichole and Jacob to see if Larissa could stay also.

Savannah had still been on the house phone to Amanda telling her the good news and making plans for their weekend letting her know that her cousin might be joining, that Evangeline was asking her right now. Pulling out her cell phone to call Rose, no one answered so she left a message asking if Larissa could spend the night over the weekend. After a few hours, there was a knock at the door not expecting anyone this evening, Lewis was surprised to find Rose and Larissa standing at the door. With a yawn, Rose explained.

"I hope you don't mind; I go to work a little earlier in the morning, she never would have let me sleep. She was already bouncing off the walls." A slight smile came over Rose's face.

Giving Larissa a kiss goodnight reminding her to behave she left her sleeping bags with her and Lewis before she left. Savannah still on the phone grabbed Larissa excitedly, both had run to her room to talk about their plans for the weekend. Only the chatter could be heard from the two until there were no more sounds at all. We guessed that Larissa must have fallen asleep, at least we hoped they had hung up the phone first. Checking on the girls we had come into the room quietly moving Larissa to the bed, taking the house phone out of the bedroom, we carefully closed the door behind us. Savannah sat in the corner window seat reading books. We felt bad we couldn't stay up with her all night. At least tonight even though Larissa was sleeping she wouldn't be alone. We tried hard enough to make sure she had enough activities; it helped the nights she was restless when the family would take her at night. Either Lucian would take her out running through the woods, not that we were too thrilled he taught her how to repel or dive off a cliff. Dinah or Lorah would take her out teaching her how to paint, swim, or do other things. Even Charlie would take her out on nature walks teaching her about tracking and sensing other creatures and distinguishing them from people. This gave us a chance to sleep without worrying if she was lonely or getting into something.

It helped that Larissa and savannah also went to the same school, except savannah had been back a grade. The day seemed to fly by rather fast with all the lesson plans. It hadn't seemed possible the girls could get any more excited than they had already been. We were proven wrong. Coming into the house quickly as they could, three little hellos as the girls raced for Savannah's room. The girls did a rather good job at keeping pace with Amanda and not running too fast. The way they usually did. After checking on them we ordered pizza and ate cookies and ice cream for dessert. Savannah faked an upset stomach, so she drank out of the solid thermos that Evangeline prepared for her. Amanda never once questioned it.

The girls played all night inventing their games. Even Amanda had come up with a few interesting games. The house had been filled with their laughter; it was difficult not to laugh along with them. Larissa and Amanda started yawning so Larissa said she was going to shower, and that Amanda could go second. This had been the plan that Savannah and Larissa concocted the night before, that by the time savannah had gotten out of the shower herself, the other two girls would be relaxed and fully asleep making it appear as if savannah had been the first to wake up in the morning. Just as the girls had planned, it worked as Amanda never assumed anything different and if she had she never let on. She was just excited about spending time with them. As much fun as they were having it had been a long weekend Amanda had stayed an extra night. At first, her parents were worried until they found she did just fine. The slumber party she had been at earlier hadn't gone too well as she had to leave to go home early, she had faked not being able to sleep being homesick but here she hadn't wanted to go home. At least it helped her parents feel at ease.

The girls had been playing on the swing set when Lucian came over, he was already warned there was a mortal visiting so he was careful to walk once he was within range of the house. Walking along acting normal he could hear Amanda whisper to savannah.

"Why doesn't he drive here in a car? Doesn't he live a long way away?" She may not have seen him running fast, but she had noticed something basic.

"He doesn't like to pollute so he refuses to drive a car. Besides, he doesn't live too far away it just feels like it." Smiling, Lucian seemed to be happy with his niece's response until he heard something he thought she didn't see, wondering how she did, when he stopped back far enough even walking a bit further than he cared for.

"How fast do you think he was running? He's got to be the fastest person I've ever seen!" Amanda seemed amazed by it.

"I wasn't watching but yes, he likes to run so I guess he would be pretty fast, let's see who can swing the highest." Savannah was trying to divert her attention which she finally had when the three of them started swinging higher trying to see who could go faster and higher. Not wanting to stick around outside to let her question more, Lucian had gone inside to see Lewis.

"I see savannah is doing pretty good out there with her friend, has Larissa been a lot of help? I know she loves it when the kids from school sleepover." I had been over at Rose's house when eight little girls were running around, he had decided to leave for Charlie's until they all went home.

The noise was more than I wanted to handle. I wasn't used to seeing savannah around others as much yet.

"Their first night went great. The two even came up with their way of covering for why she didn't sleep last night, and Amanda hadn't questioned it at all." Lewis was rather proud of savannah and Larissa for coming up with their way of handling it together. They worked very well as a team.

"On my way in here I heard Amanda ask an unusual question, she asked how fast I ran to savannah. She just said she wasn't watching so she wasn't sure. I stopped way back there so I'm curious how she saw me?" Sitting down on the couch I knew I had caught both Lewis and Evangeline's attention when I said that.

"I don't know how she would know that unless it was just a question in general? What brings you over? We were just about to pop a movie in." Both Evangeline and Lewis sat down on the other couch facing me with a bowl of popcorn between them.

"I was going to see if savannah wanted to go for a run tonight. I found a cave with a bunch of crystals, and I thought she would like to see it. I didn't know her friend was staying for the whole weekend, or I would have avoided coming over. I'm glad she's having fun." As they had watched the movie about halfway into it, Amanda had come in to use the restroom even though everyone noticed how she had stared at Lucian on her way through. Almost in a curious way not as if he was gross or anything.

Not wanting to raise any more questions by her Lucian had decided to leave a bit early. Either Lewis or Evangeline wondered why he had decided to leave but before he did, he wanted to say goodbye to his nieces. As Amanda was working her way back out, he started walking away until he heard the faintest voice. Lucian wasn't sure if he had heard anything. Turning around he could see Amanda standing next to the house with her hands clasped in front of her watching me. Barely moving her mouth, she smiled a bit when she said the next few words when she realized he had heard her.

"If you are hearing me, I want to ask you something?" Still standing there next to the house it was just out of sight of Larissa and Savannah on the swing set where they had been waiting for her to get back.

Walking back toward her I was curious what she wanted to ask in such a low voice. It was almost as if she hadn't wanted anyone else to hear her.

"What did you want to ask?" I was curious if it still had to do with the speed or something different.

I never knew what to expect when Larissa would ask me questions, sometimes it threw me. Making sure I didn't laugh in case it sounded so strange I didn't want to hurt her feelings, but I figured I might as well find out that way she doesn't ask her parents later.

"Did you have an accident like me? Most of your family is different." She asked in a hushed tone again.

An accident? I wasn't sure what she meant unless she meant we both looked pale or maybe I looked stunted too?

"I guess I don't understand what you mean? What do you mean by an accident?" Kneeling in front of her getting down to her level I wanted to understand what she meant not that I was aware of what she was about to tell me.

"I wanted to play outside a little longer, so I went out my bedroom window and played, it's when I had my accident, mom and dad didn't want anyone to know. They said it made me abnormal, so we had to move to hide it, but your family doesn't seem to think I'm abnormal. They keep calling me normal. I used to be like my parents but I'm not anymore. I'm not supposed to tell anyone, but savannah says she tells you everything." Now she had a worried look on her face as if she had given her deepest darkest secret away.

"As far as I can tell you are more normal than any of us. Can you explain the accident a little more, maybe that will help me understand better? What happened when you were playing outside?" I was getting an idea, but I didn't want to voice it in case I was wrong, I wanted to find out from her first.

"This man was sitting on one of my swings, we lived in the city, and I never saw him before, but he was sitting there and told me that he never liked kids and then he bit me on the shoulder. It hurt a lot. I didn't see him go but mom and dad thought a dog bit me and I made the whole story up, but I didn't I know what I saw." Putting her hand over her other shoulder she lowered the back part of her shirt to show two dark red marks.

They looked as if they were still new but from the circle around them, you could tell they were done quite some time ago. This poor kid felt so horrible about herself, not that I could blame the parents. They probably had no idea how to treat her, at least they were protecting her from others finding out they could have just dropped her off somewhere instead.

"I want to see how fast you can run, see that tree way over there with the white fencing near it by the end of the driveway. Run down there and back as fast as you can, don't hold back." Smiling I knew she was excited to do this.

Watching her in almost disbelief I never would have assumed she was a vampire child. Like myself, she must have had something in her keeping her human side alive so as long as it did she may grow up, whoever had bit her might not have done it enough. As she ran back there was no denying it, I could even see Evangeline and Lewis watching from the window carefully as she made her way back to me.

"I don't know how much your parents want you to know and what they can handle. This is very hard for some people to understand especially mortals. You would be more like Larissa and Evangeline; they are half part vampire and part human as you are. I used to have some mortal to me as I grew but once I hit a certain age that died off. My sister on the other hand hasn't lost hers at all. Believe me, it's not from her not trying. I bit her a lot when we were little which used to upset our parents, but it never did anything to her because venom affects everyone differently. Some people are changed for many different reasons, and some are not acceptable while some are. Savannah isn't going to change, she's going to be this way for the rest of her life while Larissa will continue to grow, and you might also it's hard to say how it's going to affect you. There's nothing wrong with you it's just that you're different. I need to talk to Lewis and Evangeline for a bit again before I go. But is that all you wanted to ask?" Nodding her head in agreement she seemed a lot happier this time than before.

She hurried off to play with the other girls. As I had said I needed to talk to Lewis and Evangeline now. I didn't have to knock on the door they already had it opened waiting for me inside.

"I never saw that coming. This whole time I was worried that she would find out about savannah when her parents must have been panicking over what would happen if we had found out? I am curious if her parents would let us talk to them? I don't want to ruin their fun especially if this is the first time she's had time to play with kids like her. Not that I feel that comfortable talking about our family letting our secret out, it might be what she needs so that she can cope otherwise if they don't know what to do to help her grow up and blend in, she might stick out too much and catch the attention of the new order or worse be stuck in a witch hunt and get hurt." Lewis had sat down thinking over his questions.

"I just want to make sure her parents don't believe it was an animal bite, find out what we are, and start a witch hunt themselves. You know how humans get. We can have them over tomorrow for tea or coffee and get to know them first, maybe feel them out a bit before we lay all this heavy news on them. After all, if they don't like what they hear you could lose your job, and we might have to move. This is all new to them and they might need help just coping. It's hard to tell without knowing them." Evangeline had sat down next to Lewis; this certainly wasn't something either of them had ever thought they would be dealing with.

But now they were right in the middle of it and not something either could let themselves ignore. Not having to say much they had wanted Charlie's advice on it even though Evangeline had guessed what her brother might say. Calling her parents, they had set up for them to come over to chat to get to know each other better.

Evangeline had tried to keep it on a very cheerful tune so that she would not worry them or make them think there was anything wrong. At first, they had still been hesitant but after a bit, they finally had agreed. Funny, how it was easier to arrange to have Amanda over but much harder to get her parents over.

The girls enjoyed the rest of the day only this time instead of holding back all three girls were just themselves, even Amanda was finally able to be herself more not worrying about hiding what she could do, they certainly enjoyed themselves much more. Then at night, no one had to pretend to sleep if they hadn't wanted to. Both Larissa and Amanda had fallen asleep as they did the night before only this time, Amanda had accepted the fact that savannah didn't need sleep. She asked her a few questions about it then after that off to dreamland while savannah picked out a few of her favorite books and started reading.

Early in the morning the girls chose their normal foods and chatted as they watched whatever cartoons they could find on the television. While Evangeline and Lewis had been set up for their lunch meeting with Amanda's parents. Lewis almost felt like it was a parent-teacher conference just much different and something he would never discuss with most parents. As the afternoon approached, we noticed the girls were much more conservative again probably worried that Amanda's parents would find out that she had talked about her secret.

We had packed a lunch for the girls to eat outside while Amanda's parents were here, that way savannah wouldn't have to fake another stomachache even though she did convincingly well last time. As we heard the car parking, we heard Amanda excited to see her parents but then she had gone back to playing. Welcoming them in they seemed rather nervous probably wondering why we had wanted to meet with them instead of just handling a sleepover and being done with it. Sitting on the couch they hadn't moved much even though we could tell they were waiting for the bomb to drop about their daughter being told what they had already been told before by other parents that she's very unusual.

"We loved having Amanda over and she's welcomed any time, it was nice having one of savannah's friends spend the night, other than her cousin usually she's the only one that stays over. We thought it would be nice for us to get to know each other. Amanda said you moved here not long ago, how do you like the area?" It always seemed easier to have a conversation with someone you didn't know by asking minor weather questions or locations without giving away too much personal information.

"The towns are smaller than what we are used to, we had moved here from the city but it's growing on us, we love the privacy." The whole time she spoke she seemed to be watching her words probably because she wasn't sure what their daughter had talked to us about even though we could say honestly, she hadn't talked to us she spoke to Lucian.

"If you ever need any help with anything just let us know, we'd be happy to help out. We have so many projects going on it's nice to have others around. Amanda's very outgoing and inventive, it was fun watching the girls invent their games." Taking a sip from her coffee mug, we knew this was a lot harder than they thought.

It was very hard to speak with people who didn't say very much let alone the fact we had no idea what to talk to them about. We did but it wasn't the sort of thing you just blurt out.

"Evangeline, can we go run with Lucian? He's taking the dogs for a run along the beach, he said he would watch us so we could build sandcastles." Savannah had been waiting at the door rather patiently before she had decided to interrupt.

"That's fine just remember no going in the water. It's too cold now, just stay on the beach and when he says to come back with then come straight back." Lewis was rather happy to say something since the silence had set in for longer than he cared for thankful for the interruption.

"Your daughter calls you by your name? There's nothing wrong with that but just not something we are used to." Amanda's father seemed a little surprised as well like her mother.

"She's our adopted daughter. She was a little more than her parents could handle so we took her in. She had a few extra gifts they just were not able to deal with. We figured we would let her call us by what she is used to and if she ever decides to call us mom and dad it's when she's comfortable or when she wants to. We would rather not push anything. She's blended in so well with our family it is rather large." The expression had changed a bit on their faces when we had let them know she was gifted almost a curious look on their faces.

"I hope I'm not being rude by asking this but what way is she gifted? Amanda had told us she wasn't going to grow much because of a birth defect or something to that effect, is that what you mean?" Not exactly what we were planning but at least now they were getting into the conversation.

"That's just one of them but she's a little different than other children her age. Yes, she won't grow very much and might not have a very long life, it's hard to say how she's going to fare as she ages but she's a bit stronger and faster than most children her age. Some feel this is unusual or abnormal, but we are used to it." Without having to give too much information the couple had picked up on what we were trying to say finally.

"To be honest we were never superstitious before or believed in certain things until recently and what I say might make you think we're crazy, at least I still feel that way when I just think it to myself. Amanda isn't a normal girl, and I wish I could pinpoint a disease on her because at least there would be hope for curing her, we just can't talk to anyone, and we are somewhat afraid that if she gets sick or hurt, we won't be able to help her because she can't see a doctor for this." This we could handle after all both sets of my foster parents were worried about me seeing a doctor when I was little so I could speak from experience.

"I understand what you mean, I've had two sets of foster parents who cared for me while I was growing up and I had the same problem. I couldn't see a regular doctor but thankfully for myself, we had one at the time we could trust not to share what was different about me. It didn't mean he could help with everything because for certain reasons I wasn't like everyone else. As I later found I had more family that shared similar traits as I have. Your daughter is much like me, and Larissa, and it can be scary when you don't know what to do if she gets hurt. From personal experience know those who are bitten by a creature or perhaps from a family will inherit traits. When people are bitten, everyone reacts to it differently. We know that Amanda was a bite, it seems that there were a few children this happened to in the larger city recently but for now, the attacks have stopped." Not that hearing that would be consoling news to her parents since there was nothing that could be done for her now, we just hoped that maybe finding out that they were not alone there is a possibility that she could still do well.

"So far all we seem to do right now is trying to help her blend in, so no one notices. We don't know anything about this or what to do for her? She seems rather normal until you see her run or pick up something a child her age and size just should not be able to pick up. I still feel overwhelmed but at least we are not the only ones. It's nice to know another couple who is facing the same issues. I don't mean to be rude, but we do need to get going it's getting late, and we start early in the morning. We appreciate you allowing Amanda out here and for the talk." Standing up we walked to the door.

"If it's alright with you we would love to have Amanda sleepover again next weekend? I'm sure the girls would love to spend more time together." Standing at the door Rose was in the distance driving her car up to pick Larissa up.

Coming up to greet our guests before they left Rose was rather cheerful this morning.

"Hello, I'm Larissa's mom, Rose", I heard the girls had a lot of fun this weekend.

Rose never seemed to have a problem getting others to talk, she was such a natural but then she had been raised to be more open whereas both Lewis and Evangeline had been more private. Rose explained how one of the caves they would give tours through was now permitted to take certified scuba divers down into a deep area. She was rather excited about this since it happened to be one of her hobbies. After Amanda had left with her parents, we talked to Rose about how the weekend had gone. How Lucian found out when Amanda approached him about her being different and how the family had been handling it. Then we waved as we watched Larissa and Rose leave for home that night. Later in the evening, Lorah had come to pick up savannah to keep her busy tonight dropping her off just before school as usual.

The next few days had gone by as normal. Dinah and Goseck had let the family know they would be out for a while and wouldn't have their cell phones available for calling them, so we had assumed they were doing more investigating which Goseck seemed to be obsessed with, when he had found out Harmony was one of the leaders of the new order. Alana had even changed her name; she knew her name but had wanted to dissociate herself from her old past that she couldn't remember. Now calling herself Sydney where she had come up with the name or why she chose it no one knew. Other than that, there hadn't been too much brand-new information the new order hadn't been on the patrol for anyone not that anyone had been throwing themselves out there to be hunted.

For the most part, they had left others alone to live their lives other than the usual very few that harmed humans, to begin with. They had even allowed the blood drinkers who preyed on humans to do so with a limit however any mass murders that would draw attention had ended rather quickly. As long as they hadn't found out about our family raising vampire children, we were still safe. Charlie and Sophie had gone to the summer cabin while Nichole and Anthony were planning on a vacation in about a week for their family. Everyone seemed to be making plans, so it was nice to look forward to Amanda's visit again.

It had been around Wednesday evening when savannah had been in her room finishing her homework and Evangeline was putting away the leftovers from supper when a knock at the door interrupted her train of thought. She looked over to see who was at the door. Lewis had gotten up to answer it. Opening the door, a much-panicked Copson family was standing there holding Amanda who didn't look like she was doing well. Opening the door wide letting them in, they came in quickly laying her on the couch. One look at her you could tell the venom was slowly taking over the last few parts of her that had been human.

"We didn't know what to do she's so sick, we hoped you might know what to do?" We hated to admit to her parents there wasn't anything anyone could do other than hope during the rest of the change she would survive it.

We tried our best to make her comfortable on the couch and reassure her parents, unfortunately, there were no promises we could make.

"I'm sorry to say there's nothing you can do to stop the venom from spreading through her system, we just have to hope the rest of her system handles it and lives, the best we can do is keep her as comfortable as possible. She is going to be a little dangerous when she first wakes up. She won't mean to harm you but she's going to get even stronger and if she tries to hug you out of fear, she could crush you until she learns to gain control. When did this first start?" Adding another blanket, not that it would soon matter but the emotional moves of it helped relax Amanda.

"We would have brought her here earlier, but we had to wait for someone to leave. This man stopped by the house saying he was taking the census which is normal but rather late to be out for this sort of thing. I don't know how often but the questions he was asking were a little strange, it was almost as if he knew about our daughter? He asked if everyone human was living in our household, and we thought maybe he was referring to any deaths in the family and we answered no there hadn't been any deaths, it's just the three of us. Then he started asking us if we noticed anything unusual with anyone or if anything out of the ordinary had happened around us. That's when we told him we didn't believe he was with the census and asked him to leave. We went to check on Amanda and she was in bed sweating blood like she is now. We wrapped her in a blanket and brought her here, it was all we could think to do. We didn't want to risk your family, but we don't think they followed us." They had looked so helpless we hated to tell them the truth, but it was inevitable.

"Your right he wasn't taking a census he was more likely a guard from the new order or another snitch of some sort for them, right now they are searching for the few vampire children that had been turned by Luther Augustus. Your daughter is in as much danger as ours is, the new order won't let her live, they don't believe children vampires are safe to let exist. Its why children are never turned because they are much more unpredictable and could be dangerous if not handled correctly. Then there are some even with training and someone constantly watching over them that can't control them. There are a lot more reasons but so far, we have been lucky not to have those problems. You may need to go into hiding if they are after you, we already know at some point we may need to also." Brushing her hair away from her forehead, savannah had come in asking Lewis what was happening with her friend.

We tried our best to explain so she would understand that she might either end up like her now or she might die, we don't know yet.

"The man who came by is he like our daughter? If he is we don't know how to fight against that. We hardly know how to recognize it let alone know where to keep going with her?" Mr. Copson placed his arm around his wife trying to comfort her even though he felt helpless himself.

We had sat there with Amanda waiting to find out if she was going to survive the night, we just never made it there. After they had been with us for about six hours Charlie had shown up at the door with Sophie in tow. The expression on his face had been nothing like we would have hoped, even though the entire family had been prepared for this moment. We had to let the Copson family know they would have to make a choice quickly or risk losing their daughter as well as their lives if they stood in the way.

"We have to be blunt; the new order will kill you for standing in the way of them, they might let you live if you hand her over because they understand as humans you don't know what's happening to your daughter, but if they find out you do and are protecting her, they will kill all of you. This is Charlie my brother, and I'm guessing he has news we knew would happen just hoped it wouldn't be for a while. You have a choice of both coming with and hiding with your daughter or we can hide her until it's safe. Once in hiding, we won't be able to come out because they will be on a constant hunt for us, one of the leaders has an unusual gift that makes it easier for her to find us when she remembers. This could get dangerous." Looking over at Charlie to see if it was time all he had to do was nod his head in agreement and say only two words we all dreaded, 'it's time' had been the worst words we could have heard.

"Can you keep her safe?" Had been the few words her parents had said.

"We would die for her." Trying to assure them we would treat her just as we would our daughter.

"Then keep her safe. Maybe someday we will be able to see her again?" Kissing their daughter and hugging before they left tearful of leaving their daughter, they knew this was the best choice for all of them.

Charlie having more experience with those going through the change held onto Amanda as we had met up with the rest of the family. We had decided it would be much safer if we hid together since so many of us would need protection anyway. Besides, if one of us went the rest of us would rather go with them as well and at least fight trying. We already had a place we had planned on staying, the one place vampires didn't live or would never really go to since there had been no need even though she could walk right in if she had wanted to. We knew we would be welcomed and kept safe there, no one would leak out that we had gone there. The entire family had known ahead of time where to meet up since we had already designated this as our safe place back when we first had decided to protect savannah.

Chapter Ten

Staying hidden

At least it didn't seem like we had to announce ourselves coming. There had already been a few people waiting for us at the city gates. A few of our old friends had been waiting at the guards' station, not that they needed to. The guards remembered us, we had been the only vampire family allowed in the shade city even after the shade queen had gone. There had been so many rumors that unless you were directly involved then they hadn't known the truth of what happened to the queen, and what her connection had been other than the fact that somehow, because of us, the shade city was still safe. We had moved in with the royals since the children were still around however now without Najee at least the important ones knew the truth.

Lewis had called the school before leaving letting them know he was handling a family emergency that he hadn't been sure when he would be coming back in. This excuse sounded much better than saying my adoptive daughter is a vampire and a group wants to kill her. At least this they would handle and believe.

It had been kind of nice being back, we had enjoyed it here before but the only person it had been hard on was Lucian. Before we had left, he kept hoping by some miracle he would find out she was alright again jumping out at the last minute asking to be taken with. It hadn't happened. We had taken several precautions only going out of the city when we had to, which for some of us hadn't been easy. We had taken over the entire second floor while Goseck and Dinah had moved back into his old house. Lucian had spent most of his time disappearing only to come out to play with his nieces every so often.

Both Larissa and Savannah celebrated their birthdays on the same day at the pub. Birthdays in the shade city had been viewed as a big deal and everyone was invited to celebrate. The girls loved it getting attention from so many different ones. Both had been given gifts to celebrate another year especially since many knew what problems they might face later in life because of what they were.

The first week we were here it was rather difficult for Amanda; she missed her parents, not that any of us could blame her. We promised once things were safe, we would make sure she saw them again. Over the next several weeks things had been rather quiet with no news about the new order and neither had they attempted searching the shade city for us. They still believed they were keeping the city pure. Something even Alana hadn't been aware of. It hadn't taken us long to blend in with the others. There had been a few nights that Goseck and Dinah had gone out to find out if they could hear anything. At one point they had mailed out a letter from a far location from Amanda for her parents to let them know she was alright even though we had her disguise some of the wording and her name but used a nickname only her parents had used so they would know it had been her, just in case someone was watching their house or mail.

The only news had been that the new order was hunting down the remainder of vampire children. As far as they had understood Luther had made his presence known in the city however most people were just looking at him as a lunatic, thankfully not taking him seriously. The children that had been changed however the hospitals were baffled not understanding what was wrong with them. When he had attacked the children in the city, they had been out playing in the park which had been where the loudest disturbance came from. Searching and checking all the children that lived nearby or had been rumored to have changed they searched for these.

Only four could not be found as the other two had been killed off mainly by Alana. Sydney had wanted to wait and find out if they were going to create a problem possibly removing them from their families and placing them into other families who might be able to handle it, however, Alana had been positive this would have been a dangerous breeding ground for allowing the way for other vampire children and create a problem they might not be able to keep up with. Luther hadn't done much however it was enough to get the attention of humans not that they knew how to take it. If he had been allowed to keep going then the secret could have gotten out and uncontrollable until a few humans started hunting again. Even in this day and age if people felt threatened, many act impulsively out of fear of doing what they felt was right even though it might not be.

Everyone had adjusted rather well here except Lucian even though he was always used to drifting between family members never really settling in a place of his own. He liked being independent but being cooped up in here was making it harder on him. Even though he understood why we were here it hadn't made it any easier. Instead of making one of the very short trips out, Goseck had taken Lucian out scouting with him one night instead of Dinah, that way he would be able to be out much longer than he normally had. Not letting anyone else know he hoped he would run into Harmony again. Not sure if she would remember him or not, he had hoped maybe seeing him would spark her memory. No one knew if she ever really had a good look at his other family members that day she was caught fighting Luther; if she had she certainly hadn't remembered them. Over the next few months, things had slowed down, no one had been talking about the new order, and no new signs of them. It had seemed they were settling into their place wherever it had been just watching out for the main signs that they would need to take care of.

Their main plan hadn't changed making sure creatures kept their secret silent, not mixing with the mortal world, only certain types of interactions were allowed, otherwise, trying to purify the different groups to make them stronger. So far, the last piece of news had been that Alana viewed shades as the highest group of creatures. Not caring if the others intermingled with each other since she felt this only weakened their gifts. However, she did not want humans being changed for vampire benefit let alone children or those who did not agree or were too young, they risked too much exposure making us all a target. For the longest time different ones were able to govern themselves after the original order was rumored to have died out, but now that there were far many more creatures out there the lines were being crossed as humans are starting to notice there's something out there other than themselves. Many were getting cocky and over-self-assured with constant struggles of power and dominance that Alana figured there should be one and if there were, she should be the lead of it.

We had left rather quickly from our homes, not packing very much. Lucian volunteered to go back and get items. Not that Nichole or Anthony was happy with this, they would have rather gone without, than have him risk his life in case someone was there waiting for us hoping we would return. It had been more of an excuse for Lucian to go out alone for a while, not that anyone liked the idea of him traveling alone. It had made sense that it would be easier for one to get away if they didn't have to worry about another person. Lucian planned on making a few trips. First, he would bring back items and safely store them where no one would find them. Then once back for the final trip making sure no one had followed him; he would take the rest of the stashed items and bring them into the shade city.

The first place to stop had been Charlie and Sophie's home. Not that they wanted much, mainly a few clothes and her mini herb garden with a few stones. Taking a large bag stuffing what he could without smashing anything, this was the first part to get stashed nearby. The second place had been a little more from Rose and Jacob's house. It felt strange being here knowing Rose wasn't here. Picking up a few things for Larissa there had been something a bit strange. They had left all the windows and doors closed to keep animals or the weather out but one of the windows was cracked open just a little. Walking carefully to the bedroom there had been clothing tossed all over the place from Larissa's room almost as if someone was looking for something. All the other rooms had been untouched except for hers.

I was going to collect their mail for them while I was here but there hadn't been any to grab. Whoever was here must have already taken it for whatever purpose I wasn't sure unless they were trying to figure out where Larissa was or what she was? Being extremely careful not to take the same path back. I had stopped in a few other areas further away making sure no one had watched. I left their items covered here until I could make a special trip back for them. Goseck's cabin had still been the same as we last left it only a bit musty smelling now. Grabbing what Dinah wanted Goseck had said he really didn't need anything but then he always kept things back at his home in the shade city saying he hated packing. This way he was always ready no matter where he was.

Lorah had always been more nomadic than the rest of us. She never confirmed or denied it but we both knew she had been friends with Augustus for a while even working for him, she was extremely private about it. Anything she could need; she already had it with her. She was very simple and never cared for owning or having very much, not that you would know that by looking at her hair, it was always done, matching jewelry, and feminine-looking clothing. She felt that if you owned more, it was simply more that others could take away, she wasn't obsessed with things, she obsessed over people. Most of the places hadn't been touched or looked any different other than Rose's house along with Evangeline's house in both girls' rooms. Everything had been tossed everywhere as if someone was looking for something. Making sure not to spend too much time here the mail hadn't been taken from here however it had been opened and spread all over the floor. There hadn't been one room in this house that hadn't been searched even a few things had been broken of Evangeline's. It was a good thing they were not here to see this; it wasn't even mine and I found it upsetting. But then I guess we had also left at the right time, at least everyone was safe.

Just as I was leaving with the bag over my shoulder, I heard a sound. I didn't want whoever it was to be aware that I knew they were there. I wanted to see if they were willing to follow me at all. Not wanting to lose them, I had started walking which it hadn't seemed like they were interested in following until I had taken off in a full run, they kept further behind but not too far where they would lose me. Instead of running them towards my family, I had run the opposite way heading towards the new mine that Rose had spoken of that her tour group was now allowing scuba diving through. Racing as fast as I could. At least the toys, clothing, and jewelry I had in the bags could get wet. I just wanted to see how determined they were to follow me.

Whoever it was that had been following me slowed down before following me into the caves, probably worried it was a trap, which I couldn't blame him. I would have assumed so also. Heading towards the end of the tunnel that finally led to the water. I could see where they had it set up for the scuba divers to enter and to guide them down along the narrow passage. Closing my mouth so I wouldn't fill my lungs with water. I went down following the thick rope that had been attached to the wall in the water, following it along the bottom. I was surprised the tunnel shaft had gone as far as it did. Then it had occurred to me that Rose had been down here doing this also, that I wasn't too thrilled with even though she was a mom and could take care of herself more now, even with Jacob to watch over her. I still didn't like the idea of where she might put herself in danger. I was pretty sure I would always feel protective of my sister.

Finally, the end had led straight out to the lake normally it would have been extremely cold to go in, but the temperature never bothered me like it had some of my family. I just wanted to see if the person was willing to follow me through all of that. Waiting on the side of the opening quietly. I could see bubbles from the water coming up. I wasn't sure if that was a good or bad thing, but I figured I would risk it, leaving the bag on the rocks. I jumped in swimming down as fast as I could. The person who had followed me almost made it all the way out on their own. I could only assume hypothermia was affecting him. He was laying restless at the bottom of the water as I grabbed him by the arm, I pulled him up to the surface trying to force the water out of his lungs without crushing his chest. His skin had turned purple and there was barely any breath in him. Swinging the wet bag over my shoulder and picking him up I ran up the lower part of the mountain to cut some time off. I had run directly to Rose and Jacob's house. Not that I wanted my family to get hurt. I certainly hadn't wanted anyone else dying either even if they didn't realize what they were doing. This could have been simply a follower who for his reasons might have listened to orders out of self-preservation.

As soon as I was in the house, I stripped all of his clothing off putting him in some of Jacob's clothing, they were a bit loose, but at least it would keep him dry. Rubbing his arms and legs trying to move him around a bit. I tried my best to get his circulation going. After messing with him for about an hour he finally started stirring even though he seemed rather afraid at first, he didn't try struggling when he realized what I was doing. The look on his face had changed from sheer terror to that of relief and a bit of shock as if he couldn't believe I was saving his life willingly. At least his heart and breath had never completely stopped even though he had swallowed quite a bit of water.

"I could have left you for dead. You were already laying at the bottom unconscious, but we prefer to preserve life not end it if possible." He could still see me as I walked into the kitchen.

I filled a cup with water heating it up in the microwave, then added the hot cocoa mix to it and then I walked back over.

"I don't know how to make coffee. I don't find a need to drink it myself so hopefully you like hot cocoa. It should help warm you up a bit. So, who are you? I'm Lucian." Handing him the cup he accepted it, at least by now if I had wanted to kill him, I would have done it already so at least he trusted me a little.

"I'm never supposed to give out my name, but if you want, for now, you can call me "Steve." I was following you because you were taking things out of the house, I hoped you might know where the family that lives here is so that I can find them. My master has been searching for them and needs to find them most urgently, that's all I know, and I was sent here to find anything that might lead to where they are. If I find them. I get a special reward from my master." He was smiling rather intently.

The reward was worth it to him even though the idea of someone calling Harmony master felt a bit sickening or rather calling anyone master for that matter had been just as bad.

"Has your master told you what they want to do with the family from here? Does everyone call this person master? Is it possible for me to meet this person?" I knew my family was safe, it couldn't hurt if I were to see her, I don't think she considers me a threat unless she finds I'm related.

"They don't meet with people unless they want you themselves then you don't have to go looking for them, they come for you. Only the invited go in and no not everyone calls them both master. One of them doesn't like it, but my master does, and I work for her." He seemed rather proud of himself when he said he worked for her.

At least I could hope it hadn't been Harmony he worked for, and it was the other woman.

"What are you going to tell them if you don't find anything?" Sitting across from him I was curious if he would report about me.

"I don't report back unless I find something. You've asked me enough questions. I want to know what you are doing here? I know you're not human and you're certainly no shade. What's your interest in these people?" Nodding my head, fair enough.

I had been asking a lot of questions already. I hadn't wanted to tell him the real reason I was here.

"I happen to be friends with the family, and I wanted to see if they were home, but you made a rather nasty mess in here, so I wanted to make sure nothing was missing. I left my traveling bag here and came to get it which is wet as you can see now. If you are fine now it's time I got going. If you decide to follow me, I won't lead you to them, but you will also end up in trouble again, not necessarily underwater. I promise I get more creative every time." Giving him a quick nod, I ran outside grabbing the bag that I had left outside and ran as fast as I could.

I almost think he listened to me and didn't follow but just in case I made a few stops along the way. So far, I have taken three days to do all of this. I know it should have only taken a day and a half, but I had taken my time checking things out, messing with that guy, and investigating a little myself. At least I knew they were watching the house, so if I wanted to catch another person, I might hopefully get someone else who might give more information or someone I could follow myself?

I figured if anyone had followed me, they would get bored following me around for a day, just going around in circles not doing much of anything, even just sitting still watching the lake. Even I was boring myself. When I was confident no one had followed. I went to gather the other items that I had stashed collecting everything. There hadn't been that much to carry back, instead of making separate trips. I had made it in one even with the wet bag that seemed to be taking forever to dry. Keeping an eye out to make sure no one had seen me go into the cave entrance of the shade city. I had bolted as fast as I could across the clearing into the cave right up to the gates, only slowing enough to try not to scare the gate guards that were still there. Once they had seen who I was they opened the doors.

The first person I had seen was Lewis, sadly it was their bag that was still damp since it hadn't dried much on the way back. I hoped it would have from all the wind rushing past it as I had run here. Even though he seemed to be surprised that it was wet then I explained to him how it got that way as if it was an everyday thing. I didn't want to worry them any more than they already were. At least now I confirmed that their home was being watched.

"Charlie wanted to see you as soon as you were back. I'm guessing they're worried since you took a bit longer than we were expecting. With things being dangerous we can't help but worry, I'm glad you're back now, Charlie should be in the main room. I last saw him talking with Goseck. I guess there's something Goseck wants to do. I haven't heard the full thing yet, probably will when they clarify whatever plan he's making. I think even though everyone knows this is the safest place. They are planning, in case we get found here where else to go after here." Lewis was trying to keep his voice calm.

I knew I wasn't the only one tired of being trapped in here. It wasn't so bad when we could come and go places, but now that Lewis and I know they are actively looking for us being in here and not going out was the best thing for us.

"If they're already worrying then I guess I should probably get up there. Sorry about the wet clothes." At least it wasn't anything that couldn't dry or be washed.

Not that I wanted to rush back. I walked all the way there since we had decided not to spook the other residents with our fast speed. Even though they could run rather fast themselves it still struck fear in them when they saw a vampire race past them. Just from past conditioning, it was all they knew for the last several centuries, so we tried our best to keep them comfortable.

Lewis was right they were still talking in the main room of the palace the only thing I hadn't counted on had been the fact there would be five vampire children running around along with Larissa. Evangeline and Rose were sitting on the side just watching the kids play until they had seen me come in the room even the children had stopped playing except Larissa had come running towards me jumping upward for me to catch her. Grabbing a hold of her I walked over towards Charlie.

"Lewis said you wanted to see me. I dropped everyone's bags outside their doors before I came over here. I notice we have some more visitors. I'm surprised everyone was so calm when I got back, it's almost like we're invading the place. Who are the other two kids?" Pointing at the remainder who had started playing chasing each other around again.

Even Larissa after saying her hello to me, had hopped down to rejoin the others playing whatever game it had been that they made up.

"They happen to be a brother and sister; they had been savannah's friends, the main reason she wanted to play outside longer to be with them. Goseck had found the two of them earlier. They had been with members of the order. They were being brought in. The order was hoping they would know where savannah and Amanda had gone. Charlie was worried since you had been gone for so long, that they had done something with you. The order is traveling in groups now rather than individually. It wasn't easy getting the kids away from them. Goseck and Dinah distracted them slightly by yelling 'hide the kids' which sort of spooked them thinking there might be more than two children. They followed off after Dinah and Lorah in their direction. When they let them catch up with them, they turned and attacked them while Goseck had attacked the remaining two keeping them busy until they realized that Aiden grabbed the two kids and ran with them." Aiden was over by Rose smiling as he heard his name mentioned feeling rather proud of himself for sneaking in without being caught.

"Sorry it took so long. I explained to Lewis that I had a bit of a run-in. They were watching Evangeline and Lewis's house. Even Rose and Jacob's house had been searched however none of the others were touched at all, just the two. I made a brief run by Amanda's parents' home. I didn't let them see me, they seemed to be going on as if everything was normal." Charlie looked concerned as soon as I mentioned the run in even though I tried to downplay it when I did.

"What kind of run-in?" Charlie crossed his arms to keep from fidgeting, he wasn't the only one interested in my run-in since Jacob came into the room also wanting to know.

Rose was more worried about the house and what damage they had done to it, not that she wasn't worried about me, but she knew me well enough that I was here, that I could handle myself just fine.

"A person was watching Lewis and Evangeline's house; he's supposed to stay out until he finds out something then he reports back. When he had chased me, I took him through the cave that Rose's company had opened for scuba diving except he hadn't taken it too well so in short, I did a good thing, I saved his life which is why he told me anything and thought I didn't know anymore then he did." Looking over at Rose, I could see her smile, she had figured out there was more to my story, but she knew not to say anything.

"I told you it was pretty amazing down there." Rose was always more adventurous the way I was sadly she was much more vulnerable because of her human side.

I was always trying to protect her or keep her from getting into danger that was too much for her.

"It doesn't matter how old you two get you still act like little kids, from now on just for safety reasons we travel in twos." I understand his concern, but I was going crazy.

It's not as if they were going after me if I went out, but then as Rose had later pointed out that if they put the connection together, I was family, they might try to use me as a bargaining tool or follow me back to the family. Usually, I had gone out with Lorah or Aiden since Dinah and Goseck were usually busy with their plans when they had gone out. I know they were out investigating, they just chose not to share everything yet, after all, Goseck was just as obsessed about the new order as I was because of Harmony.

Over the next several weeks there were more sightings of those who worked for the order, frustrated that they couldn't find the last remaining five children, they doubled their efforts searching for them. They had even come close when a pair came to the gates asking if any of the guards had seen them. Simply making a grunt towards them the guards commented, "you know how we feel about vampires" not that they still felt that way they just let them believe their views had not changed. For now, they believed it which was what had mattered. We hadn't picked another place to go to if they had wanted to search even though the royal family said the guards would never allow them through. Charlie had been talking to James when he found out something rather interesting.

"Since they had taken the stones that went to the other worlds. I wonder if they have been able to use them? After all, Harmony had the power to." Charlie had been trying to think of a backup plan to keep the family safe.

He hated hiding like this, but he didn't want to risk the family's lives but he knew they couldn't keep hiding like this, eventually they would find them. This wasn't a way for the kids to grow up constantly on the run but then there would be no end, shades lived an unbearably long time, and now that the stone was in Harmony, who knows how that will affect her? No one knew exactly how old Alana had been, but she had to be getting close to the end of her life cycle. Not that she ever looked that much older. Most lived till they were at least seven hundred.

"I need to correct you on that, she had the power to get out and take others out with her. She didn't have the power to get in. Najee had helped her get in there." Charlie had a look of concern on his face since this was the first time they had talked about their father.

"Sorry, I hope my bringing this up isn't upsetting?" Not wanting to press it but just in case James had wanted to talk about it at all.

He had been so concerned with his own family's welfare that it hadn't hit him until now that they owed Najee's family a lot of gratitude for their survival.

"We were never really close to him, after all we thought he had died a long time ago. We were as surprised as you to find out he was still around, especially to find out he was Najee. I think I'm still more shocked by it than anything. If you wanted to know if they would be able to control the portals, then you could ask Elija he knew more about that than I did." After thinking about it for a while all Charlie could come up with had been if they get attacked here, they might just have to fight and make their stand here instead of constantly running.

The next few weeks passed rather slowly since we were more aware of the time now that we went out much less than we already had been. I had been sitting staring at the huge hole in the wall that now opened into another room behind it. I was far down in the basement where the portal used to be, it looked strange with it gone. Knowing the last person who had gone with her had been Jacob. He hadn't remembered how they were separated; he did remember waking up feeling cramped when he found he was also added to the crystals that the rest of the family had been imprisoned in. At the time she had remembered enough to have us freed but now over time she could barely remember anything at all, even as some said she preferred not to. At least I was the only one who had come down here or the family would have worried even more knowing I was sinking into my depression again, and this was the only way of hiding it from them.

One of the evenings I had spent down here looking at the hole like I normally would, Elija had come down rather quietly just sitting down next to me with just as much of a thoughtful look on his face. I wondered if he was thinking about his father. Not looking like he was trying to start a conversation or even asking me anything, we sat there just relaxed both looking at the hole. We probably would have scared anyone else if they had seen this or realized we both had something in common and it was alright to mourn like this. After all, he was mourning for the dead while I mourned for the living.

After sitting next to each other for several hours not saying anything Elija had finally spoken but rather softly with not too much reflection in his voice. He seemed so laid back and relaxed. Not that he had asked anything anyone else wouldn't have, he was more curious than anything.

"This might be personal, but how did you meet Harmony? We all know you think of her constantly or you wouldn't be down here." Most people would phrase that because she was a human, why would I choose to be friends with her.

Neither of us had chosen each other it had just happened. Anyone for that matter who was able to get close enough to me outside of my family, was generally by mistake or timing.

"To be honest I hadn't set out to meet her. I was out swimming heading home and came across her yelling at the stone on this little island in the middle of nowhere. She was still learning how to use it." I wasn't sure how much more he had wanted to know, usually I didn't tell people more than that.

"First time I had met her she cleared out a group of vampires who tried to take over the city, even though now I know it was a ploy by the queen to make it look like they had taken over, she hadn't expected her people to get wiped out. Oddly she gave harmony such a strong gift, usually, it's never given to a human. Probably because she had wanted the stone also. She was very sweet it's hard not to think of her even with her memory loss and the path she seems to be following, everyone is thinking of her. Always good to prevent evil before it becomes so." Never once raising his tone of voice or changing the reflection to the sound of his voice, I had to remind myself I was older than him.

"I thought only shades born from a shade could pass on the traits so how is it that the queen had the ability to give Harmony the traits? I've lived with Goseck for a while but it's not something we talked about; we know a little but not much." I was curious since I had always heard that it was passed on and if not used the gift could be lost.

"For the most part, natural shades are born from parents of the same kind however the abilities of a shade diminish when mixed with other creatures or humans. There are those rare ones who have the ability to infect others and it's not always the same way. Sometimes it's with sharing blood, others it's simply transferring some of their power to another, most don't because who wants to give up a part of themselves like that? The queen was a rare exception, she was able to place her blood so that it would seep through an object of her choosing and just absorb into the skin without anyone knowing. Not the same if she bit someone that would just hurt! but it wouldn't change them. A shade only has powers over the elements which in some ways are a lot, however speed we do not possess, we appear to run fast however we are being propelled by the energy and wind we create around us." Smiling to himself he could tell there were a lot more questions that I had especially about how all this affected Harmony.

"Also, to answer the question you are not asking. The elements of a shade will not fight against the stone, after all the guardians before her were also shades, it was never meant to go to them, other than when she had found she was going to be killed for it, the people she oversaw she had to make it look as if she was not evil herself. She wanted control, which is not always an evil action, it depends on what you do with it. Harmony also has the stone's power in her, it is no longer a physical stone, it's the power that is absorbed into her, she will be the last guardian which makes her much more powerful and feared. It can also drive her to insanity if she does not learn to care for her power. Eventually, we all make choices however at the time we don't always know the right one to make." In the end, his voice had slightly changed a little as he sounded sad when he thought of this.

"I always wondered why mom and dad got together. After all, they were always trying to kill each other yet they would be the first to save the other if someone else were trying. Even the reasons they named us were messed up. Victoria,

Madison, Natalie, and Gabriella were all named after our father's past girlfriends. Mother was no better. She named us boys James, Logan, Lucas, and me after her past boyfriends. With the two stones that were taken, I always wondered why they hadn't taken the pool? Sure, it's wet and a bit messy. Maybe it was a little harder to move but I always thought it was far better than the stones. But then who knows maybe they just didn't want to get wet?" With that, he had stopped talking.

Why would they want water when they can get that anywhere? Besides there had only been two portals what would the water have done? I know Sophie taught me and Harmony how to scry using water, but I never felt it that useful? I was hoping he would go on to finish explaining the rest of it, but he hadn't. Instead, he stood as if he was finished looking at the hole and got up and started walking away. Jumping up quickly I wanted to ask him about the water and why he preferred it.

"Wait for a second, why did you prefer the water. I don't remember seeing any water around here? There was a waterfall at the Eurubian city, but I don't remember one here?" Turning to face me, he smiled a devilishly evil grin while he thought about why he preferred the water.

"Sometimes the absolute best things in the world are those that are not so heavily protected because others don't realize their value. And you're correct, it's not here. It's in the Eurubian city. Each city had its own to protect but the Eurubian people never felt threatened because no one understood how it worked. I found out from another person in another world which no one else can learn from anymore because he's dead. In seven ways, it can give you the very things you want yet make you earn them at the same time. I always thought someone with a pretty good sense of humor invented it. Probably why I love it so much. Besides, there is no special power needed to work it other than Cerebrospinal fluid, it's detected in the brain, so I don't know if you still have any or not. The one portal could bring you to the center and there were two worlds you could look directly at and enter, one of them was my father's original world, which was destroyed, that one is a charred door, and the other is still glossy looking. The second portal only brought you to a third world. Remember when there were numerous worlds beyond the portal? Ever wonder where those were? If you are ever near the water, feel free to take a dip. You might want to take your family with you when the time comes, and it will." Walking away from me I stood there trying to understand what he had just told me.

The first thing I wanted to do was race over to search for it to make sure it was still there, not that I could explain my sudden urge for needing to go there. I swear from the time they had stayed without the family being protected to being locked up in the crystals with us. When Elija was talking to me, I wondered if I was speaking with the same person who stayed with us for several months, he acted like an adult instead of the young children we had gotten to know them as. Who knows, maybe this place brings that out of them? I was curious what he had meant by saying whoever invented it must have had a sense of humor?

I was excited to search but needed to keep that in and not show any expression or everyone would know I was about to do something. Not that I felt it was wrong to check out this pool, but it would be taking a chance at being found there and being out longer than we agreed to for safety as a family. The main ones I had to avoid were Dinah, Goseck, Lorah, Rose, and Charlie since they know me too well and would know I was up to something, especially Dinah or Charley. I could never hide anything from them. I was planning something. Mom and dad never read me quite like the others, it wasn't that they didn't try. I was just too good at hiding it from them.

Instead of spending so much time hidden away. I had figured if I spent a day or two out in the open, they might not be too suspicious except now I had the entire family watching me so that plan had backfired. Even when we had gone out, instead of going with just two. The family made me go out with four relatives to make sure I hadn't taken off. So, I told them fine. I'll go back to hiding myself away again, that I wasn't planning on taking off. I figured I would try to take their advice and get to know people since they were always trying to encourage me. So, I did exactly as I said. I would and had been for the last few months, I hid in the basement along with Elija, even the family had known he was with me, but they didn't know where.

At least sitting down here. I had a lot of time to think even from my silence Elija knew what I was thinking, scheming, and trying to accomplish something. I hadn't wanted to admit it out loud because I didn't know if I could pull it off or if it would work, even though he said it didn't need to be controlled by magic. I just had to find it and hope my head wasn't empty, I know it sounds bad, but I never gave thought to the condition of my brain. It worked but would it still need cushioning like the living? Instead of trying to blend in, which I guess I should have assumed would have been too easy for them, I would wait until Charlie had left with Nichole. Then as soon as they had been far enough, I would make my break for it. As I was thinking this, I heard the slightest whisper almost not hearing it.

'Don't forget me.' As I looked down at him, Elija had still been staring straight ahead.

I wasn't sure if he had spoken to me. Maybe I was thinking too hard? Did he need a reply? Besides if I were to make a break for it, this would be a lot harder with two. Besides, I didn't want to take responsibility for anyone else in case anything went wrong.

'You heard me; I'll be responsible for myself but you're not going without me." Looking back at Elija his expression and position hadn't moved until he realized I was looking at him.

"Did you say something?" I wanted to make sure I wasn't imagining this. I know Charlie; Nichole and Anthony could hear each other's thoughts along with any one of Charlie's brothers or sisters however Rose and I were the only ones who could speak to each other that way. Mom always thought it had been because of a special twin connection.

"No, I have said nothing however I hear your friend speaking to you, possibly if he could lower his voice, I could meditate much better." Giving me a light smile he returned to his trance state staring straight ahead.

All I could think had been if he spoke any lower, I wouldn't be able to hear whoever it was. I knew there was no way it was Rose since she had Larissa, even though she was still adventurous she took fewer risks.

"Fine, meet me in the tavern in about twenty minutes." That was the last time I had heard the voice better.

Not wanting to risk not finding out who it was I excused myself leaving Elija to relax as I went to the tavern. I wasn't sure who I was expecting. I had sat in the far corner booth that Harmony and her friends used to sit at together. Many of her old friends still hung out at the booth in the corner however they started drifting to other groups and corners since some still couldn't quite get used to having vampires around. It always felt strange we were called vampires. I never once felt like one not that I would have had a personal distinction between living and dead. I just personally grew with whatever living humanity I had inside until it died off, not that I ever noticed a difference. I had still felt the same.

Waiting around feeling impatient I wasn't sure how long it was going to take this person to show up. I had already been sitting here for thirty minutes now just sitting pretending to relax and listen to the music. Maybe the person didn't know who was thinking of checking out the pool or of sneaking out? Maybe I missed them already? Then I shook my head slightly as I had thought to myself, it had been barely ten minutes since I heard the person speak to me. Not wanting to raise suspicions with the rest of the family. I had gotten up and started walking out when I saw Goseck walking toward me.

"Follow me, I would talk to you at the house or palace, but at least one of your family members is in one of those places." Nodding I followed Goseck up close to the gates.

We had turned to the right where there had been a store selling clothing, extremely bright skirts were hanging along with shirts, jewelry, and dream catchers. Sort of a Native American splashed with a bit of gypsy; I had to admit if I had known what this store was in here. I would have been hanging out here earlier. Goseck had known everyone around here as we walked past the shopkeeper, they had simply nodded their head towards each other as Goseck made his way to the back of the store and then into a separate private room. As we both entered, I closed the door behind me as he had instructed. Sitting down at the table I could see he was ready to start talking to me now that he had himself comfortable. Sitting down since I knew it irritated him when I just stood around, he certainly had never minded what my family or myself had been, he just wasn't used to the constant standing or no sleep part.

"I used to talk to Harmony in her thoughts, sadly I couldn't do it with others not even you at first, I wasn't sure why? Then lately without even having to try your thoughts keep ringing in my ears. Since you had lived with me for a while in the cabin, that's when it became stronger. I didn't want to invade your privacy but for some reason, I just couldn't shut you out. I figured no one would know if I just never said anything. To get to the point. I want to find this pool with you. I agree with the reasons for trying to work and control it if that's the way it works. We can keep an eye on Harmony if it works and we can use it to hide the family if it works the way Elija was thinking.

The only reason he sat there not talking with you had been that I was talking to him." Goseck stated.

I thought Elija was rather silent because he didn't have anything to say, not that he spoke that much at other times but even for him he was rather silent just to sit there humoring me.

"If you take off with me won't Dinah notice or wonder where you're going without her? She usually likes to be in on your schemes." Smiling I had known they had grown much more attached than that.

Besides, she not only shared the same interests. She had also grown used to him as well no matter what she said about him. Then I stopped for a second, was Goseck hearing this now too?

"Sadly, yes I hear that. Charlie has told me that once a certain connection has been made with his family it's more of an automatic thing rather than the trust angle. I taught Harmony. Besides, I already knew how Dinah felt about me, she doesn't need to say anything. I want you to hang out in the palace until Charlie and Nichole leave tonight to head out, then make your way down but don't let them know you're coming, Dinah is going to be with Lewis and Evangeline tonight. I'll just meet you at the entrance of the Eurubian city, that way we won't be searching over the same spots." Not really looking at me I could tell he was slightly blushing; he was listening to someone else's thoughts.

Such a huge intimidating-looking guy blushing wasn't something you would assume he was capable of mainly just from the looks of him. After living at his place for a while I had gotten close to him, Goseck was a pretty good friend.

When we left the private room, we were in, I had gone back to the palace while Goseck went home acting as if nothing was different. He could still guard his thoughts against Dinah for now but there would be a time he might not be able to do that any longer, unless he learned control like the rest of the family. Strange it hadn't hit me until now if he was connecting to the rest of the family as Charlie had said, he was bonding much stronger with the family. The next few hours were easy to pass by when the kids had come into the main hall of the palace. Victoria and Madison had been playing with the two other vampire children or as we found out they liked being called Philip and Phoebe. Savannah had left when Lewis came in to collect them, they were having family night while the other two went with Rose and Jacob to spend time with them. Everyone was trying to make sure the kids hadn't felt left out, sort of just adding them to our family also. We seemed to absorb quite a few people.

I had been sitting in the main part of the palace when Charlie and Nichole had gone past heading for the gates when Lorah decided to head out with them. She usually went outside with Aiden; it was a bit strange if all three of them decided to take off tonight?

Chapter eleven

Gateway

As the gates closed behind Charlie, Nichole, and Lorah. I had watched rather closely making sure they left. I was rather talented for sneaking up on Charlie. I hoped I could hide as well since he was looking around so much aware of everything around him. Even though the family wasn't assuming I was going to try to take off. I was sure that Charlie kept his eye out for me. As soon as they had been out of sight. I went for the gate, none of the guards had known about our arrangement acting as I normally would, they opened and closed the gates for me. I hadn't seen Goseck however he did say he was going to meet me there. Perhaps he had to make an excuse for what he was doing? Heading out of the tunnel rather slowly in case they had stopped at the end, there was no sign of anyone. Usually, they would stay away from the Eurubian city not wanting to risk being near there in case it was being watched for our family. We were sure by now even if the guy who was ransacking the houses wasn't sure what he was looking for, he would have connected the two families through personal pictures.

Once across the clearing and into the covering of the trees, I had taken off as fast as I could running for the city, I knew it was going to take a while to get there, and eventually, the family would notice we were missing. I could stay gone longer unfortunately they would notice Goseck missing much earlier. Dinah would be curious where he had gone, not that they went everywhere together but they generally told each other when they would be back so they wouldn't worry about the safety of the other. I doubted Goseck said where he was going otherwise, I had a feeling the rest of the family would have joined us. He told me not to worry, that he had it figured out which might be why he was going to meet me there? Instead of taking the route I normally would, I had taken the path straight to it not that I had ever gone that way before. Rarely would we see others from the creatures who lived outside, we had assumed very few of them had survived.

Passing through trees and running closely between the two mountains, I kept my attention on anything around me in case someone was watching or something I might run into. Not that running is difficult for me. I always find myself getting bored when running long stretches. As busy as I was staying alert, there hadn't been any signs of anything along here, but then I had also noticed there hadn't been anything either. Stopping in my tracks. I had been curious why there were no animals? Usually, they ran from me which I was used to except there hadn't been any scents for quite a while and the ones that had been had aged, I was guessing the last animal I had sensed around here had been about six months ago. What would have scared them away from here? Did the Lipedians populate somehow? Usually, their tempers and fighting amongst their people had led to their demise. Only a few that had gotten away survived, even then they would kill each other off when they ran into each other.

Almost to the entrance I had stopped back a short distance to look around in case anyone was close by. I had noticed Goseck already by the waterfall, he had taken the plunge to get in instead of the dry route. Looking towards the other entrance, I realized why two people were standing there watching the entrance and two outlooks standing guard in the trees further ahead. They were not aware of another entrance since none of them looked this way. Being careful not to catch any attention I leapt over the side not that I could land as gracefully as a shade would. They could slow their momentum while falling. I was just hoping not to create too much of a splash. Aiming for the base of the waterfall the splash would blend in with the rumbling of the already landing water. It had been a good thing since my splash was rather huge.

Swimming in a little then pulling myself up along the side, Goseck was lightly laughing to himself as he motioned with his hand to point out how dry he was. Smiling back, I walked up to him patting him on the shoulder.

"Yes, you managed to stay dry, good for you." Then I grabbed him quickly throwing him into the water.

I watched with satisfaction as he swam to the end to get out, as I grabbed the corner of my clothes to wring out the water.

"Are you happy now?" Not that he was angry, he even sounded amused.

"Yes. I am." Nodding in agreement we both started walking in being careful not to be seen from the other end of the tunnel yet.

"Did you see the watchers outside? I'm guessing they assume we will come back here; I wonder if they are aware of the pool also or if there's some other reason they need to watch over this place? I haven't been inside yet so there might be others in there." Agreeing we had been extremely careful keeping watch.

Elija had said most overlooked the pool that sometimes the most important things were not always what was guarded. We had been all over the palace here and never found anything, so instead we decided to go to the wishing well on the further east side of the city. Both cities were very long in design as the palace had been at the far end of the shops. At the entrance and straight up the middle while the homes had been built into the sides on either side all along the way from front to back.

The only difference had been the shade city had a second floor up in the palace as well as another floor deeper. The Eurubian city had been a little larger utilizing an additional area between the two mountains, instead of going up, it was more of an underground tunnel. There had only been a few homes back here for larger families. We had spent a few hours searching through each room. After a while I was beginning to feel this was hopeless, I just wish Elija could have told us where it was. Why hadn't he said since he was the first one to let me know it existed. If he hadn't wanted us to find it then he wouldn't have told us about it. I was trying to think about anything I could remember about the place, then it occurred to me as I remembered, I don't know why I even forgot. Finding Goseck had been a bit easier, we had to stop for a second to be quiet as a group of people from the order walked through the center of the city. Making our way along the stairs that lined the sides of the city, we followed it staying low trying not to be noticed. We worked our way to where Harmony had first been brought here.

They were using the palace side, we watched as several walked in, we hadn't seen anything set up in there. It must have been relatively new, not that it explains why the animals were missing from the outside, they were not afraid of shades. Now we were wondering if they were working with any other kinds of creatures even though it seemed Alana wanted to keep strict control over who was in their group. As the last were to leave, we finished making our way across to Harmony's room she had been staying in. I hope I was correct about its location. The people hadn't feared her at all placing her here, it was as if they already knew who she was and what she would be doing.

Once in, we started looking around the place, it had been a public wishing well for a while until they had to close it off from being accessible. If anyone dropped change into the well, it would come flying back out. The people on the other side would throw the change back through. To keep it from being used as a wishing well they had closed it off and covered it, so we had to look for something covered but not protected. Searching around the room there were only two other rooms off this one. The main room had been set up as a relaxed family room, the second room was the private restroom while the third had been the bedroom. There was no kitchen since most ate together down at the diner or pub here. Also, her place had only been a transition place, not a regular apartment. This was extremely frustrating, where could it possibly be. I could have sworn it would have been in here. There was a small closet off the bedroom I had looked in not that I expected to see harmony's clothing. It brought back memories of her standing here deciding what to wear, she might not have stayed here long but it had been gifted to her hoping to encourage her to visit longer when she did, the people living here felt safer with her around.

She used to have such unusually designed carpets here. Now there was absolutely nothing around or on the floor. The city had cloaked a few belongings while the others had come to claim them later when it was safe. Now that it was gone there were only a few pieces left everywhere. Even here, only a few things had remained on the floor. Harmony had left a few pieces of clothing hanging in here. If I hadn't been looking in the closet for nostalgic reasons. I never would have seen it. There was a dark circle outline on the floor, feeling around it, there were slight ridges showing. In the center, there was a separate piece of the floor and not just a circle stain or anything else. Calling Goseck into the room we both tried to open it. Sadly, it had not wanted to move.

We tried almost everything; it did not want to budge. There wasn't enough of a gap, there had to be a way of getting this up even for as strong as we both had been it still wasn't moving.

"You could try twisting it instead of pulling at it?" An extremely unexpected voice, rather soft-spoken came directly behind us as we jumped back away from it.

"Crap," I almost yelled, "when did you get here?" I know I was good at sneaking up on people, but I think I might have been outdone by Elija, he's so silent no wonder why no one caught him before.

"I thought you might need some help; I was also interested in checking out the well again. It has been some time since I've been here, there are friends I would like to make a quick visit to on the other side. I thought you might want to know Dinah found out you were missing, she read Goseck's note about checking something out, and that you'd be back in a few days. She didn't buy it and was going to look for you, so I told them I wanted both of you to do me a personal favor which is why you both hadn't told them where you were going. It bought you some time, so are we going in or not?" Elija explained himself in such a matter-of-fact way even though this was the first time I had seen him get excited about something.

Twisting the cover off as he had suggested. It did start to move upward until we were able to move it aside. Not quite what I was expecting as I looked down, I expected to see a well filled with water. Instead, there was a ladder along the side wall as we watched Elija lower himself. Being the first to climb down. He was eager since he was going first. I followed him as Goseck slid the cover over the best he could, then followed us down the narrow shaft.

I couldn't help it. I was wondering what kind of well this would be if it had been down this far? How would people be able to go down here just to throw change or tokens of thanks if it was so well hidden? I didn't think it needed to be guarded because who would even have any idea it was down here. The temporary apartment we had entered. It was set up along the second row of homes from ground level as we followed the shaft by now, we could have easily been down in the subbasement of the city. Maybe the well dried up? But then if it had it seemed Elija would have said something by now. Stepping off the ladder at the end it had been a wide-open dark cave with absolutely no light, at least not until we had gone a little further into the cave.

There were tiny little bugs as we passed them, they had lit a slight green glow that lit the cave only to stop as we passed.

This reminded me of a cave that Rose and I explored when we were little. The only difference had been the way we found it. She had slipped into a small hole and slid down. This hadn't been it, but the rock formations reminded me a lot of it. As we walked to the end it had been a large oval-shaped room with a few bricks placed around the center outlining the well. Standing over it the water hadn't looked like water. It looked thicker, almost like blood rather than water. Poking at it with my finger, the liquid was rather warm, thick, and almost greasy feeling however it had slid off my finger rather quickly leaving no trace as if I had never touched it. In my experience with blood, it wasn't common for it to feel greasy unless there was a high level of fat in the blood or as Lorah would tell me, the person possibly had lipemia. The majority of my blood came from animals but the few times I took a little from people, there was a lot I could tell about their health.

"The best way of learning is by doing, you both might not end up in the same place but every time you come through you will end up back here without trying. Just be careful not to let others see you use it, and make sure you memorize where you came out, otherwise you won't be able to find it. It's not as easy as this side is since it's marked with bricks. On the other side it could be a certain spot in the lake, as a hint it's always a spot in the water, somewhere you can even get to is the bottom of the palace using the water, but remember you must originate from here to start in the first place. Once in the well, you enter a whole world in itself, like the portals it has various areas to go anywhere. Once you get used to it, it's much easier to get lost if you go far. I'm off, I'll be back in a few days." As he said that Elija jumped feet first, and we watched him disappear into the thick red goo.

I hadn't wanted to risk swallowing any of that stuff making sure my mouth and eyes were closed when I jumped in. I had expected it to instantly pop out somewhere, instead, it almost felt as if I was standing in the center of thick jelly. I didn't have much of a choice but to open my eyes and look around. All I could see was this thick goo around me, the goo made everything slightly blurry. I wasn't stuck. I could move around easily. I could even see the light green glow from the room I had just come from. I was curious if this was close to the same concept as the life stone when Harmony used to focus on it. Elija must have already passed all the way through since he wasn't still in here. Moving forward even more I found as a bright flash of light hit, I was expecting to feel instant pain as the stone had inflicted on me before, except this time no searing pain and no torn body parts as I was feeling around myself, I was still intact much to my relief.

I knew that Goseck jumped in right after me except when I wound up out of the pool, I was floating in the dead center of a lake looking around me. I hadn't seen him anywhere. Swimming down to the bottom I hadn't seen him in there anywhere, at least I know he wasn't drowning but where had he gone? Maybe each person wound up somewhere else? There had to be a trick to this or a way of making sure everyone wound up at the same place. I would hate to send my family in here and have everyone scattered almost everywhere. Wanting to make sure I could get back. I swam back to the area I had come through. It took a while surrounding the same area to find it, however as soon as I reached it, I was back in the red glowing goo. This time Goseck had also been in here. He must have had the same idea I did wanting to test it to make sure we both made it back.

After a while of coming back and forth, I found I could travel to quite a few places in our world but then there were a few I knew were not our own from the way it looked. Some were much more exotic than others. I liked the overgrown jungles. There were no humans or creatures around until you came to certain areas, even though they were far stretched apart and kept to themselves in their colonies. One of the places looked like it was in eternal darkness not that I had been around for very long but there had to be some light at a certain point even for the grass to grow. I popped out of a watering hole in the center of nothing but blades of grass surrounding me. There was a lot of moss, so the ground was extremely wet; the trees in the far distance had grown to an amazing height. There had to be a sun even though as I looked around, I couldn't even find the moon but the light in the sky had to be coming from somewhere no matter how dense it was. As much as I would love a place like this never being stuck indoors, it would depress Rose being here. Besides, I kind of like seeing the sun out, for some reason as great as this place looks it also looks rather depressing even for a vampire.

We left a piece of cloth on the floor in the main room of the well, that way we would know if we were still waiting for anyone. It was much harder to keep track of time in these worlds since they seemed to go by much slower than the earth had. Goseck left after being gone already from Dinah for two nights, he didn't want to risk her coming looking for him. I stayed behind waiting for Elija, I wasn't sure how much longer he would be if he had known our own time ticked by so quickly? Sitting down in the corner, finally, Elija popped out with a huge grin on his face, I wondered what he was thinking.

"I thought you might be waiting for me, I wanted to let you know I'm staying for a while longer. If you wish you may head back. I'll be fine or you can stay however if you stay, I doubt your family will look for you quite yet since they know you are with me and I'm sure Goseck has assured them that we are both alright. I'll be back in two earth days." Not taking much time he was off again in the pool. Wherever he was going he was certainly happy.

Still sitting here, I wasn't sure if I wanted to go back in again or wait here. Either way, the time was going to go by slowly. I wasn't in the mood to be trapped in the shade city even though that's sort of what I was doing down here. Standing up, I walked over to the pool jumping in. It felt strange to jump in going down and then be able to move around and walk in any direction once I was in. The ground felt soft except it was still solid enough to walk on, it would be easy to lose your balance in here, the only object that came to mind were pillows. It felt like walking on slippery pillows. Feeling around at the goo it had created enough space away from my body that it no longer touched me as I stood here. I had been thinking of Harmony when I heard a voice; it wasn't coming from outside the well. It was coming from in front of me. Leaning forward to listen, but not enough to go through in case I didn't want to risk whoever was seeing me. Then I recognized the sound. It was her. I would know her voice anywhere.

"I can't believe we haven't been able to find the rest of the children. They can't be that good at hiding. The ones we found were exactly the way Alana described them as, dangerous, attacking, and making a scene. I can't seem to focus on them. They have to be hidden away somewhere with some sort of magic otherwise there is no reason they should still be unfound by us. Enough about that. I have the training to commit to right now, I must be ready in two weeks. We will be visiting the shade city. There are rumors they have vampires staying with them, it's most unusual. Something that has never been allowed before so we must check it out." Her voice had trailed off a little not that they had left where they were standing, whoever she was speaking to started talking, a voice I did not recognize.

"Alana made it clear when the others were to find who the vampires were, she wanted you to stay here. I think there's something about it that worries her; she knows you are vulnerable to a vampire's venom. Shades can burn off the venom's attack but because you have the other power that may kill you, she doesn't know yet. Besides Luther is not dead yet, he may be setting up a trap, and if he's ready this time you might not be so lucky as you were last time." The other voice was of a woman who seemed very worried.

"Yes, I know there is danger, there will always be some threat. It's what we deal with. I can't hide from it forever. I can't fight that feeling that there is something more to this. Something I should know." As she spoke, I wished I could step out and tell her and hope she would remember everything.

Knowing my luck, it could either make it worse or have her not remember and call in the guards assuming I was there to attack her. Besides, I could never present myself while she was with someone, I would never get the chance to speak or explain anything.

"You know Alana looks out for you, she's very protective of you. Perhaps training will help you focus better, and you will be able to think better." As reassuring as this woman had sounded it didn't seem as if Harmony was buying it.

"Perhaps" had all she said to the woman as their footsteps now echoed.

I could hear the other woman in the distance call out to her

"Any time you need to talk Sydney you know where to find me." Then their conversation ended with that.

It felt strange having someone call her by another name. Must have been how Jacob and Harmony felt when they found out Dorina's original name was Sophie. I know Charlie said he felt strange having others call her that instead of the name he had always known her by, even now he tries to accept her other life had been as this other person. Either way, I would have to make sure I made it home before two weeks. If they were planning on checking out the shade city but then they might be doing that now.

After a while, there was silence with no one coming or speaking. I stepped forward now into a hallway. Strange, I wondered where the water had been as I looked back there was a picture on the wall with a woman holding the bowl as the water in the bowl seemed to swirl around. How was I supposed to get back in there? I was hoping this wasn't the sense of humor that Elija hinted at. If I had my time to practice it would be fine but if I had to hurry. I might not figure it out. Even though my curiosity did get the better of me. Walking down the hallway when I heard Harmony's voice trail off to, I wasn't sure if I would run into her or not, but I was curious about where she was training. The hallway had gone down quite a distance until there was an open door that led into an even larger room. One part of the room looked like it could be sectioned off while the other was wide open. No one had been in that room as I peeked in a little further. I could see through the very tiny slit that let me look into the sectioned-off room. Inside, harmony was in there with a rather tall man dressed for what looked like combat. I did think he was overdressed for practice fighting until I saw that Harmony hadn't held back but then neither had he.

I assumed he was her teacher; any time she had made a mistake he would send her sailing into the wall. Each time he did this I had to fight the urge to go in and finish him off. I hated seeing her get hurt but then I was shocked she hadn't let it stop her. She would simply get right back up going back for the attack. She kept trying to hold back from using any powers to keep fighting as a human would. She made it look as though she was trying to conquer the physical art of fighting first. From my guess, they were using various fighting styles, but I could only guess a few of them. I had visited Burma years ago, so I knew the one style was Bando Thaing and Kajukenbo, Kajukenbo was founded in nineteen hundred forty-seven at Palamas Settlement on Oahu, Hawaii by a group called the black belt society.

I was entranced by the art style, basically watching, I lost track of time as they were finishing up, and her instructor started talking with her again.

"Work on your timing more. Don't be so eager to get in there, the saying patience is a virtue is not just words full of hot air. There is a reason for it. You also did quite well at controlling, and not using your powers. Many of my students do not fully master these skills because they are so reliant on the skills of a shade. Perhaps you were more human at one time than you realize? We will pick up again tomorrow Sydney." As soon as he said that I realized I needed to hide right now, he was the last person I wanted to get caught by.

I was sure that I would be stronger but if Harmony had not remembered me the first action of me attacking her instructor would not be good. Besides, I think this guy could outmaneuver me if he has speed, he could take me regardless of my power. Being a vampire didn't mean I was invincible.

The only place I could go had been on the other side of the partition hiding in the far corner hoping no one was coming in here. As I had seen her teacher leave, I sighed, relieved that he had gone straight out and not into the room I was in. Harmony on the other hand stayed behind. It had sounded like she was still practicing after he left. Then nothing but silence until I heard her speak.

"There's no sense in you hiding there whoever you are. I know you watched my practice not that I'm sure why you would want to?" She seemed rather surprised that I had hidden but then I wasn't sure if I wanted to reveal myself.

"I didn't want to interfere in your training, but I was fascinated by watching you. Sorry I bothered you. I'll leave you to your practice. I think I should be going anyway." As I said this, I tried to leave heading down the hallway except she was quicker which I had forgotten since she hasn't been around me for a while.

"I don't recognize you. You're rather strange looking for a shade, what is your name?" She seemed curious but also ready to defend herself since she held her stance taking a step back for a second when she realized she didn't know who I was.

"I am strange looking for a shade. I would have to agree with you there, sorry for imposing. Usually, I don't just stare but I enjoyed watching you train, it's been a while. My name is Lucian. I'm sure you don't remember me." Even though I was hoping she would it hadn't seemed like she was from looking at me.

Not that I wanted to admit I wasn't a shade at all. I was a vampire; we had heard was not allowed in their confines. Not even half breeds were permitted. Harmony had been the only one but then it had been because of the power she possessed.

"I know every worker and you don't work for me; how did you get in here? Are you one of Alana's friends?" As she had asked her eyes narrowed a little frowning at me.

"No, I have to be honest with you there. I'm not one of Alana's friends but I'm also someone who won't hurt you. I could explain myself to you, but I doubt you would remember or understand. I mainly got lost and should leave since I don't belong here, I'm sorry again for bothering you but it is good to see you doing well." Taking a few steps backward she didn't seem nervous.

I was slowly inching away from her, not that she made any attempt to follow me, at least not until I was standing in front of the painting. I turned and she was already behind me. Almost more with a curious look on her face as she watched me.

"You look familiar, but I can't place it? How do you know me? Why don't you want to explain yourself? It can't be that complicated?" She was curious now how I knew her.

I could only hope that if she did not like what she heard I could escape fast enough through the picture, my only hope had been that if I touched it that it might send me through.

"I didn't know you as Sydney, I knew you as Harmony from your past. I wasn't planning on coming here until I heard your voice, sad to say my heart speaks louder than reason. I should get going before I'm missed." As I raised my hand towards the picture, she had asked one last time.

"Will I see you again?" She seemed willing to see me again, she was curious and not upset with me being here.

I couldn't help but feel happy she wanted to see me even if it might not be for the reason I was hoping for.

"I doubt that would be a good idea no matter how badly I would want to see you again. Unless we could meet somewhere else? You pick the place, and I will meet you there." As I leaned against the wall with my hand on it knowing as soon as I slid it over the water, I might disappear.

Not that I wanted her to see me leave this way, but I didn't know how else to get away but then I also didn't know if simply touching it would work either since it wasn't physical water but a drawing of it.

"I'm leaving early with two guards of mine to the Eurubian city, do you know where that is? Perhaps you can meet me there. At least it will be a neutral place, and we can talk without being interrupted." She seemed sure of herself even though I was worried about meeting her there.

"I know where that is, exactly where in the city do you want to meet or perhaps by the waterfall? I could even meet you in the basement of the palace. That might be better. I doubt anyone would be down there to bother us." As I looked at her decision she seemed curious how I knew there was a palace let alone about the basement.

"I'll see you there in the basement if you know where it is." Smiling back at me I couldn't help but feel excited.

I still had to be careful, but it felt so good to know I was going to see her again. I wasn't sure if she would fall for it as I looked past her and then pointed with my free hand.

"Who is that?" As I nodded over behind her, watching her turn to see who was behind her.

As she looked behind her, I slid my hand over the water, and to my hopes, it worked. I was pulled in instantly as panic had set in. I could hear her say 'There's no one there, where did you go?' I kept silent hoping she would not notice where I had gone. Stepping back, I followed the green light shining from the pool as I followed it stepping out. I could see that Elija had stuck to his word; he would be gone for a while. Even though it would take a while to get here again. I needed to find out what the family was doing in case they were about to be under attack with the others checking out the city. I had to at least warn them about what I heard. But then I would make sure I also made it back here even if I had to convince Goseck to help me out which I knew with him. I wouldn't have to convince much.

Heading back up the shaft the way we had come. I didn't get very far before I could hear people talking from the center of the town. There was a group down there with guards around them as I heard a small voice I was familiar with. What would Larissa be doing here? Did they search the city already knowing that Harmony had wanted to go? Walking out onto the steps to get a better look, my family was already down there lined up even though Goseck had been with them. How did they get caught? My only guess had been they grabbed the children, and my family had come willingly with them not wanting to be separated. Looking around I was trying to find a way of distracting the guards. If anything, I could lure my family down to the pool and get them to a safe place, even if I hadn't mastered it yet, it would be safer than where they were now. As I watched I could see savannah looking directly up at me now smiling. She didn't let on that she knew I was up here to anyone else, but she looked me directly in the eye knowing I was here.

Eventually, they started taking them to the palace from what Goseck told me. In the past, there was a strong area they could take them that they would not be able to break out of because of what the walls had been reinforced from. As they worked their way back, I followed them as carefully as I could. I knew Charlie picked up on the fact I was nearby. Even Lorah noticed. I wondered where the others were, I hoped they hadn't been harmed. I guess if I had the chance I might eventually find out. As I suspected they were put in the furthest part of the basement as the door closed only one guard had stood outside keeping watch as the others departed. Staying back to stay hidden observing to see who might still be in close range. I had to wait quite a while for the guard to relax himself assuming there was no danger. He sat down on the chair beside the door he was guarding. Checking the pathway out, there hadn't been anyone standing there. I wanted to make sure it was clear for leaving.

Heading back, I could see the guard falling asleep in his chair not wanting to risk waiting any longer. I took the first opportunity that I had. I snuck up on him as I had so many others, I hit him on the head rather hard. I hoped I hadn't broken anything as he slumped over falling to the ground. Taking the keys off from him I placed it in the keyhole opening the door. I knew once I had them out and hidden, the others would be searching the city for them but hopefully, they won't find the pool. Opening the door my family at least was relieved when they had seen me.

"We don't have much time; he won't be unconscious for long and there may be others soon. We need to get you to a safe place; you're going to have to trust me but if I have to distract the guards you can follow Goseck, he can show you the safe place." As I said this Goseck nodded in agreement.

I could tell the family was wondering what we knew. Following us out we had made it halfway through before they noticed they were missing. One of the other guards went to switch with him when they found he was lying on the floor. Trying to move along faster we went along the side as the others ran towards the palace probably assuming we were still in there. Getting everyone into the temporary apartment wasn't too bad, it would be getting everyone down the shaft. Charlie had a rather questioning look on his face but didn't say anything other than to help the girls down and Goseck helped the young boy. Out of my family only Rose, Jacob, Lorah, Lewis, and Evangeline were missing.

At least it hadn't taken us as long as I thought it might get down. The slow ones of the family were not here but then I worried if that was why they were not with the rest of the family? I know there is no way Rose wouldn't be with her daughter unless something happened. I was almost too scared to think of the possibility even though I think Charlie would have said something if he knew, even a way of passing the news to me without Larissa knowing. As we had gotten to the pool Goseck said a few words.

"We were surprised and attacked by Alana. We happened to be with the kids so she could justify why they took us, however the others just disappeared, so we don't know where they are or if they are okay, once they are safe, I'm coming with you to search for them." Nodding it was what I had thought but I hoped my connection with my sister was still as strong since I hadn't noticed her being gone, I hoped she was alive.

I knew he was thinking of Dinah being worried about her. Now to explain to everyone else to let them know what the plan was.

"I need all of you to trust me, as long as you are holding hands, I believe you will end up in a safe place. I will go in first, I am hoping to lead you to a particular place then I'm going to search for the others." Just as I had thought I knew Charlie would insist on going with me only I hadn't planned on taking him.

Not that I wanted Goseck to go but I understood his need was as strong as mine had been. Not only Harmony was planning on meeting me here, but even though it would be with her group, it was no longer safe for me to meet her. Having everyone hold hands as we jumped into the pool, we were surrounded by the red goo. Goseck stayed out opting to wait for me to come out. He figured out what my plan was for dealing with Charlie. I simply told him for the benefit of the kids I still needed his help moving them to a safe place. As I thought of the place that seemed as though it was in eternal darkness. I could see a slight light where we needed to go. Walking in that direction holding everyone's hand, we walked out into the forest surrounded by trees instead of showing up in the marsh as I had the first time, we were all at the far end in the distance.

As Charlie spoke to the others reassuring them, we would be back. I hadn't wanted him to see how I would take off while he was distracted. I took a step back stepping on the puddle and in a flash, I was gone. I could hear him calling for me not knowing where I had gone. I couldn't help but smile when he said out loud 'this is very typical of you if you can hear me, get back here.' I had to stop myself from laughing. I was surprised he hadn't been wary enough to keep holding my hand to make sure I didn't ditch him. I swear in the future. I wouldn't be surprised if he never trusted me again! Following the green glow of the light, I popped out then following Goseck we made our way out making sure to securely close the lid so that if they went looking for them in here, they would not find them. Grabbing some leftover tattered rugs that had been left on the floor we threw them over the lid to cover it.

We hadn't been able to go very far. In the center of town, we could see Alana standing there yelling at her guards for their incompetence in watching the prisoners. Out of sheer anger, she killed two of them telling the rest if they failed in finding the vampire children and the other traitors they would be killed also. We tried moving downward cutting through one of the stairways that led to the back of the little shops that the Eurubian people had set up. They didn't have as many as the shade city did but theirs were much closer to the exit. As we made our way out it had been clear to the waterfall until I heard my name said. Turning around I looked and there stood Harmony walking towards us. Goseck whispered to me 'does she remember you?' But sadly, I had to dash his hopes and say no.

"Come with us. We need to talk somewhere else. We can't stay here but you're going to have to trust me." I hoped she would trust us; we couldn't stay here with Alana especially since we didn't know what Harmony would do or what side she would take even though I was positive she would protect Alana first. I motioned for Goseck to go check the rest of the path to make sure it was safe to take off.

"Why isn't it safe? But then I don't understand why Alana is here. I wasn't expecting her in this city, not that she was supposed to go to the other one yet. What's going on that I don't know about?" She looked very confused trying to figure out what was going on and why Alana hadn't told her the truth about where she had gone to.

"She's trying to kill my family, and I need to find the others which is why I need to leave. I know you will be safe but watch your back even to her, if she can, she will kill you. She's been seen with Luther. I don't know what they are planning but if he bites you, it could kill you and she might be hoping your power might absorb into her." As I was saying this sadly Alana came out hearing us speak.

I tried to keep it down, but the tunnel had such an echo. As she walked up to Harmony, I knew she would not harm her but that was no guarantee about me.

"Where are the vampire children? If you do not tell me. I will hunt every one of you down and kill you until I find them. Now tell me and I might spare your life." Alana was growing angrier by the minute.

"I won't tell you; they don't deserve to die." At least Goseck knew to stay hidden.

Alana wasn't aware of him being close by but then neither had Harmony given him away. As Alana raised her hand, I could feel the air swirling around me getting hotter. It hadn't taken an expert to guess what she was going to do. She was going to kill me on the spot. What I hadn't expected had been to be shifted from one place to the other, apparently, harmony called me to her away from the firestorm that Alana had started creating around me. Placing me behind her she faced Alana speaking to her in a cool but firm tone.

"If he knows where the children are we stand a better chance at reasoning with him rather than killing him. Besides, there are other reasons I will explain to you later that I want him alive. I also expect an explanation as to why all our guards are covering this place. I had been by the shade city, and it looks as though you were already there." Watching and waiting for an answer, Harmony wasn't sure what to expect.

"I was out doing exactly as I said I was, but we had urgent news that could not be put off. We chased them from the shade city to this place, he is one of the traitors protecting the children. We already have a few in custody and they are being moved to the compound to be questioned. The other adults tried to get away with the children and this one helped them. He is a risk and a traitor and needs to be dealt with. I highly doubt he would give you any honest answers if you asked him other than to prolong his life." Alana was so angry she was waiting for Harmony to move out of her way so that she could finish what she started.

The firestorm still in the corner was brewing, as I watched, Harmony only glanced at it as she dowsed the firestorm into nothing but smoke.

"He is to be kept alive until I say so; we will bring him back to the compound as I now have questions for the others you have said were in custody? We will deal with them as each problem is solved and perhaps, we can find out where the children are. But I highly doubt he will give that information right now. Besides I am sure he can be reasoned with." As soon as she had said that Alana put her hand down.

Almost as if there was a secret code being spoken between the two not that I had known but Harmony was having a silent conversation with Alana in her mind to calm her down, reassuring her justice would be met at the right time. Alana was worried she would find out the truth, but Harmony wanted to find out the truth not that she wanted to distrust Alana even though she started having her doubts she certainly wasn't showing them.

Chapter Twelve

Alana's deception

Only a couple of the guards were left behind as Alana told Sydney they were there to clean up the place, even though I knew they were there looking for the missing family that was hidden. This had to be eating at her knowing she couldn't keep moving on with her plan when she had to go back to the rest of the clan to prove or explain herself and her actions. Along the way, we had made a few stops that I wasn't sure what they were for, however, Alana seemed to be talking with people as Harmony stood back letting her take care of what she needed. Then instead of heading above ground we went underground using tunnels that were connected and many that I could tell were added much later. Many storm drains looked closed off with heavy lids protecting them until Harmony simply walked up to them barely moving her hand to open them. We had been a long way away from the city, so I was wondering how we were going to get there unless they had another portal to use. Then as I found out we had come close to where we were going. Instead of taking me to the city as she had been earlier, we came to a stop. They had a temporary holding down here closer to the Eurubian and shade cities.

There were not many rooms however it certainly looked more than a temporary base, it looked rather permanent to me as we walked through. We passed one enormous room as we entered, the guards who had come with us blocked off the exit as I was told to sit in the chair in the center of the room. Not wanting to start a fight yet I sat down as Harmony and Alana stepped into another room. Sydney as the others called her explained they would be right back after discussing a few things. As they left, I was there watching the guards as they had with me never taking their eyes off me. As hard as I tried, I could barely hear what they were discussing in the other room. The walls were thicker than I expected them to be.

"I need to know why you were over by the Eurubian city Alana; you have to admit if this were in the reverse you would be angry seeing me there. I was there to meet up with an old friend who remembered me from the past. I was going to question him and if you had been back when you said you were, I left a note. I tried contacting you, but you never returned my messages. Now please explain what is going on?" Knowing that Lucian was in the other room she was still trying to make sense of this while Alana was trying to think of an excuse Sydney would accept when it came to her.

"When I was out scouting as we usually do, we ran into Luther. I realize that I should have let you know except I didn't want him to know you were alone and possibly vulnerable. He was looking for something he wouldn't tell us, so we followed him, and he led us to the shade city. It's why some of the guards are still there. The two guards that are dead in the Eurubian city were killed by that man sitting out there. He was protecting the vampire children. It was just him and the children. There were no others. There's not much to explain, but who was it that you were there to see? Have I met this person before?" Alana was rather interested to see who Sydney would be visiting in the city that would know her from her past.

Not sure how much she remembered from her past she didn't seem overly friendly but treated him as she would have with anyone else so maybe there's no reason to panic yet?

"The man out there is the one I went to see. He claims to have known me from my past and he used my old name. True that could be public knowledge, but I felt I could trust him. I wanted to find out exactly how he got into the compound and how he got out without my seeing him. One second, he was there and the next he was gone. No one saw him come or go. I was in the main compound training when he showed up, I don't know how he got in or left but he said he was only there because he was lost and heard a familiar voice, so he followed it to me." Alana shook her head not wanting her to find out the truth now that she was too close.

At least if they were exterminated there would be no more fear of her finding out. The only ones left had been a few adults and children.

"I planned on filling you in on everything when we got back so instead of waiting you might as well know now. I guess I should have taken you even though I just thought the last few days' scouting would be routine. There are a group of vampire half-breeds that are questioning our authority and threatening to wipe out everything we have worked hard to start. We must take care of it now before it gets out of hand. I have some locked up in the main compound, I know you like to question them so they will be waiting for you if you had been there, you might have been informed earlier about all of this, you must have just missed them." Not sure if Sydney was buying this, her expression had failed to change but then since she had absorbed herself so much into her training, she rarely gave way to emotion or expression being very well guarded from it.

Once explaining that your emotions could be used against you, this had been her main cause for contemplating and reacting. Alana missed when she used to overreact and panic looking to her for advice and now, she was so sure of herself and much more in control it was difficult to know what she was thinking or doing.

"I have no reason to distrust you, Alana; if he is as loyal to his friends as I think he might be then he will be judged and possibly executed along with the others. You and I have something else to deal with while we are here so if he does not want his friends killed, then he will not try anything while he is being transported over." This wasn't what Alana had wanted to hear but at least it was heading the same way helping her feel she still had the support of Sydney.

Walking out of the room showing no expression as I had watched them both come out together Alana had a bit of a sneer on her face which didn't make me feel too confident.

"We have decided that you will be joined by a few others whom we feel you know, we will not be joining you however if you try anything then they die. Your fate rests with them. I will see you again in a few days. Guards escorted him to the main compound. Alana and I have some work to do before we get there." As soon as she had said this both had left the room.

The only others I could think of would be my missing family members. Standing up I followed the guards on our way there, at least I would find out if they were alright. The last week went rather quickly, the guards never spoke to us even though I thought Harmony would have been back by now. Every so often I would hear guards either side with Harmony or Alana about how we should be handled even though we all had the clear idea they were afraid of Harmony because of her powers.

At least I knew the others were alright. Rose, Jacob, Evangeline, Lewis, and Lorah had been here however no one still knew where Sophie had disappeared. She was out collecting herbs for her garden when the others attacked. I filled them in on hiding the family in the pool. At first, my sister looked at me as if I lost my mind putting them in water since Larissa still breathed until she understood what kind of pool it was. I had to admit I thought the same thing when I first heard of it. Elija had been right that you had to originate with the pool first as we had walked past the familiar painting, I had run my hand along the moving water, and nothing happened. Every so often food would be sent in for us, but nothing else was done. Then the guards showed up requesting that I go first. I wasn't sure what they were going to do but I had to find out.

Being seated the two guards stepped out of the room keeping watch to make sure no one came or went. I wasn't sure what I was waiting for or if this was to be my execution? Then the side door opened. I wasn't sure why I hadn't remembered this room; it was the fighting room except the partition had been taken out. Harmony walked over in front of me as I noticed a door was sliding in place behind us.

"Alana will be listening, but she won't be in here with us depending on your answers and how this goes you will either live or die today. First, start with the vampire children, why are you protecting them?" Speaking as she stood, she hadn't brought another chair for herself to sit in.

"To start, my niece who is only half-vampire, half-human and will continue to grow into an adult as my sister and brother-in-law have. And the three actual vampire children are the most loving, sweet and compassionate children, yes it sucks they will never grow to be adults. We don't know what to expect other than to know they will be frustrated as they get older but it's something we are willing to deal with as a family and we are better equipped than anyone else to handle them. They are no threat and never will be. We have taught them to blend in and to hide their secret. That they have done quite well so they have not broken your codes. The only one who had was the one who changed them to begin with, and that was Luther." I wished I had known what she was thinking, her expression never changed once. I couldn't tell if she was angry or pleased with what she was hearing. Sitting in the far corner now she was sitting there silently not changing her expression then I heard something I wasn't expecting.

"Only speak in your thoughts right now, you are the only one allowed to enter my mind, how is it that you know my past?" As soon as she asked this, her eyes looked directly at me.

I wasn't sure if she was speaking to me this way because she didn't want Alana to know what she asked? Either way, I wasn't going to make her wait long.

"I am a large part of your past. I first met you when you were arguing with your stone alone on an island trying to figure out how it worked, as much as you hadn't wanted to practice on me. I finally got you to do it, mainly because you had seen what it did to me was the reason why you didn't want to hurt me with it again. We have been together for a long time, then we were separated when Katherine Hawthorn died otherwise known as the lady in black. Then you lived with Goseck and after a while, you had adopted him as your father, he could speak to you the way you are doing with me now. We found each other again and lived together with Goseck and my aunt Dinah. The ones you have jailed are our family. You and Lorah had become close friends. I just wish you could remember." I tried to sum it up as best as I could, it wasn't as if we had time, and I could lay it out all slow.

"So do I. There is so much I don't remember, or certain things seem familiar but then I keep thinking what if I was a monster. Do I want to remember that? I have so many responsibilities here I don't have time to find out my past and right now it's just not important."

"Alana is using you, is there anything I can do to prove to you that my family and I are safe? Harmony you were part of our family, do you remember your childhood friend Beth? If I didn't know you personally, I would never know about her, go see her and find out the truth of what made you run. She may not know everything but it's where it all started. You all came back to find friends of yours killed." Standing up I wasn't sure if I had made an impact on her or not as she nodded her head and left the room.

The guards moved me back to the holding cell with the rest of the family not saying anything to me. For once I couldn't think of a way out, besides I didn't want to risk my family getting hurt if I had. It had been a few days since we heard anything. It was getting exhausting waiting in here doing nothing. I wondered how the kids and the others were doing.

One set of guards who dropped food off again had been talking to each other down the hall a short distance. With nothing else to do we all eavesdropped on their conversation.

"I don't know what Harmony did but I'm staying out of Alana's way, she's extremely pissed off. Whatever it is. I'm guessing it has to do with those people we have locked up. Normally Alana would have had them taken care of by now." Not much else had been said other than to wait for the next round.

We were beginning to think they would never come back for us. Maybe they had forgotten we were here. It was difficult keeping track of days here when you had no view of the outdoors. The only way we had for judging time had been the guards declaring they would only be feeding us twice every twenty-four hours. So, when the second meal came, we counted it as another day. Rose and the others walked around in the cell to keep from getting stiff and too weak. We had even tested the bars, but they were prepared for keeping vampires in, I wasn't sure what the material had been made of however we could neither break them or budge them.

Then after a short time from seeing the guards come back early with keys in hand not to let us all go; however, they were releasing Lorah. Mia, a Eurubian had been in the shade city when she spoke up saying she did not understand why she was taken when she was simply visiting her and had permission to be in the shade city. She had been the only one she could convince the others that had no connection to us or the vampire children. Against Alana's wishes, Sydney decided that she be freed. Not that Lorah wanted to leave us. We let her know it was less to worry about for her to keep safe until the rest of us could meet with her again.

Then again not too much later. I had been escorted to another room as I could hear furious screaming from Alana, she had been so angry. I could only assume her anger was directed towards Harmony. As we walked to the room, I was being taken to the main room. I heard Alana talking to someone about how she felt, 'they could use Luther to flush out the others. Make him feel comfortable then they would make him pay for his crime except harmony was not accepting that option.'

"At the beginning, you made it clear you did not want to work with vampires saying they could not be trusted. Now you want to work with the very one that started this mess? We are to keep order and not make it appear that we are weak by using someone that should be condemned to death, otherwise what was the purpose of making the law? You were a strong supporter of that. I know the ones we have here should die, but I also feel that the children were not given a choice and so far, have done nothing to need us getting involved. There may be allowances but it's a very thin line. There is no need for you to get so angry. This is very much unlike you unless you can explain to me why I can't help." Sydney had spoken rather calmly but to the point of making sure that Alana knew she was not making her choices based on emotional ones.

Not bothering to talk with her Alana stormed out of the room with Sydney watching her completely confused. Before they had spoken about every step they had taken and now Alana was keeping something from her that she could not figure out other than the fact it started with this family.

Alana walked straight to her chambers where three guards were waiting for her. Making sure no one was around she closed the door to speak with them silently.

"Keep Luther hidden until I tell you otherwise. I will have it set up as soon as she makes her move. I will have her finished. I no longer need her. Luther is a much more willing participant; besides, I have nothing to hide from him." The guards looked a little surprised but then figured this had been her plan all along.

"Even if we keep him hidden how are you going to get the power transferred, we don't even know if it will work if she dies, the power is lost. The guards and I can spend some extra time wiping out her past, she would never know. How do you know that Luther will work with you and not turn on you?" The guard seemed rather hopeful with this prospect.

"If she lives, I still have to deal with her. I would rather the power be gone than anyone holding power over me. If she ever found out I wanted her killed to get the life stone, she might not look too favorable on that. Besides, Luther and I go way back. He won't risk it, especially once I get the power. Eventually, we will wipe out that family for getting in my way. I don't care if the stupid vampire children live or die, I want revenge if things had worked out. I should have had the life stone already." The guards seemed puzzled since they thought she had the stone when she was last in the city of the shades.

"To answer your odd-looking expressions. I never had the life stone. Sydney made it appear as if I had, she somehow still called it to herself or it came to her, either way, I don't know how she controlled its power when it was no longer with her. The life stone I had was just a plain cloudy crystal stone, nothing special about it." As she spoke her temper rose, leaving the room even angrier than she had been before.

Still sitting patiently in the other room. I expected to see Harmony, but instead I saw Alana walked into the room. She had a smile on her face that made my back creep with disgust. Watching her walk around in front of me, leaning against the wall, crossing her arms in front of her never taking her eyes off me.

"I have a proposition for you. There's not much choice in the matter however it will determine if and how your family dies. You won't be going back to your cell. I have you held here for a reason. I may not be able to kill you right now but later nothing will stop me, not even Sydney. For now, enjoy being the punching bag for my trainers. I've told them all about you. How dangerous and hateful you are to Sydney. How you hope to kill her and when she does die, they will believe it was you. Right now, they think she has disappeared. She hasn't, she had gone to check out something you said to her. She will be detained on her way back and she will think it's you, but Luther will do your dirty work. He will bite her, and it will all be over. Your family will endure watching you suffer for a while, then I will execute them. You get beat up, it's easy to explain it was an escape attempt, you'll be beaten so badly you won't be able to explain yourself. You hurt them and you don't look good to Sydney, that is if she lives. Enjoy your beating." Walking out through the side door it had been sealed after she left.

The trainers entered from the other side, concentrating on me. I wasn't sure how I was going to survive this. The one I had seen training Harmony walked in. I've been in fights before but never where I was personally beaten up. I knew this wasn't going to go well. The only reason they could control elements in this room at all had been from the vents above. If I harmed them Harmony would assume I attacked them while escaping. This was a no-win situation for me, not that I could do anything about it because Alana had all the control at this point. The best I could do would be not to attack but to protect myself.

They certainly weren't taking it easy on me. Soon as they entered the room. I was immediately picked up by a gush of wind and slammed into the wall. As strong as these walls were. I was leaving dents. I used to wonder who was stronger, a vampire or a shade. Even if I didn't hold back, I was sure a shade was stronger. Simply because they didn't need to touch me to cause damage. The wind would pick up around me, squeezing me. Blood started seeping through my skin slowly drying before it could go far. The heat from the fire was intense. I might have been a vampire, but it didn't mean the fire didn't hurt. Feeling almost consumed by it; they would douse me with water before starting again. I think they were even surprised by the fact I never once tried to attack them. I only defended myself when I had to or shielded my eyes when they shot fire at me. Either I wasn't the opponent they assumed I would have been or perhaps, they were stunned enough that I didn't once try to attack them. They didn't stay very long leaving out one of the doors. The last one had taken a long last look at me shaking his head as if he wasn't sure of something before leaving. I had been left in there for quite some time, my skin badly burned, and I had a few bruises. I hated knowing my family was going to see me like this but no way I could hide it and besides this might work. They can focus on me all they wanted, at least they wouldn't be hurting my family yet. I hated that I couldn't protect Harmony, what if Alana was correct and didn't make it back, if she did would she trust Alana still or me. I just had to hope harmony got back soon.

I was almost beginning to think they were going to leave me in here until they decided to go another round but with no such luck, I was brought back in with the rest of my family. Smiling at them I hoped it would relax them a little. If they looked too worried the guards might get too much of a thrill from it and pass on the news to Alana or the instructors. I knew they were worried, but they held it until the guards left. Rose was the first to greet me being careful about touching me, not that it had hurt as much as I expected. Or at least not until she touched me so I tried to hold back as much as I could. I did explain my method and why I reacted the way I did and how I was hoping they would keep reacting. Lewis agreed, thinking this might slow down the assaults, he was only worried they might come after the others. Not that he was worried, he could hold his own, he didn't want to risk anyone else getting hurt. The idea of my sister being in that situation made me angry. Something had to be done.

Before they came for me again and I was sure they would since Alana was holding a personal grudge against me. I sat on the floor leaning against the wall; at least it felt nice and cool. Closing my eyes relaxing the best that I could I tried to concentrate on Harmony. Even if it took forever there had to be a way of speaking with her the way she had with me. If my family could connect and I could read her when I had met her, if Goseck could reach her when she was nearby then I had to try. I wondered where Goseck was hiding or what he was doing since he was smart enough never to show himself when they took me. It hadn't worked the first or second time I tried. I knew it might take a while, even Sophie used to say sometimes things took a while but to keep practicing and never give up. I couldn't help it, but I was missing the trapped feeling I had of the shade city than being trapped here. So far, they had taken me out three times not taking any of the others. I went through much of the same, they never once touched me with their bare hands, but I had felt much of the power of the shades. They seemed to like throwing me more than anything. Fierce wind whipping around turning into firestorms. I wound up burned a lot.

The trainers tried enticing me to fight, verbally and physically, but they were not getting any reaction, especially the violent reactions that Alana warned them about. I was brought back. I would sit against the wall relaxing focusing on Harmony saying her name repeatedly when I finally heard her speak back.

'What do you want, for the last few days I keep hearing you call me. How are you doing this? Alana can't even call me?" She seemed surprised but also irritated that I called her so often.

"Are you able to see me? You used to be able to see people with the life stone. Can you still do that? If so, look for me and tell me what you think." I knew it would help if she could just see me.

"What the hell happened to you? It looks like you've been in a raging fire, did the place get attacked while I was gone? Have you seen Alana? Is she alright?" I guessed this would be the way she would respond, I also hoped for it.

"I'm sure Alana is just fine. The last time I saw her she said enjoy your beating, I've been getting free fighting training from your instructors except I have to say I'm a rather poor student since I refuse to participate. If I did it would only look bad if I hurt them. It's fine if they want to keep doing this to me or even use me to pay for everyone else's crimes, but there must be a way to let my family go. I can't stand back and watch them get harmed like I have and so far, thankfully it hasn't happened, but I know you won't trust me if I fight back even if it is to protect myself and my family. Please just do what you're planning and be done with it, no more toying around with us. Be careful coming home." I was worried I had lost connection with her until I had finally heard something else from her.

"I am on my way back already. It won't be long. I had to check something out but if my visions are true then I might need you if you're willing to work with me? I promise I will release your family. I see no threat from them." As soon as she said that there was no more communication, I just had to wait through the attacks until she got back here.

There weren't too many more. I think the initial wanting revenge wore out when they didn't get the reaction they wanted. I was thankful they hadn't decided to trade me out for another family member. As she said Harmony came back earlier than they expected her, only the one trainer Jaron knew she was back. She had called him to meet with her, she wanted to be here for a while without anyone knowing she had come back. She physically called herself to him. Checking on Alana through the ring, she was surprised to find her still wearing it. It was given to her to wear as not only a gift but also a false sense of protection, not that harmony ever shared that part with her.

Making sure no one else had been aware of her being there. Not that anyone could have sensed her when she popped in. Another trick she had hidden from Alana made her believe any magic used in the compound would be easily detectable and even if Sidney used any, Alana would know. She didn't want her to know every time she used it. She used to feel guilty for hiding secrets from Alana until she found out there were many being kept from her. Several she learned from Jaron, one of the few trainers she fully trusted. Looking at Jaron in the face hoping he would still be honest with her.

"What has been happening with the prisoners for this last week? I saw something completely against what I wished for them. I had left for a reason. I needed to find out the truth about something, so I brought my assistant with me. She was questioning a woman who was supposedly my friend before when I had just been a human. I was listening from a distance as she filled her in on the murders and the fact that I disappeared, and my body had never been found. She seemed broken up about it still even after all this time. I wanted to make the trip back so that my decision would not keep holding things up. But on the way I kept hearing this voice speaking to me, I know who it is, but I need to know the things I was seeing. Who and why did they happen." After filling Jaron in on so much I stood there waiting for an answer.

I could tell he was nervous about saying not that he has ever held anything back from me before which worried me.

"We didn't know what happened to you. Alana came to us asking if we had seen or heard from you and she felt that the guy in the cell had done something to do with you missing. I was a little skeptical, but I didn't have any reason not to trust her, after all, you trust her. She told us she was worried you would remember them, that they had traumatized you before, that they had been abusive, and she was worried it would affect your confidence now. If he had done something wrong, he should have been punished with death, but I thought we were supposed to work the truth out of him. She never came to find out if he spoke or not. He never once attacked us he just let us attack him. It just all felt strange so I ordered the others to stop, that we would handle it later if Alana said anything further to us." At least he was telling the truth and acting on what he had been ordered to do.

Not that I agreed with the fact he had gone along with such brutality to begin with.

"Alana knew exactly where I was, I had told her why I was going there. I knew she was angry about it since I delayed our decision, but I wanted to make sure, I wanted to find out if they were telling the truth. If the children were not a threat, I felt they should be let go for now, but Luther should still pay his debt for what he had done. My guess is these families wound up with the children somehow and are responsible enough to care for them. One of the children isn't even a vampire child, it's a half-breed. We have no laws against that. I have seen Alana with Luther, not in person but I have been keeping an eye on her. She cannot be trusted, there is something wrong." Jaron didn't seem upset or surprised that she had been keeping tabs on Alana.

"There are rumors you should hear then. I dismissed them because I did not believe there was any truth in them because it came from vampires, however, I feel there might be now. Alana is working with Luther. I'm sure she will get rid of him when she feels he is no longer useful. He could be a danger to you if he infects you. We heard rumors Alana wanted to kill you but there are so many false rumors out there, it's difficult to tell which are true and what isn't." Jaron sounded frustrated.

"Alana wishes to meet me in the fields which for her would be the right opportunity to set me up. Before I fill you in on my plans, I need to check with someone. I still feel a bit unsure however at least I know he can tell me some truth. Has Alana said anything about coming back here?" I had a plan however it would work much better if Alana stayed out in the field until I was to join her.

Mentally called to one of my guards who had traveled with me recently but had not been back to the compound. I let him know to find Alana, to let her know I would be out until I met her in the field, that I would try to cut short my visit by two days to rejoin her. That I ordered the execution of the prisoners, and it should be done before I joined her. As he agreed he left immediately, not questioning his orders. Then Harmony turned her attention back to Jaron.

"Do not fill the other instructors in that I am around yet however let them know they are to meet me soon. I will not be taking any guards with me. For now, I do not know which I can trust and which ones I cannot. After I speak to this person, I will let you know where to meet us, just do not let anyone else know that I've talked to you or where all of you are about to go, if anything, I might have you leave at separate times so that it's not figured out. Bring in the one who Alana blamed." Eyeing her curiously but not questioning what she was asking him he hurried to collect Lucian.

Standing in front of the cell he opened the door, no one questioned it since he has done this before except he had guards with him the last time. This time he had come alone. Walking Lucian to the training room we both stood inside. Sydney's back had been turned momentarily before she turned around, she was pacing the floor in deep thought.

"Do you wish for me to stay; you have no guards with you?" Jaron knew her fighting style better than anyone, not that she ever needed a guard, it had only been customary to have one present more as a witness than anything.

Waving her hand signaling she wanted to be alone he left without another word leaving me standing there wondering what was going on. As Jaron left, however Sydney had spoken to him as he was walking out telling him to take the rest of the ones who were in the holding cells with this one and to free them. To make sure they were at a safe distance, to let no one know they were being let go, that Alana is under the assumption they have all been put to death. Agreeing he set out to fulfill his order.

"I didn't know that Alana would risk doing this. She had never gone behind my back before. For some reason, she wants to destroy your family and I'm not sure why but somehow, I almost think it has to do with the fact my past is tied in with you. I feel she may be choosing to take me out if I thinks she's working with Luther. There may not be much I can do if he gets past my attacks. The only way he could was if she helped him. I've been learning a lot about Luther; he doesn't get involved unless there is something he wants or benefits from it." Harmony Leaned against the wall while she looked like she was concentrating on trying to figure out what exactly she wanted to do.

"What do you want me to do? I will do anything to keep you safe. I have in the past and I will continue to do so." I truly meant what.

I knew the person I had fallen in love with was still in there she just had to come out. No longer leaning against the wall looking frustrated she had an interesting look on her face as she walked over to me.

"I wish I could remember you. I had your family set free; Alana won't be looking for them since she will be under the assumption that I had them killed. Jaron is setting them free now but under my orders to make sure they are safe before he lets them go. You are free any time you wish to leave. I will take you anywhere you wish." Walking away from me for a moment before she stopped in her tracks to speak again.

"This is my fight against Alana. I still have an order to run with many people under me. I firmly believe in what I am doing and what I believed Alana had been doing, only now she's far too harmful herself. She's too eager to kill. There is reason to but not just to kill for power. Many are already fearful just because of the power we hold especially me, but we have to follow our rules. They are nothing new and we keep to ourselves if they are kept for any creature. To keep our secrets hidden and not to create dangers that will expose us. Eventually, I will have to kill Luther, and I hope he is not family or friend to you. But he has committed a crime, and I cannot let it go. If anything happens to Alana, it must be me doing it otherwise, too many excuses might be made for her." Sad to say I understood what she meant; in a short time, they had taken control of many senseless deaths.

More were being cautious. Before they feared nothing and answered to no one. Before there had been constant rumors or sightings where humans were trying to prove we existed, things had slowed down dramatically. There were still a few smaller royalty systems among some of the creatures, even vampires that controlled their groups but then they respected having the new system in place.

"Where is Alana supposed to meet you?" I don't know why it hadn't hit me until now, but I had a plan that could work to help her out.

"Not far from the Eurubian city. There is a cave that has had some disturbances attracting far too much attention and some human sacrifice area that needs to be closed. Alana is working her way there. I am to meet her there, why?" Looking even more curious since I could tell she knew I was planning something.

"It's difficult to explain. I would rather show you; can you take me to the Eurubian city? Without any of the guards seeing us. If you do get attacked, there is a fast way out and I can pop in and help if needed. It gives more chances. At least it's something, perhaps we should have anyone that is helping you, meet us there. They can all have the same exit if everyone needs to. That way there are fewer people you need to worry about if you are unable to assist them. If you're ready we can transport there now, I don't know how it works now. I used to stand behind you with my hand around your waist when we poofed, but now that the stone isn't physical how do we transport?" I was curious how she did it now even though it would probably be easier for her not to have to hold onto the life stone anymore.

"You remember transporting around with me and the life stone? I don't even remember the stone itself. If we are still around later, I have a lot of questions for you." Smiling she simply reached for my hand, thankfully with no painful explosion since the light seemed to be shadowed simply from the power being in her now and not exposed.

We were in the Eurubian city within seconds. This time it was much different. Before it had been so bright you could not see anything other than feeling the wind swooshing around, this time it had darkened with the wind still there, but it was almost as if we had just stepped through to where we wanted to go, like the pool only a different center and the fact that you couldn't stay in the middle.

We appeared at the bottom of the steps to the palace. Instead, I directed her attention to follow me rather quietly. We could both see guards walking around down below thankfully no sign of Alana. We made it across using the same path that Goseck and I used earlier. I wasn't sure if this was going to be a mistake to show her the pool, but if she could see I wasn't afraid of sharing secrets like these, then perhaps she might trust me more? Either that or I screwed up a good thing and would pay for it in the end. Either way, I had to try to take a chance with Harmony. We walked into the temporary room as I was leading her to the closet when she stopped moving in the center of the room. Looking around her quickly, I was trying to figure out what caught her attention.

I watched her as she walked over to the tiny window of the living room peeking down, she could see almost everything, the apartment had been centrally located.

After she stopped for a few minutes looking around the room. I could tell something familiar had kicked in. She wasn't sure how to take it. Now following behind me I removed the blankets; Elija still hadn't come back through since the cover still had the rugs on top the same way when we had left. Twisting the cover until it had come off, Harmony seemed rather curious.

"Do you want to go down first, or I can?" As she nodded towards me, I stepped down onto the steps so that she could see where they were.

I wasn't sure if she could take such a long drop or not. Goseck and I dropped straight to the bottom once we were sure Elija had gotten out of the way. Standing in front of the pool she stared at me waiting for the big surprise.

"I'm not sure if I should have followed you down here, what are we doing?" Curious, even the look on her face made me smile.

"I wanted to find a way to show you that I can be trusted, this is something that makes me incredibly vulnerable if you don't. Not to worry, you're safe down here, not that I ever could have used the life stone because of what I am, but it works almost like that. When you jump into the pool you see thick red goo that looks nasty, but it doesn't stick to you, and you can breathe in it. Focus on where you want to go, and you simply walk towards the other light. When you want back you go back to the exact spot you popped out of but the only way to get back to this spot is if you originate from here. It doesn't require any magical skill, the pool does it all for you.

"Show me exactly how it works." As she asked, I set out my hand for her to hold, motioning for her to step on one of the bricks.

We walked in at the same time now standing with the goo around us. Not long after we had been in there Elija came through with a huge smile on his face looking directly at Harmony, feeling nervous she had stood a bit further behind me.

"I see you found harmony or rather Sydney as you prefer being called now. It's a pleasure to see you again. I would chat, but I am on my way out, not to worry. The rest of your family has been rounded up with Goseck and are together in the Iralemin world." Soon as he said that Elija was already on his way out.

Focusing on a place that looked like a lush jungle. I pointed directly ahead of where the glow was. Taking her hand, I led her as I went first. Looking around she seemed amazed but then I knew the feeling when I first saw this place. After practicing so much beforehand. I was getting much better at traveling. Walking back leaving the place and back by the well. I knew Harmony had been impressed.

"This could work, I'll be right back, now that I know where this place is. I'm going to locate my instructors and bring them here; will you be waiting for me?" She had sounded more hopeful than wondering.

"I don't plan on going anywhere, I may be free, but I promise I am here to help you with anything I can." To prove to her I had no plans of going anywhere, I sat down leaning against the wall waiting for her to come back.

I wasn't worried about anything else now other than how her instructors would take seeing me here. I didn't have to wait for long. Harmony had already popped back, at least she had come back with Jaron. She purposely brought him first so that he would keep the others from attacking me when they saw I was there possibly thinking it was a sneak attack.

The next two people she brought were Daniel and Jordyn. They were surprised to see me taking guard of Sydney as soon as they popped in until they had seen Jaron standing next to me. Calming down they still seemed confused. Daniel was rather intimidating to look at, not only was he tall. I was guessing six foot four. He was also rather built. Jordyn looked so short standing next to him but then anyone would have. She was rather slim, with dark brown hair, fair in complexion, they almost looked like they could be brother and sister. In a way, they reminded me of James and Gabriella.

Then I was surprised by the fourth instructor not that he expected to see me there. Smiling at me he put his finger to his lips as if to say not to let the secret out. He hadn't been one of the instructors who was attacking me in the room; I never once knew Nikolai was working for her or around all of this. Then the last of the instructors was brought in, and him, I remembered. He had not wanted to quit. He was simply known as Roman. I could only guess he was called that because of the intimidating way he looked, almost like the old roman soldiers. Now she had the people she wanted. I hoped it was enough. I knew it was painful having a shade attack me, but I wasn't sure how nasty it could get when they fought each other. This would certainly be interesting.

Chapter Thirteen

Lucian versus Family

Every eye had been focused on me except Jaron who knew the truth already. As we stood there, Sydney as they knew her filled them in about Alana pretending not to know where she was but also why we were there. A few voiced concerns in case we were misjudging things however most of them agreed that Alana had overstepped her bounds, even for her position. Even though she was one of the top commanding powers, she had broken her own rules, always making new ones just so she could punish those she saw fit to punish. Not living up to her end was making it so that many were not as loyal as they once were to her. However, now many more rallied behind Sydney because she lived according to her rules not making more, but at times making for allowances, avoiding punishment for others based on various reason. Alana had to start using outside help to back her up getting angrier that Sydney had such a stronghold on their organization.

The others had never once shown a sign of impatience while waiting. They had grown accustomed to waiting for Sydney to be ready while she watched for Alana. Something the pool had been able to do. I was curious if Elija had been aware of it. Even with its special ability all on its own, Sydney was able to watch from above and see right through, she would have this figured out long before I had myself. Years ago, she used to be freighted easily and now she commanded others with such confidence. Even from the time she was with me, she has changed so much, but then I guess having to fend for yourself and not having anyone else you can completely rely on does that to yourself.

During the long silence Harmony asked me a question speaking to me again mentally, 'why do you insist on calling me, Harmony? Please call me Sydney.' As she waited for an answer all I could think of had been, 'I will call you anything you want but to me, you will always be the Harmony I fell in love with but as you wish, I will call you Sydney.' Jordyn had been the first one to speak asking Sydney a question.

"Are we taking him with us or is he staying here?" Nodding over towards me.

I couldn't exactly tell if she was upset with the idea of me tagging along or hoped I would stay behind. I was sure after finding out I hadn't done anything still didn't make them trust me any more than they had before, even though they were surprised that Nikolai was so receptive to the whole idea.

"Yes, he is coming with in case Alana has Luther with her. I want another vampire with us, at least one that is on our side for help. In my past, he's looked out for me before so I'm hoping he'll do the same again." I knew she still hadn't remembered me even Nikolai picked up on that fact.

At least she showed she trusted me. It was at least a start. We seemed to be waiting for the right time to head out as no one had been in place waiting for us on the outside yet since we were still early. I had shown the others by going through how to end up where we wanted to go, at least to give them the feel of the place. Then while we were talking beside the pool the others stood immediately in front of Sydney to protect her as a smaller person dropped down the shaft along with two more people not so small behind him. Giving a light wave to Elija, he and his siblings made a quick move for the pool and were gone as the others stared at him not sure if they should attack or prevent them from going in the pool.

"Was that Elija, James, and Gabriella, the royals from the shade city going into the pool? I wonder where they are off to?" Nikolai voiced his interest even if the others hadn't had the chance yet.

"Yes, that was. What they happen to be up to, who knows? Could be anything. Elija's rather addicted to using the pool." I could tell the others were curious about the three that came by so quickly.

But I couldn't help noticing the smile on her face when Elija stopped for a moment saying 'hello again Harmony' before he jumped into the pool. I couldn't help it, but the way Elija smiles you wonder what he's getting into or what he's planning? For a split second, it looked as if she remembered him.

The time came. Alana had her back turned away from the small stream that had gone along the field. Sydney had chosen this time to jump into the pool appearing not far from her. Not saying a word until everyone had been with her. Alana seemed rather startled looking back, she could have sworn she hadn't seen anyone. She would have noticed Sydney coming up, especially with a group with her. She hadn't spotted me; I was standing behind them all keeping an eye from behind and the sides looking for Luther.

"When did you get here, I never noticed you came? Why aren't you traveling with the guards? Did something happen with them?" Alana didn't look concerned she was more curious.

"We just got here a second ago. I thought I would give the guards time off for now, after all, you already have some with you. No need to overcrowd the place. My instructors are enough for company." Smiling waiting to see how Alana would respond to that.

"We were waiting for a few of the guards to catch up. We were going to meet you here and then head over to the Eurubian city. There seems to be something going on, the guards said they couldn't quite explain it but there's something written on the wall that we need to see." Alana trying not to be too noticeable looked around trying to spot someone.

Quietly focusing before Alana were to see me, I told Harmony in her mind, 'I sense Luther, and I believe he's going to attack the Eurubian city. I can get in without him knowing through the pool and be prepared and keep him from attacking you when all of you get there. That is if you wish for me to go?' I wasn't sure if she would prefer me to stay with her or move ahead.

She hadn't taken long to respond to my request saying, 'it would be rather foolish if all of us were ambushed, yes it would be a good idea that you go. We will see you there and please take care.' As she finished her hand slid behind her back waving goodbye to me. Not knowing what was going on or sharing any information with the others they noticed her waving to me as I stepped into the water disappearing instantly.

Once I arrived coming out of the pool, I left the little temporary apartment moving down toward the stairs when I couldn't help but look straight ahead at the usual large black wall, there had been a picture drawn on it with a few words underneath it. I had to cover my mouth to stop myself from laughing. I recognized the writing. It was characteristic of Elija; he had been up to something. The center square, which is normally a rather large area had a water fountain in the center with a new statue made of the vampire children looking like they were playing in the water. On the wall had been a picture of the ocean with each of my family members either looking at the water or posing in another area of it. The words were spelled out in Italian especially for Alana as it read, "il mio regalo speciale a voi Alana, sapevo che hai amato questa famiglia." If Alana hadn't been angry before. Wait until she sees this. Translated into English the message said, 'my special gift to you Alana, I knew you loved this family." I was curious if she would translate this to the guards or not? One main point I noticed was that he purposely set areas for water to be accessible.

Not far in the distance in one of the empty shops I could see a dark shadow moving around, being careful not to be seen. I moved down further keeping an eye on it. As I had gotten closer, I could see it was Luther waiting, probably hoping that when they passed them, he would attack Sydney from behind. At least I knew she could take care of herself as long as I kept an eye on Luther just in case he was to leave, except he seemed rather content to stay in the shadows of the old store.

There had been some commotion as I watched a few guards assemble inside walking through acting as if they hadn't been inside of the place for a while. Alana came through with her group followed by Sydney and the others not far behind. Concentrating on Sydney, I told her as she was entering, 'Luther is in the second shop on your right. He might not come out right away until there is more commotion, but he may be planning on attacking from behind. Just be careful. I'm still keeping an eye on him.' As I told her this, I moved closer staying in the shadows myself making sure not to be seen. I had only taken my attention off him for a split second looking at Alana for her reaction. She kept taking glances at the pictures. She was extremely angered over it.

One thing I hadn't been hoping for had been Luther spotting me, but then I guess if he was as good as I was at hiding, he would be keeping an eye out for anything. After all, he had been around longer than any of my family members, even Charlie. Backing up he disappeared, maybe he wouldn't try anything while I was here since I'm sure he can guess why I'm hiding in the background. Luther knew our family rather well which is why I was surprised he was willing to help Alana. It seemed as if he wanted to restart the old empire, he would have tried to get together with Sydney rather than Alana. At least the same old rules and alliances would have been held up.

Keeping an eye on the store there hadn't been any movement not that I had ever seen him leave, keeping an eye on Sydney. I quickly looked around trying to spot him before he tried making a move on her. Feeling nervous about not finding him now that I was frantically searching around, I couldn't find him anywhere and Sydney was standing even further behind making herself more vulnerable to a quick attack. Looking at her I said, 'I lost him. He spotted me and disappeared. I can't find him. It's safer if you stay in the center of the group than out,' keeping close as they moved even further into the city it was getting harder to hide in the shadows without being seen. Then it hit me, his plans had changed. He was no longer after Sydney; he was going to eliminate me first before he got to her. probably assuming he had time to wait for her. As I watched Sydney safely move out of the way they headed towards the palace. All I could think to say is, 'be careful in there. Luther is waiting out here for me. Protect yourself. I'll keep him busy until you are in a safe position to get rid of him, I might be strong, but he has more experience than I'll ever have. Luther had been around for so long giving him the advantage not only in fighting styles but also in knowing the personalities of vampires well enough to have the upper hand. That and he knew my family rather well, especially Lorah

Sydney and the rest of the group were soon out of sight. I could smell a certain scent getting stronger from behind as I launched myself out into the open, I knew he was standing right behind me. I didn't think it would take long for him to be after me once I was out in the open let alone when the others were gone for him to come after me.

"This should have been over already, out of respect for Charlie and your uncle Drezin, I will give you a second to leave calling your being here an act of insanity. After all, we all know how you feel about the little wench. This is my time to take over." Luther seemed angered but he controlled it rather well by keeping his tone unchanging only the slight coloring in his eyes gave him away.

"How could you possibly think that helping Alana would be your chance to take over? If she has the power, she will only kill you, she doesn't plan on having you help her, so why kill Sydney when it's Alana you should be after?" This still confused me.

How could he be after Sydney if he wanted power unless he wanted it to himself? Alana had been very powerful and certainly hadn't trusted anyone even if she was using the help of a creature she despised.

"I don't need lessons from a child. There is not a move I make that has not been planned out. I never planned on letting Alana take over or Sydney. No one has the right to take over the old order. If anyone is to be in power, it is to be from the true bloodline, direct descendants of Lilith. One that has not been corrupted by half breeds. Vampires ruled all at one time. There is no way I will ever let a shade tell me what to do let alone tell me the laws that my family and I set up. Besides, I have been handling things just fine over the last decade." Luther seemed rather sure of himself.

I knew my family certainly hadn't heard of Luther still ruling. If he had been taking care of things, then he kept the fact he was still around rather silent.

"You can kill Alana if you want but I can't let you kill Sydney." Shaking his head in disgust he couldn't believe I would still stand here against him.

"You are a fool. Do you think by protecting her she will come running back? Do you think she will leave her position for little old you?" Before I could move, he had been a lot faster than I thought he was.

I was slammed into the wall with such force. I had to peel myself away from the it. If I thought Sydney's instructors beating me up earlier was painful then this was going to be far worse, and I hated to think it, but I was positive after this. I wasn't going to see my family. As self-assured as I had been, I knew I couldn't outsmart or outfight him. I wasn't sure what I was going to do. I just knew I was going to try to keep him away from Sydney. Even if it meant my life, I knew I might never get her back but keeping her alive was worth it to me.

As he slammed into me again, I almost felt like he was toying with me since he could finish me off rather quickly. Then as he raised his hand in the air with a grave digger's spade, I had seen the object disappear from his hand, even surprised himself he looked behind him. All I could see had been a shadow that disappeared rather quickly. The tiniest hint of a voice spoke, 'stall, but don't get yourself killed.'

I wasn't sure who it had been that spoke to me. Normally I can distinguish voices but then the pummeling my head has been getting, sounds started to be a little off. Only Goseck or Sydney had been able to speak to me. But then Elija heard Goseck talking to me once before when I realized it was Elija speaking to me.

"How did you do that? You were never behind me. Who else are you in here with?" Keeping an eye on me while he surveyed the rest of the area searching for another person not just by sight but by sensing.

Since he couldn't find anyone, he turned his full attention back to me.

"I'm here on my own." Luther could have figured that out without my explaining it to him.

"At least I know Sophie isn't cloaking herself to help you. She won't be bothering me anymore." Lucian sneered at me.

"What did you do to her?" Standing up slowly I could feel my anger and a rush of adrenaline kick in.

"I have her buried six feet underground." Luther smiled as he made a run at me.

Moving to the side I was ready for Luther as he went for my neck trying to break my neck, I dug into his shoulder taking a chunk of skin out. As I did, he stepped back momentarily wincing from the pain not that it stopped him.

As he was about to come at me again something flew and hit his head, as he turned to see what it was, there was nothing there, then from another direction another object was flung at him as if flying with no thrower. Only leaving me temporarily, he chased after the area it had come from finding no one. Keeping me in sight, not leaving far I knew it would be pointless to run since he could catch up to me in no time. Standing in front of me again he kept watching around him.

When he came at me full force, I had gotten lucky moving aside only he whipped around still catching me, throwing me into the air colliding with the wall again. As I had this time, part of the picture shattered but a very small spout of water had leaked coming out of the wall now. Before I could even get up, he had grabbed a hold of me again throwing me into the wall again. This time I barely looked down to see my arm had been broken. Not my day or should I say hasn't been my year? Reaching into my pocket I pulled out a few little beads that I picked up from one of the other worlds I had been in earlier with Sydney. Throwing them at Luther as soon as he swatted them away, they exploded into little fireballs. They hadn't lasted long but I figured anything to delay him attacking me again. I knew I needed to delay him but then I wasn't sure what Elija planned. I was learning he was rather sneaky but even he was limited. He had powers of a shade and could do a lot however for the time I had known him he never needed to fight, he was rather slow, unlike his brother Lucas. I couldn't keep an eye on him since he was so fast. Lucas and Victoria used to practice sparring with each other since they were close to each other's level in fighting and style. I might have been a good fighter but there wasn't much of a chance with a seasoned pro like Luther.

At this point, I was looking severely battered and bruised already with one arm broken, not that I was too worried. I knew it would heal. That is if I lived long enough for it to heal. I still felt weak from being beaten by Harmony's guards.

But then I wondered what happened to Sophie, no one had seen her. I was beginning to worry something horrible happened to her. It's not like her to hide this long especially if she knows her family is in danger or needs her. She's always in there trying to figure something out, maybe Luther was right, he might have done something with her. Feeling fear that she was harmed not that I wanted to allow myself to think she was dead, it gave me enough strength to keep fighting.

Elija popped out behind him not even needing to say a word. Luther spun around to attack him, as he had I jumped on his back trying to distract him so he wouldn't hurt Elija. Not that he seemed too worried, he disappeared as soon as he touched the water. Flinging me off his back Luther struck out again, striking me across the face. I knew this one was going to leave a permanent scar. As soon as I looked up after being struck to the ground again there was a large crowd of people standing behind and all around him. Not that I wanted any of my family to be hurt. They had all been here except the children, Sophie, Emma, Rose, and Jacob.

To the left of him had been Charlie, Goseck, Dinah, Lorah, Nichole, and Anthony. To the right of him had been Elija, James, Gabriella, Victoria, Lewis and Evangeline, Mathais and Lily. Now popping out behind me on my left were Aidelle and Aiden. Andrew and Charlotte are two people our family hasn't seen in a long time. Then on my right had been Iuliana, Jelizaveta, Katarina, Anatolii, Mikhail from the Petrova family as well as Bridgette, Zoë, Tara, and Mia. Another batch of fresh faces had been Forrest, Ivy, Luna, Daniel, and Marcheline. On either side had been filled in now with Madison, Lucas, Natalie, and Logan.

I didn't want to get cocky, but I was positive we were going to survive this now. Not just new faces but also experienced ones as well. Luna had grown so much since the last time I had seen her. She visited my family a while back, she had always been quite a bit older than me even though she still looked younger. She was just taller now. Speaking up Charlie had been the first to speak breaking the long silence as Luther realized he was surrounded. At least this was what I loved about my family, if any one of us needed help the rest would always be there even if they didn't always agree with you, they wanted you safe.

"We thought you could use some help kiddo." Only Charlie could call me a kid without it sounding like an insult.

"Saying I could use some help is a bit of an understatement at this point." Most of them hadn't seen us since we disappeared but then they might have thought Luther did all of this to me since I still hadn't recovered that much from Sydney's trainers beating me up.

Luther must have felt trapped by now since his quick move was to attack me, getting me into a hold; it was starting to piss me off at how fast he could attack me before I could even do anything. I used to be the one who fought off the vampires and other creatures to protect Rose, yet now I could barely stay in one piece trying to protect myself. As he tried to fling me at the rest of the family, he made his path between the youngest in the group trying to outrun everyone escaping from the place. However, everyone hadn't let him do that as we chased after him.

The veterans in our group were able to keep up with him with no problem. After a while, I had lost sight of many of the others. About half of us had come back to the Eurubian city waiting for Sydney to come back out while the others were off taking care of Luther. At least he wouldn't be attacking her, but I still had to worry about the others now that I didn't know what was going on. Even if I tracked them Luther was sprinting like mad to get away. I hoped he wouldn't lead them into a trap. At least Goseck could call me if they needed help. Before he disappeared, he had said 'stay back' as we listened, we came to a stop. We figured he must have had a reason for asking us this.

Instead of waiting around to find out when Sydney would come back, I concentrated on her asking her, 'are you still alright? Do you need me up there?' I hoped she would be able to hear me or still want to. I knew I may never have the same person back again, but I hadn't cared what she turned into because even then she was still the same person I loved. I was beginning to wonder if she was okay since she hadn't responded to me for a while. Then finally I heard her reassuring voice, 'sorry, Alana was speaking, and I was trying to concentrate on what she was saying, did you take care of Luther? I've been stalling in here hoping to hear from you. I hope you're still safe?' I could tell she could see me even if she hadn't seen what was going on.

I couldn't help but smile to myself since I could picture the look on her face. It would have been rather close to what she expressed the first time she had seen me. Answering her now, 'Luther is taken care of, and yes I do look much worse than before but don't worry I'll heal, and if you do come out with Alana, you're safe, there are several of your old friends and family here now also to help protect you.' I hoped this would help her feel safe, not that I was sure how she would respond, at least I know she had trusted me. I hoped she would trust them also.

Waiting for a few more moments she had spoken to me again asking 'when we come down, make sure everyone is hiding. I will call you out if I need you otherwise I don't want anyone else getting hurt when Alana tries to lash out. Another question can anyone else speak to me this way? I've done this with Alana only when I'm controlling it, but you seem to contact me without my permission?' She seemed rather curious who else could hear her but then I guess I would also if I didn't remember too much. I would be worried about the wrong person hearing my thoughts or speaking with me using it against me.

Responding, I simply said, 'as far as I know only Sophie, Goseck, a couple of trainers and I can speak to you like that, mainly the ones who taught you to use the life stone. I'm not sure if he wants you to know but Nikolai is one of your teachers from when we all knew you as Harmony, he can speak to me also like the others. But I think I need to start talking to the others here because only Elija has figured out what I'm doing, the others are very curious.' As I tried to think about what we were going to do in case we were needed to, there wasn't much we could prepare for.

"Sydney wants us to hide out of the way for when they come down, she's not sure if Alana is going to start something on the way out when she realizes that Luther is gone and isn't available to do what they planned. But then again, he might have spoken to her as I was just now speaking with Sydney." After explaining this, different ones either hid inside of the old, abandoned stores or any crevices they could slide into or shadows they could blend in with. Even a few disappeared deciding to wait next to the pool watching and waiting until they were needed.

Chapter Fourteen

Judgement

First, the guards had come with Alana following behind them. She seemed more nervous this time with Sydney following relatively close behind her, with her instructors filling the back area not allowing any space for anyone to invade. This had been the plan to make it seem she was being cautious however for Alana, she didn't like being this close to the others just in case there was a mistake. She knew she wasn't going to use Luther after this. She hoped he had not switched sides, and she hadn't known about it.

Stopping for a moment in the center squire as Alana looked around trying to find something, the place looked like a tornado struck the place. The city had been destroyed back by the palace, even though much of it had been intact upfront. However, now there were large pieces of stone laying on the ground with huge cracks and even holes formed in the walls. One of the store's fronts had been destroyed. Alana seemed rather shocked when she saw how damaged it was out here. Not seeing Luther or myself she must have been wondering who won the fight and where the winner had gone unless the winner was hiding waiting for his chance to attack again? Not wanting to take chances Alana turned to face Sydney. Listening as carefully as I could

"I think it would be safer for all of us to transport back to the compound, I'll travel back with Sydney to keep her safe, then the guards can travel the usual way since they can secure the place before they leave. I'm sure your instructors won't mind a bit of travel. We are the main ones that need protection;

besides, it would be rather time-consuming coming back for each one, now that you can only bring one person at a time with you." As she tried to reason why she would be traveling with Sydney hoping no one would think it is strange she would insist on traveling alone with her. Sydney turned to face her instructors looking at each one of them to see if they objected at all.

"Do you want me to come back for you?" Asking the question carefully, to let them voice how they felt especially if they thought it was too dangerous for her. Not that she questioned herself that she could protect herself, especially against Alana.

"It won't take us that long to get there, Alana is right the two of you should get there first, besides, things are waiting for you back at the compound." As Nikolai said this, I wondered why he was risking letting her leave.

I know she was much more powerful than before, but she could still get ambushed. As I watched her turn toward Alana and Alana took her hand, I wasn't sure if she heard my silent 'no.' I didn't want to lose her again especially to have her out of my sight. How much longer was she going to risk being around Alana? Within seconds they were both gone as the guards started making their way out looking around them wondering what exactly happened to cause all this destruction. They knew it had to do with Luther, but they hadn't exactly known about me. Even Alana didn't know yet if Luther was still around or what happened to him.

As they had cleared out leaving no guards in site the instructors ran past us heading for the water, that way they could reach their destination much faster. The others waiting back there had taken a step back not wanting to put them on the defensive, only watching them as they had taken off. Even I had run back to the pool with the rest of them. Nearing the pool, I was going to take off when I saw that Nicolai had stayed back for a moment to speak with me. The others had already taken off even though he had voiced that Sydney would not be getting there right away. She had wanted to make a stop first with Alana. I felt instantly sick to my stomach when he said that. I was worried about her being alone when Alana tries to attack her.

"Don't worry. She's going to be fine. She can certainly hold her own against Alana which is why she hadn't made a move against Sydney on her own yet. I hope you don't mind I found this box earlier when I was here, and you were showing the others how the pool worked. I was interested in this place since I knew Harmony had been here. I looked at it. I assume it's the helmet you made for her years ago?" Smiling at me holding the box in his hands.

"I figured she would have understood back then, it was kind of a personal thing but now that she doesn't remember me, I guess it doesn't matter. She might find it too strange or possibly mean if I give it to her now?" Not wanting to deal with it I had let him keep it since he seemed rather interested in it still.

"Not to worry she will still need it in the future. As a shade, her balance still hasn't improved. There are times you should see her run! I will make sure she gets your gift." As soon as he said that he was off in the pool along with the box.

I couldn't help but smile to myself when I thought about it, I had seen her run, she had been far from elegant but certainly had enough determination never to quit regardless of if she wasn't perfect. I found that with her flaws she was better than perfect.

I asked the others to stay here so they could find out if they caught Luther or not. Jumping into the pool the split second I was in the in-between part I felt a hand grab hold of my good arm slowing me down.

"I'm hoping you were the worst of the fight. Charlie was getting worried about Sophie since no one heard from her and her things were left exactly where she said she was going to be as if she vanished. Then we heard what was going on with the three of you. Did anyone else get hurt or did you try to take it all on like you usually do?" Smiling at me I knew Jacob was serious, but he also looked worried since I did look bad.

"Charlie, Goseck, and some old friends of theirs were with them, Luther got away, so they chased him asking us to stay back. They haven't come back yet but the others are staying. I'm heading to the compound. I have to know what is going on." Before I could get going Jacob refused to let go of my arm.

"I'll come with. You shouldn't be going alone. I'm assuming it's why you're so battered because you tried to handle it alone? Rose, Larissa, and the kids are safe where they are and if the others are waiting for the group to get back, you should have at least someone come with you. I'm not letting you leave alone again." Holding on making sure he didn't lose me we both stepped out landing in the hallway of the compound.

"Where's the water? How are we supposed to get back when we need to? Looking around Jacob hadn't been too experienced yet with using this system of moving around.

"Just touch the water in the painting, you won't get wet, but it will instantly move you. If it is a sign, symbol, or actual water you can pop out or back into it. Elija said the person who created it had a humorous side to them. I'm curious what other things we could drop out of?" Smiling for a second as I pictured a person with a cold and runny nose being shocked seeing people pop in front of them.

"Perhaps we could surprise someone with a cold?" Jacob had gotten the same look on his face before he gave into a shiver of disgust at the thought.

No one made it back yet. Instead of wandering the halls possibly running into anyone, we waited in the training room, at least no one would be coming in and out of here. I heard before from Nicolai that it had been the private training room for

Sydney. Only she used it. I hated sitting here wondering what was happening not knowing if she was alright or not? Not that I had much of a choice so we sat and waited until we could hear voices or have some sign that she might be back.

When Alana and Sydney reappeared. Alana was rather shocked to find they had not popped into the compound as she expected. Feeling rather defensive not sure what Sydney had planned, she took a step back not that it would have been enough to defend herself if she decided to attack right then. Looking around, not familiar with the place trying to figure out exactly where they were, Sydney had looked rather relaxed. Taking a few steps away from Alana she looked around quickly to see if Sydney had anyone ready to attack her.

"I wanted to show you where I was going to move the compound too, I agree that being in the city helps quite a lot, but a lot of the tunnels are caving in and some of the tunnels have had to be closed off because the humans are noticing them. Besides, this city is much larger and not much attention is paid to the tunnels here. More centrally located and easy to get anywhere from here. Besides, I already know how I want some of the rooms designed since I plan on adding to it a little more. Make it more appropriate for what we need it for." Speaking in a relaxed tone trying to put Alana at ease, as if she hadn't expected anything to happen today giving her a bit of a false sense of security.

"Where is this place? I can't even recognize it? What city are we under?" Alana had still been trying to figure out where Sydney had taken her to. The place had already looked like it was being assembled looking so much more official than their headquarters had been. It felt almost as if they were standing inside of a courtroom the way it was set up. As Alana asked Sydney had walked over putting her hand on Alana's shoulder.

"Not to worry we can talk more about that later. I have another place to show you." As she said that they instantly reappeared in another place. This one Alana had remembered but wasn't sure why Sydney was taking her back here. It had been the large house she built when she was much younger with a young vampire. There had been four floors only. The first floor had been finished. While her life stone had been missing all she had known was that at some point it would come back to this place somewhere in this town, she wanted to be ready for it. Life changed in a way she hadn't expected and was prevented from waiting for it. It's when Katherine Hawthorne took over waiting for the life stone.

This had been the house Alana had taken the chunk of rock after she found it. As she trained with the sorceress who guided and protected her, she sensed the strong power from the stone warning, Alana, to be cautious around it. She imbued protection spells to the life stone hoping to help her. Alana knew it had power but learning how to connect or tap into its power hadn't been easy. She spent every minute working with the life stone not even fully harnessing its full power. Working on it day and night preparing to use such a strong power. Her significant other helped her practice with the life stone. He had been a rather powerful sorcerer, one who used to be physically joined in the stone.

This house represents to her where the infamous fight with her sister started over the life stone. Katherine left her there for dead when the life stone vanished from the area. Leaving in frustration and Alana thought she was about to die from her injuries, she called out to a friend of hers, Najee, with whom she had a relationship, even had a family with him, she called for him to save her. Not remembering much other than being placed in the other world to heal to hopefully start over. It always seemed something prevented her from getting out to look for the life stone. She was angry never letting anything go, even though her relationship with Najee hadn't been what she wanted, she stopped her relationship with him once she realized he wasn't going to release her from the world that became her prison.

Looking at the house now she hadn't thought of any good that had come of the place other than how she felt she would get revenge someday for it all. Looking over at Sydney trying to figure out why she had brought her here. Sydney reached out her hand to Alana not sure if she was going to take her to another place or what her plan had been. Taking her hand Sydney simply started to walk along the beach with her.

"Let's take a walk, I always thought this place was beautiful not that I had been here for very long, but it certainly has had an impact. See the house in the distance. I lived there so long ago. It had been my first place away from home. I had no clue what I was getting into or how my life would be changed. Just like the house back there that somewhat ended everything for you. This place started everything with me. You and I are not that different. I was fortunate with the help that I had and I'm sorry you didn't have the same, you had a chance however you killed the hand that protected you. Why did you start the organization? Why now?" As Sydney asked this the wind started picking up over the water leaving a chill in the air.

Sydney waited to see how Alana would answer.

"I needed to establish order. I was tired of other creatures taking advantage of me thinking they could run me over. Doing whatever they wished. It's why you should never own something. The second you do they have power over you, because it can be taken away. You don't know how lucky you are to have a power inside of you, so powerful that no one can take it from you. You and I can weed out the good from the bad. We alone can decide who lives or dies, we need to throw out the old vampire rules. They don't apply to us! We need to keep them separate from us and control them more. They will fear ever overstepping us or doing anything without our permission. We can get revenge on those who have wronged us. We alone will be able to decide how they can or cannot live their lives and if they fight it, we finish them. We do not need those who do not follow us. We would be gods!"

"I don't want to be a god. I understand keeping rules for protection or helping those who have nowhere to go to get answers. But who are we to dictate exactly every rule or how they live their lives? If they harm no one and keep our secrets safe then where is the harm for the majority? Punish the wrongdoers but is it necessary to harm all of those who have done nothing wrong?" Continuing to walk as she spoke to Alana.

Past the second house following along the path into the woods that she had taken so many years ago with her friends, as they adventured exploring the area. Until they came to the little cottage in the swamp surrounded by the trees that changed her life. When that flash of light had been let out as she took the stone from under the tree roots.

"If you do not want to be a god then you will always be under everyone. You will always have to answer someone else. No one ever does anything, and creatures are running around on this earth that don't deserve to be here." As soon as she said that I knew there wasn't convincing her any other way.

We had been standing outside of the little cabin that started it all. Walking in through where the door had still been left open. The place weathered so much more now over the years with the elements being allowed in the door. The broken part in the roof that was there intentionally years ago makes it appear as if it had been abandoned and broken down, even though it had been occupied. I climbed under the table and made my way to the other far part of the room. At first, Alana had not followed until she realized I was not coming out. She didn't want to get left behind in case it was an ambush.

Before she finished following me where the desk had been against the wall that I first heard the music box. I opened the drawer to find a small box. Lifting it for a moment I had seen what I needed underneath. Taking the object out. I placed it inside my pocket as Alana made her way into the room. Not placing the music box down, I handed it to her as I finished walking down the makeshift steps leading down to the bottom of a tree where the roots were exposed.

"This is where the stone was hidden. No one could pull it out other than the guardians, did you know that Nikolai was one of your guardians? I always wondered why I was chosen for the life stone to go to when you had chosen one at the time. You thought you would retrieve the life stone at some point when you were able to. Your main reason for sending it off had been so that your sister could not get a hold of it, and it wasn't left behind for your mother to get, yet you couldn't get it either, because you were locked away in another world healing. I found I am a direct descendant of him. The stone went from one person to another in the line until it had been disrupted, so it found another line to follow just as close. This music box was why I bothered looking in this room at all." Walking back up the steps Alana had been looking over the music box.

I wasn't sure why I could explain it but at that moment we left the Eurubian city I had taken a long look at the pictures of the family by the beach on the onyx stone wall as it all came flooding back to me. Standing next to Alana letting out a sigh of frustration it was amazing how something so massively good can come out of anger and wrong motives. Something I hoped I would never allow myself to get to. Surprising Alana since she had not expected it, I wrapped my arms around her hugging her.

"I could have used a sister to rule with." Without saying another word, I knew time was passing, I had to know if there were any chances left or at least to find out how determined she had been.

Transporting directly back to the old compound for possibly the last time. I hadn't shared it not that I was going with her. I intended on appointing Philip, Phoebe, Jaron, Nikolai, and Lorah, and if he would accept Lucian to co-counsel along with me. If not, I had two others in mind, they would be unusual but given their history would do just fine. I might not have noticed how much time passed even though our simple trip felt so quick to me.

Lucian was watching the time waiting for the moment for us to be back so that he could stop worrying. Lucian and Jacob had been hiding inside of the training room even though now Lucian left only once to check on the others by transporting them through the water on the picture except no one had been there. Lucian could see a few waiting around in the center, and Lucian was worried they should have been back by now. Going through the picture again now looking both ways of the tunnel leaving Jacob behind for a moment to move much more quickly he had still been standing waiting by the picture.

Lucian would usually go towards the training room, but instead, they went in the opposite direction. Not that he was familiar with this place. Lucian hadn't wanted to run into any guards but at least he knew her instructors wouldn't try to kill him anymore. With Jacob following close behind he was doing his best to listen for voices. He heard a familiar voice. They came back much faster than we had since they probably knew what room to pop directly into. I had been curious if we would run into them while we were searching. Following their voices down the long hallway that seemed to curve. There were several closed doors until we had come close to the far end where it led to a large meeting room. This had to be the biggest room I've seen so far. There were tables in the far back with at least one exit on either side and one large one leading down a large tunnel. On the opposite side of the tunnel and past, all the tables at what looked like the head of the room had been a platform slightly raising two chairs at the end with nothing else around them.

Alana was sitting in her chair with Sydney in hers, there had been two guards standing before them explaining to Alana what orders Sydney had given them to execute the prisoners, however, the trainers handled it first. Looking off to the side I could see shadows hiding in a side room. I could tell that Nikolai was in there with the other trainers. At least I did feel better knowing he was nearby. I wished I knew what they were planning. Sydney had been acting as she would normally act as if nothing was wrong. Did she take the threat earlier seriously?

As we sat there watching, Jacob tapped me on the shoulder pointing out the end tunnel as one of the guards walked up with a woman in front of him, walking up the center aisle. It was difficult to recognize her since she looked filthy, even battered quite a bit. As she was presented in front of the two of them. The instructors had come out of the side room to stand behind the guards. Alana watched them amazed they had come here so soon, and Sydney had not left her side once to bring them. No one else spoke other than the woman who had been hooded not until we heard her voice had we known who she was. We both looked horrified.

"You called for my services? I am not entirely sure how I can help you?" The woman seemed surprised that she had been called for not that we knew which one she had been addressing using no name when she spoke.

Alana stood up walking directly in front of the woman looking her over before she spoke. The expression on Sydney's face seemed more than shocked, she seemed horrified. At that moment we knew she remembered this woman also. Trying not to change her expression even though the initial shock had somewhat given her away. Alana hadn't been looking at her to notice it.

"I know that you had been trained by Maddie. A gypsy from long ago. She left a box in her wagon which she had given this to you; by any chance do you know where we can find that box? It's a rather personal item that I want to find." Alana slowed during her talking almost thinking of the words before saying them.

Jacob and I guessed she wasn't prepared for what she would say in case Sydney had still been there.

"I don't have that wagon anymore. All the items that would have been left are gone from it now. I don't have anything from it any longer. I have moved around too much that if anything still existed it would be doubtful it would either be useful or intact." We hadn't been sure if she meant what she had said or if she was hiding something.

But she certainly sounded convincing to us. Alana looked like she was thinking over what she had told her or rather planning what her next move was going to be. Either that or she had been stalling waiting for the next woman who walked in. She looked rather interesting as she stood out from everything down here, even from the human world, she couldn't have blended in with them. But Sophie seemed to know her.

"Hello Dorina, it's been a while. You've changed a lot since the last time I saw you. I underestimated you. From the time of your change, I didn't think you would last very long. I guess you were smarter than I thought. I know from the way that I trained you that you would not have lost anything of mine no matter how old it had gotten." As she had stood there the gypsy had given her a rather strange look as she waited for Sophie's response.

"If it meant so much to you then why did you leave it in the wagon to begin with? Didn't you ever think I might lose whatever it is or not know what it was in the first place?" As she asked, she kept her expression from moving at all.

At least now I knew where Sydney learned that one from.

"I've heard enough. Put her back in the cell. I will deal with her later." Alana tried ordering the guard to go put her away, not wanting to give away what her intent had been.

Now that she felt her first plan had backfired, she was using her backup plan.

"Guard wait, I don't see any reason to detain this person any longer. If she does not know where this item is that you are asking for, she might not know. What do you need to question her for later Alana?" Sydney walked over near Dorina.

Not wanting to say, Alana had not spoken as she then smiled which we found out after.

"Will you stop poking me in the ribs?" Jacob looked serious as he said this to me.

"Why would I poke you in the ribs?" Looking back, I knew we were no longer going to be able to hide as he stood there with a cocky expression on his face looking down at the two of us eavesdropping.

Walking out into the center of the room to join the others all three of us had joined them.

"Nice to see you give up so easily Alana, and hello there, Maddie, it's been a long time since I've seen you, I thought I killed you? I'll take a personal note that you do well in high places." Almost hissing at him Alana was getting angrier by the minute.

As she was reacting Luther had taken out the knife, which he was holding to his back now, bringing it up to Jacob's neck so that everyone could see.

"I would say we have some trades to make, who would like to start and don't bother covering Alana. No one believes you're here for the greater good, especially when you wanted me to kill your dear Sydney. And Sophie if you haven't guessed. She wants the round crystal that you use all the time, it lets you know where the stone is and draws you to it. We all know it's in Sydney dear here but what she doesn't know is the power will not disappear. It will go back into the lesser stone when she dies. If the lesser stone is no longer then it dies with her. Pathetic little Luchie, I didn't have the time to kill Sophie earlier, besides she's quite enjoyable not that it's a promise I wouldn't in the future or depending on how this goes. Now, who wants to make a bargain worth my not killing all of you?" Now I was worried about what happened to Charlie and the others.

Did he kill them, or did he get away? No matter what happened now, it looked like we were all screwed at this point. Luther kicked Jacob behind the knees forcing him to land rather forcefully on his knees on the ground while keeping the knife at his throat.

"No sense in threatening those things we do not need, for once you have no bargaining tool Luther." Maddie seemed rather confident in herself until Luther started to laugh to himself but loud enough for everyone to hear how amused he was.

"Still over all these years and you still have yet to learn. I never make a move unless I know exactly what I am doing. I'll give you a hint. These are Dorina's nephews, there is a reason Dorina may not have it. Think about it." Continuing to smile Luther seemed to enjoy frustrating Maddie and Alana.

If he wasn't holding us hostage or the one who agreed to kill Sydney. I would have almost like the guy. Not that I could see what it was, Alana pulled something out of her pocket holding it rather closely in her hands, keeping it covered not that no one noticed her. Some of the guards at this moment had been making up their minds about who to follow and who they thought they should protect. We had been separated into three groups now.

"You can say anything you want we know you're full of hot air. You may have been a powerful entity at one time but that was when you had an entire force behind you. Now all you have behind you is speed." As soon as she said that Luther shoved Jacob aside now shooting himself behind and pulling her away from the group, everyone assumed he was going after Sydney when instead he grabbed Sophie.

"Yes, but speed also gets me what I want, besides, I do have other talents my dear, or have you forgotten them already? Very sad if you have." Pulling Sydney into the center of their group her trainers tried to keep her protected from the others whispering, 'take us out we will deal with Alana later' Sydney had simply shaken her head no.

She hadn't wanted to leave the others here behind especially Dorina. I could tell how stressed she was feeling as she was trying to make up her mind. Her thoughts were so scattered it was hard reaching her. Finally, when I had she looked over at me, 'take off with the others, they can hide you and keep you safe until this is settled, they want something from Sophie, so they won't hurt her until they get it, she's smart. She won't let them and maybe it will give us enough time to get her away?' As she nodded silently there was a quick whoosh as Sydney and her instructors disappeared somewhere hopefully far enough away from here.

At least I knew she would be safe. I had most trusted Nikolai as he was in the group, he was also holding the small package I meant to give to Sydney. I just never had the chance.

As soon as everyone had been distracted Luther had taken off with Sophie with Alana and Maddie following close behind him. Not that either could keep up, we frantically tried to find a way out. There were so many rooms and tunnels. Some were very small, and others led into large rooms and one room hadn't been such a good choice, it held several of the guards.

We originally tried to follow Luther and the others out except there had been so many turns we couldn't keep up and neither could Alana and Maddie, we stopped quickly running in another direction trying to get out of this place. There were so many tunnels. I swear they must have had the entire underground of the city down here. Who knows possibly even the next one over could have been connected. Several tunnels had gone even deeper underground than the ones we had already gone through. Few had water resting at the bottom from leaking in and nowhere else to go.

This was not going the way I hoped as we tried to run back in the direction we had come from. Rushing into the hallway looking for the painting we dropped out of only to find the piece where the water had been torn out with the words written above it, 'my gift from Luther' our only way out had been going back through the way we had come. Now that it was gone, we had guards searching for us now along with Alana and Maddie. Racing down the hallway hoping we might find another way out there were strong winds that were almost burning to the touch as we kept trying to stay ahead of them. It hadn't taken long for Alana to find us. Racing through one room after another we hoped to give them the slip. At least the hallways kept going, it felt like they would never stop even the ones that had been filled with water that felt like they were further out we could only guess they did not use these anymore. As we swam fast as we could to get up out of the tunnel and back into a dry one.

Alana had given up much earlier than Maddie with all the turns and dips the tunnels had taken. We found one that dropped us straight down, we could have avoided that tunnel if we hadn't been running so fast and found out late as we plummeted to the ground. Not wasting time, we jumped to our feet taking off again when finally, we knew no one was following us anymore. I had stopped as Jacob was out of breath from all the running. I had almost forgotten that he wasn't like myself, he was more like my sister. As he dropped to the floor to catch his breath. I leaned against the wall. At some point, we were going to have to find a way out of here. But we certainly couldn't go back. I wished I knew how the others were doing.

Chapter Fifteen

The start of the chase

While we were busy contemplating our next move Elija gathered everyone else together while they waited for the others to get back. First had been Forrest, Ivy, and Luna after chasing Luther for so many miles, they guessed Luther was used to being chased. We lost track of Luther for quite some time. We didn't think we would pick up on his trail again, but everyone was determined to find him. After a day of him missing, Goseck picked up on his trail again.

Running through caverns, if you were not familiar with them, would slow you down or run around trees, even jumping off the side of a cliff using the clothing on his back to slightly impact the air to slow him down until he was too close to the ground. Then coming down to a halting crash landing on his feet he hadn't waited long taking off again as he knew the world far better than any of us ever had, even with all its changes. Many of us kept up only after having to find various ways around obstacles like the cliff. At one point while Luther was running through one of the caves there had been so many twists and turns that we had been shocked when we were bumped against the wall only to find he reversed his moves almost running over the top of us. When we realized he turned back we shouted back to those behind us that he was coming their way, as soon as he stopped right in front of Lucas and Victoria, they lunged out to grab him only to end up falling down a deep hole with him. Grabbing a hold of Victoria, he had flung her behind him as he tackled Lucas the way a linebacker would in football. Falling to the ground Lucas grabbed a hold of his ankle being dragged by Luther until he knocked him off on the rock down below.

Trying to escape out by the water's edge, Marcheline and Daniel had been waiting down there for him forcing him to scale the wall to get away. Instead of heading up where we had Katarina and Jelizaveta waiting there, he scaled along the side of the wall with Marcheline and Daniel trailing behind below. Then he dropped downward as Jelizaveta shot a strong gust of wind knocking Luther down into Daniel. As soon as he landed on top of him Luther grabbed Daniel flipping him over onto his back, he pushed Daniel up and over him launching him into the water but not before Daniel left scratch marks along his skin from trying to hold onto him. Luther's sleeve along with the top layer of skin tore off.

Taking off with Marcheline right behind him he came to where the beach started. A group of people had been there either playing volleyball or a few other sand building projects, no one had been in the water since the weather was too cold for it but no snow. As soon as he walked up to another woman, he put his arm around her leaning in and talking to her. They walked rather quickly along the edge of the water with our family watching from a distance. Looking around the young woman seemed rather nervous as they both got into her car, she slid across from the passenger side. Trying to be careful not to harm her or have him hurt her by escaping us we followed as closely as possible while she drove through the streets. At one point there was a lot of traffic. Charlie, Andrew, and Goseck tried to pick up on his trail again, at some point he ditched the car moving in traffic hidden by the other vehicles.

Andrew had been the first to pick up on his trail even though it was getting old as he had decided to turn back, it would already take him quite a while to get back. With the rest of us still chasing him we hoped we would catch the elusive Luther. If we didn't have to scatter so much from each other, we could circle him, but not once had he let us get that opportunity especially when he used humans to disappear on us.

Running through a few towns greatly slowed us down, not wanting to catch attention from humans, or any others, he simply took to the building tops crossing from one after another. As he sprinted across, making it out of the towns with very little effort. On one rooftop, there had been other people on top, a group of teens drinking, they watched in amazement as Luther ran past them assuming they would think they were drunk and then charlotte ran past the teens snagging the alcohol from their hands dropping it over the side of the building crashing to the street.

There was one point they thought they had him caught. He had run into a building full of humans. We hoped he wasn't going to start up a fuss when we realized that these were not normal humans, as they had come out now chasing after us. Only a handful was able to keep up after Luther as soon as he had taken off. We had to split up as his friends chased most of us in directions away until they had gotten out of the city and turned to fight. Not that his friends stood around for it they had also turned to run. For being around as long as he had. Luther certainly was clever at getting away. Charlie grabbed his jacket only as Luther stopped suddenly letting the jacket slide off from his arms as Charlie passed by turning around and running in the opposite direction now.

Almost nearly running in front of a bus Luther had run across the street with the bus driver blaring his horn at him after the close encounter caught our attention again. Running through the back-alleys Luther hadn't been too worried about who had seen him as he made his way across heading for the water as we all had been in different areas. We tried to catch up surrounding the sides. The only way he could go was straight ahead. Unfortunately, it gave him the advantage especially over the half breeds when he hit the water. He could have gone anywhere when he disappeared going deep under the water and swimming rather quickly, there was no scent or trail to pick up on anymore.

Andrew hadn't been fast like the rest, but he certainly hadn't given up. He kept tracking Luther as soon as he lost the trail of him and the others. Speed certainly hadn't been a gift he had other than enough determination. After a while, even Andrew came back. Only a handful had stayed behind. Nichole and Anthony soon came back after several hours of chasing when they lost sight of the others and Luther. We only lost him because of water, watching along the coastline to make sure he hadn't swum downward to come back up, we never saw him resurface.

Only a few had gone into the water trying to keep up, but it had been harder to see him giving up, the rest decided to make their way back. We had spent an entire two days nonstop tracking him. Eventually, everyone slowly trickled back to the Eurubian city waiting for everyone to show up. Not wanting to explain where Jacob and Lucian had gone, Elija decided to wait until everyone had come back. Different ones had been talking to each other as the last few walked in all looking at them wondering if they had caught Luther, which to no avail they had not.

"I must say there's a reason he has lasted this long, he knows the earth; the way humans think and act, he's had a long time to observe everything, and he had been in power before where I'm sure he had to preserve himself." As Charlie looked around the large town squire there had been so many here, many of them were ones they last saw when they grouped to attack the old Doc.

The one who worked with Katherine hawthorn. It was beginning to feel like things would never entirely settle down. Speaking with Daniel, Goseck, Andrew, and Mathais they had come up with the best plan they felt might help each splitting everyone into groups to head out and search not just for Sophie but also for Jacob and Lucian but also to find Luther. After getting the rest of the family together even Rose, Emma, and the kids from the pool were all discussing what they needed and when exactly they needed to head out, making plans there were so many speaking to each other. As Charlie shook his head in wonder Goseck had walked over to him.

"Don't worry, we will find her." not sure what else to say Goseck had grown fond of Charlie's family.

Especially after the way they had accepted him into it.

"I know we will find her; I told her when I first met her, she would be the death of me and so help me Lucian and Jacob are her replicas, if one doesn't kill me, I'm sure the other two will do me in." Smiling as he was proud of them, he finished making plans with his group.

****

The full moon had been out when she slowly walked down to the beach sitting on the soft sand not worried if it did get in her shoes. From her side knowing he was there as he walked out from the shadows coming over to her sitting down next to her staring out at the water.

"I know he spoke to you before you left, what did he say?" Looking at Sydney with interest as he wiped the small piece of hair that strayed along her cheek.

"He told me to look out for myself first, that he would handle getting Dorina back. I know I will see him again. He'll find out eventually, and so will everyone, I miss my father Goseck. It was easier when I didn't remember," speaking in such a hushed tone Sydney seemed rather serene almost lost in her thoughts, "I understand as a shade we control the elements in the air. There's not much else, we still age, but it takes so drastically long, technically I haven't aged a full year yet since I changed. What good are we?" Letting out a slight sigh still not content with the change in things.

"The fact we simply exist as humans exist. We live our lives whether it be nomadic, in self-made families, or simply connect to those who share our same goals and interests. We keep our secrets to keep from harming others and ourselves. We keep ourselves hidden from others' fears of the unknown and if we can we make a difference most likely no one will ever know or see. We are certainly not perfect, or death would have been final, but who knows if death should be the end? Every group has its good points. It's how it's used. It's not a cure." He had always been good at expressing his opinions.

"What are we doing with Dorina? Her family will look for her. what do I do when Lucian finds out about you?" Sydney looked at him for the answer that not even she had known other than wanting to keep her safe.

"Maddie had a lot to teach Dorina still, she has much to prepare for in her future especially if she wishes for her family to survive. Not to worry. She's going to be fine. We will worry about that when the time comes, just like you have chosen to let Alana live. I still cannot believe you let her go. She could keep coming after you. Even though I promise I will be here to protect you." Placing his arm around her waist pulling her towards him as he held her.

"She's not an evil person, she hesitated too much. She's just hurt and if she does come after me again, we will deal with it then. It helps that she has no true power behind her now. I think being out in this world she needs time and maybe there might be hope?" Leaning more into him now knowing there was so much more to come.

"I have to ask what is in that box you keep holding in your lap that Nicolai gave you?" Smiling Sydney looked down at it, she hadn't taken it out even though she knew what it was. Lifting the top, she turned it so he could see what it was.

"A steel helmet with padding on the inside? Is that supposed to be a threat?" Luther had looked at her with morbid curiosity.

"No, it's more of a personal thing since my head seems to get banged around so much. He felt this would keep it safe so I wouldn't keep forgetting what was important." Giving her a tighter hug for reassurance.

"I know it sucked for the way we had to do this but trust me when Maddie makes a prediction it happens every time. This was the best for everyone involved. We have tested people for centuries this way. At least the original order had, and it worked. We need to find those who will stick by us. And stop looking at me as if I'm being evil. Being in power, you can't trust everyone. You've put Alana through her test, now I will put Andrew and Charlie through theirs." Turning to face Sydney, Luther placed his hand on her cheek pulling her into him and kissing her lips. Pushing back as he did and looked at him disgusted.

"Do we have to have this talk again? I'm not yours." Pulling back but still did not leave his arms.

"I highly doubt he's going to want you after you've been friends with the devil who attacked him, besides you belong with me not him." I knew Lucian would never leave his family and it certainly wouldn't be safe once time went on. He would be stuck, and I doubted what I had responsibility for he would want a part of.

"Did you have to beat him up that badly?" Looking pissed off that Luther carried it that far.

Smiling back at her rather evilly before giving her an answer.

"Yes, I did. I had to show him how powerful I was." Luther was proud of himself and for personal reasons felt vindicated.

www.ingramcontent.com/pod-product-compliance
Lightning Source LLC
LaVergne TN
LVHW050535160826
845677LV00011B/2040

* 9 7 8 1 9 3 9 9 8 5 5 3 8 *